Love Points to You

Also by Alice Lin

Fireworks

Love Points to You

Alice Lin

DELACORTE ROMANCE

This is a work of fiction. Names, characters, places, and incidents either are the product of the author's imagination or are used fictitiously. Any resemblance to actual persons, living or dead, events, or locales is entirely coincidental.

Text copyright © 2025 by Alice Lin
Cover and interior art copyright © 2025 by Jacqueline Li

All rights reserved. Published in the United States by Delacorte Romance, an imprint of Random House Children's Books, a division of Penguin Random House LLC, New York.

Delacorte Romance and the colophon are trademarks of Penguin Random House LLC.

GetUnderlined.com

Educators and librarians, for a variety of teaching tools, visit us at RHTeachersLibrarians.com

Library of Congress Cataloging-in-Publication Data is available upon request.
ISBN 978-0-593-81482-6 (tr. pbk.) — ISBN 978-0-593-81483-3 (ebook)

The text of this book is set in 11-point Tisa Pro.

Editor: Alison Romig
Cover Designer: Ray Shappell
Interior Designer: Ken Crossland
Copy Editor: Colleen Fellingham
Managing Editor: Tamar Schwartz
Production Manager: CJ Han

Printed in the United States of America
1st Printing
First Edition

Random House Children's Books supports the First Amendment and celebrates the right to read.

Penguin Random House values and supports copyright. Copyright fuels creativity, encourages diverse voices, promotes free speech, and creates a vibrant culture. Thank you for buying an authorized edition of this book and for complying with copyright laws by not reproducing, scanning, or distributing any part of it in any form without permission. You are supporting writers and allowing Penguin Random House to continue to publish books for every reader. Please note that no part of this book may be used or reproduced in any manner for the purpose of training artificial intelligence technologies or systems.

Love Points to You

1

DUSTY ROSE IS a color I like to use when I paint. It's subtle and earthy, great for undertones. Like many colors, though, dusty rose doesn't pair well with everything.

A prime example is the floor-length taffeta dress I'm wearing, handpicked by Amy, my stepmom as of this afternoon. The fabric is stiff, the silhouette suffocating—and the ruffled collar? Atrocious. My stepsister, Josie, is equally unlucky in a teal monstrosity that makes her look more like a butchered fish than a mermaid. When hosting a summer wedding at an orchard known for its apricot jam and succulent peaches, you'd *think* a person would want to dress their bridesmaids in pastel tones and airy chiffon to combat the July humidity. But no.

I wipe sweat from my brow and pluck an ice-cold glass of water from the tray of a passing server. As tempting as it is to pour the contents of the glass over my head, I politely sip my drink instead. The reception hall—or outside tent—is massive, sheltering nearly two hundred guests and staff on this scorching day. The pearly white fabric draped high above us provides a respite after we languished under the five o'clock sun for the ceremony. What truly tested my patience, however, was the hour-long photo shoot that preceded it.

Amy hails from an overgrown family tree. The photographer wanted a variety of group shots with all her relatives, no matter how distant. Many flew in from Singapore and Taiwan to attend. I've never met any of them until today. In fact, over half the guests at the wedding are strangers to me. Contrary to the bride's inflated guest list, Dad's list mostly includes friends and workmates. His extended family lives in Taiwan, and everyone was either too busy or too elderly to venture to the States. Since his parents passed away years ago, the only immediate family he has left is Aunt Mindy, his sister.

Cheers ripple through the hall as Amy and Josie step onto the raised platform in the center of the tent for their mother-daughter dance. I reluctantly join everyone around the dance floor to watch the pair as they waltz along to a symphony I've heard one too many times, their movements synchronized and rehearsed.

Dad emerges from the crowd to stand next to me, and I notice the patch of foundation blended into his jawline, concealing the old scar he acquired from a shaving accident. For the sake of photos, he traded his glasses for contact lenses, despite having a chronic case of dry eye. He also grew his hair out to achieve a sideswept look I've never seen him sport until today.

"You look lovely," he says for the umpteenth time.

I snort. "I look like I'm wearing a paper bag around my neck."

"Don't say that. The dress suits you."

"Sure, if I were a PB&J sandwich wearing an Elizabethan ruff." I sent Aunt Mindy a selfie after I got my makeup done this afternoon. She told me to wear the dress and suck it up for one day, but even she acknowledged how unflattering it is.

Dad claps a hand on my shoulder. "Relax, today's a special day. You should enjoy it."

"Easier said than done," I murmur, tugging at my collar, my skin suddenly prickly.

"Lynda." He's whispering now. "Be a team player."

It takes everything in me not to roll my eyes.

Let's not forget who designed, printed, and mailed the wedding invitations, and correct me if I'm wrong, but bridal showers don't plan themselves—and that welcome sign outside with the watercolor lilies that says *Amy & Brian* in flawless calligraphy?

That was also me.

Happy bridesmaid I may not be, but I've certainly been a team player.

I met Amy last spring. She'd been dating my dad for five months by the time he introduced her to me. The news wasn't particularly shocking. He'd been single for over a decade, after Mom passed away. It made sense for him to put himself out there.

Four months later, though, he proposed.

That caught me by surprise.

The news shook the ground beneath my feet, plummeting me into a hole I'm still clawing my way out of. I was a high school freshman when I met Amy. Now, the summer before junior year, I have a stepmom and a stepsister. How is one supposed to cope?

You grin and bear it, according to my dad.

Don't get me wrong. Amy and Josie are perfectly nice. Anyone would be glad to have them as family. If the wedding weren't for another year, maybe I'd be in a more comfortable place, but who can really say? Sadly, I had no say at all.

There's a smattering of applause as Amy and Josie clear the dance floor to make way for me and my dad. I spot Aunt Mindy among the crowd. She and her husband, Uncle Ben, are the only ones here I'm excited to see. They used to live within walking distance from me until they traded Fallbank, Virginia, for Chicago, Illinois.

Aunt Mindy gives me a thumbs-up, as if to say *You've got this!*

Unfortunately, I don't.

Piano music begins to play from the speakers overhead. Dad and I sway, our hands slippery with sweat as we try to match each other's pace. Although the pointed-toe heels Amy gifted me are the right size, every step I take is like walking barefoot through a cactus field. My feet are begging to be released from their prison; yet, somehow, the awkwardness of this moment surpasses the pain. While Josie might look like a fish in her mermaid dress, I feel like a fish flopping around on land, unable to tell left from right. Maintaining eye contact with my dad during a slow dance is . . . embarrassing, so I focus on his bow tie, wishing I could be anywhere but here.

Then I hear him sniffle.

Dad's teary-eyed, just as he was when Amy walked down the aisle. He's looking at me as if I *am* lovely, as if this moment is precious and he wants nothing more than to share it with me—even though I'm waiting for it to be over.

I suck it up and finish the dance.

• • •

In his speech, Dad's best man, an old college friend of his I haven't seen in ages, prattles on about how overjoyed he is that Dad found love again, while avoiding all mentions of my dead mom. After a climactic toast to the bride and groom, dinner is served, and a cacophony of clanging cutlery and drunken laughter descends on the reception hall. I'm seated at a table with Aunt Mindy; Uncle Ben; his sister, Aunt Elle; and her son, Peter.

"When Brian told me they were hosting a big wedding, I wasn't sure what to expect," Aunt Mindy confesses as we all tuck into our first course: a peach and spinach salad. "They certainly outdid themselves. The venue is gorgeous."

We have Amy's wedding planner to thank for that. Once you strip away the tent and decor, the orchard grounds themselves are quite bare. Amy's first choice was a private estate that had been fully booked for the year by the time she phoned them. If she'd had her way, the wedding would've gone from semiformal to black tie.

From the photos I've seen, Mom and Dad had a back-yard wedding with no more than thirty guests. Mom wore a white tea-length dress and a handmade crown of daisies on her head, a glaring contrast to Amy's bejeweled ball gown.

What would Mom have thought about all this?

I don't have any memories of her—breast cancer took her when I was four—but if I had to guess, she would've found this wedding to be a bit . . . much. Just to be clear, I have nothing against lavish weddings. If you can afford to splurge, go for it. Except, Dad's always been frugal. I guess if you didn't go all out for your first wedding, you compensate for it at your second. . . .

"Lynda." Aunt Elle taps her champagne flute to get my attention, short of snapping her fingers. "You're going to be a junior this year?"

With a mouth full of peaches, I reply, "Yup."

Junior year is *the* year colleges care about most, as every adult likes to remind me. Aunt Elle loves to talk academics, and nothing is more impressive to her than Ivy League sta-tus. Peter goes to UPenn. He and I aren't close, but we have this running joke where I pretend to think he goes to Penn State. Just to piss off his mom.

"Still thinking about art school?" she asks, twirling her fork between her fingers.

I push some spinach around on my plate. "Yup. My first choice is RISD."

Aunt Elle stares at me like I'm speaking gibberish.

"The Rhode Island School of Design," I say.

"Brian's okay with that?"

Dad prefers that I leave art as a hobby in favor of a more stable and lucrative profession. He doesn't want to shell out thousands of dollars for a degree I'll never use, and I get that. The art world is competitive. Not everyone can make it to the top, much less break into the industry. But Dad knows I'm committed, so he's willing to help pay for art school under the condition that I keep my GPA above a 3.8 and apply for scholarships.

"We've talked about it," I finally say. "He supports me."

"Hmm . . ." Aunt Elle squares her elbows on the table and squints at me.

I sense an incoming lecture.

"Well, Lynda, I for one hope you're applying to SAIC," Aunt Mindy cuts in. "You're welcome to stay with Ben and me."

She gives my hand a reassuring squeeze, and I match her smile with my own. I can always count on Aunt Mindy to have my back.

The School of the Art Institute of Chicago isn't my second or third choice, but I can't deny the appeal of free housing.

"The guest room is yours to decorate," Uncle Ben adds. "I'm almost done renovating the basement. Feel free to use it as your art studio."

Aunt Elle gives him a withering look before turning back to me. "Why not stay close to home? UPenn isn't too far. Assuming you get in—"

"I'm not interested in UPenn," I tell her.

Or staying close to home.

She huffs with indignation. "You should keep an open mind. It would be such a shame to leave the nest so soon after Brian remarried. You're not an only child anymore. Think about your new family. You need more time to bond."

"I'll think about it," I say, just to appease her.

"Please do."

I sweep my eyes toward the front of the room, to where Dad and Amy are sitting alone at the sweetheart table. He feeds her a slice of peach before leaning forward to whisper into her ear. When he pulls back, they stare at each other adoringly, oblivious to everything around them.

I want to be happy for them, but when I envision the future, all I see is an art school anywhere but here.

2

BORA, MY BEST friend, is sprawled across my bedroom floor, scrolling through wedding photos tagged #Brian&Amy on Instagram.

"I wish I could've been there," she says. "It would've been the perfect opportunity to wear that vintage gem I found at the thrift store."

"You mean that silver dress?" I ask. "The one with the violet beading?"

"The one and only." Bora rolls onto her stomach, kicks her legs up behind her, and strikes a pose for an invisible camera.

The wedding was two days ago. I'm still salty I wasn't allowed to bring Bora as my plus-one. Dad thought she'd distract me from my "duties"—which he correctly assumed. Had Bora been at the wedding, I would've hung out with her the whole time.

How could I not? We're practically sisters. We had countless sleepovers throughout middle school, and when Bora wasn't staying the night, she'd come over after school for homework and snacks (Aunt Mindy always stocked our apartment with shrimp crackers and egg tarts—Bora's favorites).

Aren't weddings as much about the families as they are about the couple? Dad and Amy seem to think so, yet they wouldn't let me bring my best friend.

I have a suspicion that Amy didn't want Bora at the wedding because of her fashion sense. Some consider it garish, others eccentric. I call it *Bora*. I employ bold colors in my art, whereas Bora likes to wear them, as evidenced by her turquoise hair and sparkly magenta eyeliner.

"How did your dad and stepmom meet, again?" Bora asks.

"On a dating app," I say. "My dad wrote in his profile that he was looking for a biking partner as much as a life partner."

"Aw, that's sweet."

"More like cheesy." I don't know how that line worked on Amy, and to think he reprised it during his wedding vows. "Can you believe my dad borrowed money from my aunt to pay for the honeymoon?"

That, I overheard behind closed doors between Dad and Aunt Mindy. A trip to Singapore isn't cheap, but Dad makes decent money in recruiting, and Amy outearns him as a data analyst at a hospital. How much could they have possibly borrowed?

Bora winces. "Nothing like starting a marriage in debt. I mean"—she swipes through her phone and produces a photo of a four-tiered cake embellished with fondant roses—"their wedding must've cost mad money."

"More than fifty grand."

"Yikes, that could've gone toward a new house." Bora eyes the packing boxes scattered around my room.

I trace her line of sight and sigh.

Tomorrow's move-in day. Dad and I will officially be living with Amy and Josie in their house so we can all be one big happy family.

I knew this day was coming, and I've been dreading it. The boxes have been gathering dust in my room for months now. Even with Bora here to help, I haven't made much progress. I emptied out my closet and the stuff under my bed, and that's about it.

Part of me is glad that the wedding is over. I was losing my mind from all the talk about centerpieces and tablecloths. But another part of me wishes my dad were still single. Then I wouldn't have to say goodbye to this apartment. The upstairs neighbor can be obnoxious with his weekend karaoke nights, but this place has been my home for sixteen years. Aunt Mindy moved away four years ago, but her presence remains—in the powdery shade of blue she picked for my bedroom walls, in the mermaid mural we painted together in the bathroom, and in the narrow eat-in kitchen she retiled because our landlord couldn't be bothered. (If you search hard enough, you'll notice there's a single tile where she and I etched our initials.)

I've made countless memories here, and now I have to leave.

"You'll still come over, right?" I ask Bora.

"Of course!" she replies, outraged that I'd even ask. "I

mean, our sleepovers won't be the same now that there's Josie, but we'll make it work. We always do."

"And I'll always have shrimp crackers and egg tarts waiting for you."

"No doubt you will." Bora winks and shoots an invisible bullet at me. "You know, moving in with Josie is kind of like having a perpetual sleepover."

Josie and I are both incoming juniors at Fallbank High. We were in study hall together freshman year but never talked. I simply knew her as the shy girl with the long silky hair always tied in a gingham scrunchy. I wasn't thrilled to discover my dad was dating my classmate's mom, and now I have to share a roof with her.

"Are you and Josie hyphenating your last names?" Bora asks as I assemble a box with heavy-duty tape and then set it aside as if it'll magically pack itself. "Lynda Fan-Koh has a pleasant ring to it."

"Amy and Josie are taking mine," I tell her.

Dad asked if I wanted to hyphenate or take their surname. My answer was no to both. I refuse to give up my name on top of everything else.

"Josie Fan . . ." Bora taps a finger to her lips. "Not sure I like it."

"Good thing it's not your name, Bora Lee-Carter."

"Hey, I like my last name. It highlights my Korean and English roots."

"Lee-Carter sounds way better than Fan-Koh."

Even though I've barely started, I give up on the boxes, wheel the chair out from under my desk, and remove Henry, my iPad Pro, from his protective sleeve. (Yes, *he*—not *it*—has a name, and he's my baby.)

"Ooh!" Bora leaps to her feet and hovers over me as I wait for the drawing app to load. "Any new Buncleaver content?"

Buncleaver is a cartoon beaver that wields a cleaver and wears fake bunny ears. Soft, pudgy, and a little menacing, he sincerely believes he's a rabbit. Ever since he came to me in a dream last winter, I've been posting drawings and short comics of him to my Instagram. What started as a silly side project turned out to be my golden ticket.

People love him. I gained tons of followers and started an online sticker shop all thanks to him. Before, my Instagram mostly consisted of fan art and celebrity portraits. I'd receive a few DMs every month from people seeking to commission me. Far too many influencers asked me to draw for them in exchange for exposure and then got upset when I said no. I didn't need their endorsement. What I needed was Buncleaver, and now my DMs are inundated with paying customers.

As much as I enjoy drawing animals, I draw people on request. It's how I control my brand. Cutesy animals for stickers, and human subjects strictly by commission. My rates are fifty dollars for a headshot, one hundred for half-body, and two hundred for full-body illustrations. Additional fees are calculated based on the complexity of the request. I used to charge less, but as my art improves, so do my rates.

Art school isn't cheap.

I don't want to be too reliant on my dad, so I need to make money somehow.

RISD costs about sixty thousand dollars a year. That's three hundred full-body commissions (and carpal tunnel) just for tuition. Buncleaver would have to become the next Pusheen for me to afford my dream school. Bora did suggest that I try selling plushies, but I'm not *that* business savvy. I wouldn't even know where to begin.

"Lynda. Are you going to answer or ignore me for eternity?"

"Sorry," I say, finally snapping out of it. "I don't have anything lined up for Instagram yet." I had to close my commissions to focus on the wedding. As a result, my fun money has dwindled, and my college savings have plateaued.

"Bummer." Bora pouts. "I'm, like, starved for Buncleaver."

"You won't be hungry much longer, my friend." I tap open a file and pull up a rough sketch I did this morning, of Buncleaver chopping green onions on a tree stump. "You can expect a new post soon."

Bora claps her hands and squeals. "How I've missed you, Buncleaver!"

I've missed him, too.

It's good to be drawing again.

3

AMY INHERITED HER house from her previous marriage, which ended more than a decade ago, after her ex-husband walked out. I don't know all the sordid details, but at least she got to keep the house in all its cozy tarragon-green glory. I've been over plenty of times at my dad's insistence. The place certainly beats our cramped two-bedroom apartment.

As for everything else, well, time will tell.

Thanks to my procrastinating, I stayed up late last night to finish packing. Dad sold most of our furniture, so the move shouldn't take too long. As I haul my first box out of the rental truck, I take in the low-pitched roof and decorative dormer windows of the house. Starting today, I get to call this place *my* home. Unfortunately, it's far from mine because I have to room with Josie.

The house has three bedrooms, the smallest one reserved for Josie and her violin. The walls are outfitted with soundproof padding, and the space is furnished with a love seat and desk. The room isn't wide enough to fit a dresser and bed, but with some imagination, I could've made it work. Still, my dad thought it would be too much to ask of Josie. I've pleaded my case, but the winning argument is that if Josie wants to get into the Curtis Institute of Music, she needs a private practice room more than I need my own bedroom.

Curtis is a conservatory in Philadelphia with an acceptance rate of four percent. Tuition is free and admission is based solely on artistic promise, which means you need to master Mozart, Bach, Paganini—and I can't recall the rest. I don't know much about classical music. The little I do know I learned from hanging around Josie. She spent freshman- and sophomore-year summers at music camp, and the only reason she didn't go this year is because of the wedding.

"Do you need help with that?" Josie asks as I lift my knee up to support the bottom of the box I'm carrying and then shimmy my way into our bedroom.

"I got it." I deposit the box on the floor and take a moment to stretch.

Amy kindly bought a new bedframe and mattress. Both are waiting for me, made up all neat and tidy with nautical-themed sheets I wouldn't have chosen for myself. Josie's bed is by the window, while mine is closer to the closet. A nightstand acts as a demarcation line between us, and across from all that will be the dresser and desk I brought over from my apartment.

Sunlight filters in through the curtains, lending a warm glow to the pragmatic furnishings and sparse decor. I've already been told I can't personalize the room with prints or decals, much less paint the walls anything besides eggshell white, to accommodate Josie's minimalist taste. I've ranted to Bora countless times, but other than that I bite my tongue. After all, Josie was here first. Although she's never complained, she probably isn't too fond of me intruding into her space. She hasn't given me a hard time, so I try not to give her one. Since she has her own music room, I suppose I should be grateful that I don't have to listen to her practice violin every day.

Still, I need time to get used to this arrangement. I've never been self-conscious about snoring or talking in my sleep, but now . . .

"Well." Josie throws her arms out in an awkward welcoming gesture. "Make yourself at home. Let me know if you need anything."

Oh, there's a lot that I need. But Josie can't help me.

• • •

Once all the boxes and Bubble Wrap are recycled, Dad and Amy go to buy some last-minute items before they fly out for their honeymoon tomorrow. I don't know why they scheduled their flight so soon after our move, but I won't pretend to understand how my dad thinks. At least with them gone, I'll finally have some quiet time to myself.

Just as I'm settling in, the doorbell rings.

I wait for Josie to answer it. When the doorbell rings six

more times, I realize Josie must be practicing violin and open the front door, only to come face-to-face with Amy's sister, Val, and her eight-year-old nephew, Luke.

Arms laden with groceries, Val trudges past me in a thick plume of perfume and unloads the bags onto the dining table before collapsing into a chair. Meanwhile, Luke turns on the TV and plops down on the living room couch.

"Tea would be nice," Val says, side-eyeing me. "Amy should have those jasmine leaves I gave her. She keeps them in that red tin. You know, the one above the sink?"

Demanding tea is the new hello. I know where most things are in the house, but I haven't explored every nook and cranny.

"Would Luke like something to drink?" I ask.

"He'll drink tea as long as there's honey." Val gestures widely at the groceries. "Organize these while you're at it. I wanted to make sure the fridge was stocked while Amy and Brian are away."

First day in my new house and I get to play host. Fun.

I grab as many bags as I can and head for the kitchen.

"Aren't you forgetting something?" Val says loudly behind me.

I stop in my tracks and take a deep breath. "Thanks for the groceries."

"Thanks for the groceries, *Aunt Val*," she tuts. "Now that—"

I leave before she can finish and take my sweet time organizing everything into the fridge and pantry. From the moment we met, Val's been nothing short of insufferable.

As for Luke, well, he's just *there*. The kid doesn't do much except stare at a screen.

Once tea is served, I retreat to my room and pull out my sketchbook. Just as I'm about to sharpen my pencil and start an exercise on how to draw dragons, there's a knock at the door. When I don't respond, the doorknob rattles against the lock.

"I'm busy!" I shout. For a moment, there's silence. Then the knocking continues, incessantly. "I said I'm busy!"

"Luke's hungry!" Val shouts back. "I need your help with dinner."

I reluctantly open the door to say, "Why don't you ask Josie to help?"

Luke is her cousin, not mine.

"I don't want to interrupt her," Val says. "It's not like you're busy with anything."

"I was about to be."

"Whatever you were about to do can wait." Val crosses her arms. "I don't think Brian would appreciate how disrespectful you're being right now," she says, arching a brow. "Is this any way to treat your—"

"Okay, I'll help." But not because I'm scared of getting in trouble. The less resistance from me, the faster I can get this over with.

· · ·

Halfway into dinner prep, as I'm browning the garlic and ginger in the wok, Josie graces us with her presence.

"Look who's here!" Val reels her in for a hug. She peers at me over Josie's shoulder and says, "You can drop in the chilis now. Don't let them burn."

"I know what I'm doing," I grumble, dropping the chilis and chives into the wok. Not sure why Val demanded my help when she clearly doesn't think I can cook.

Dad's job requires him to work overtime, so Aunt Mindy and Uncle Ben used to babysit me, starting from the time I entered preschool. They taught me how to swim and ride a bike, how to tie a three-strand braid and a necktie, and how to read a recipe and follow it—starting with what they grew up eating in Taiwan: xifan and dan bing. I learned to be quite self-sufficient by the time they moved to Chicago when I was in seventh grade.

Luke darts into the kitchen and latches onto Josie's waist. It's kind of sweet how he nestles his face into her abdomen.

Josie ruffles his hair. "Hey, kiddo. Did you have fun at the wedding?"

Luke puckers his lips. "It was boring. Aunt Amy looked like a giant cupcake. Anyway, can I play with your iPad?"

"Sure, it's in my room." Once Luke's gone, Josie comes up from behind me. "Smells delicious. Anything I can do?"

"Can you pass me the eggplant?" I ask, cranking up the burner. "Also, can you please clear the drying rack?" Josie gets right to it. "Thanks."

"Now, isn't this beautiful: sisters working together." Val places a hand over her heart as her eyes mist over, her expression somewhere between endearing and patronizing. "If I didn't know better, I would've thought you two were related."

Josie and I scan each other from head to toe. We both have black hair. Mine's shoulder length and choppy while hers falls to her midback and is usually curled. Our eyes are the same dark shade of brown, but I have double eyelids. She doesn't. The biggest difference between us is really our height. At five six, she has four inches on me.

The air fryer beeps.

"Chicken's done!" I announce as I plate the fried eggplant.

Val checks the chicken with a thermometer. "Looks good. Now go—"

"Time to change!" I make a big show of flashing my sweat-stained shirt and even take a whiff of my armpit. "I'm going to freshen up. Josie can handle the rest."

Before Val can protest, Luke reappears at the doorway, hands tucked behind him. We all watch as he lingers there, quietly worrying his bottom lip as he stares at his feet.

The telltale signs of shame.

Josie stoops to eye level with him and says, "Talk to me. What's wrong?"

"Promise you won't be mad?" he mumbles.

"Promise."

I get a sinking feeling in the pit of my stomach as Luke slowly brings his arms around. In his hands is an iPad riddled with cracks, the worst of the damage concentrated in the center of the screen. I'm not a forensic scientist, but damage like that doesn't happen from an accidental fall.

"That's . . . bad." Josie's having trouble concealing her disappointment.

"Can it be fixed?" Val asks, shaking her head at Luke.

"Probably not . . ." Josie takes the iPad from Luke and traces a finger over the dent in the screen. She holds down the power button for a few seconds. Nothing happens. She then flips the iPad over to reveal a Buncleaver sticker on the back.

"Oh."

...

Henry Fan. Time of death: 6:25 p.m. Cause: Blunt force trauma.

I had Henry for three years, bought him with my own money, and now he's gone.

Dinner passes in silence. I wasn't hungry earlier and I'm not hungry now. Despite my protests, Val insisted I join everyone—because being in the same room as Luke is totally what I want to do right now. Instead of borrowing Josie's iPad, which she keeps in her practice room, Luke took mine. An honest mistake. However, instead of using a stylus pen, he used a real one. It didn't work, but boy, did he try to make it work!

Luke did apologize to me, and yes, he's a kid and kids do stupid things, but sorry doesn't cut it. Val hasn't offered to replace Henry, and I know asking won't make a difference. If she was going to do right by me, I wouldn't have to ask to begin with.

"Maybe the Apple Store can do something for you," Val says without a hint of shame, "assuming your warranty hasn't expired."

I've finally had enough and return to my room.

. . .

After Val announces her departure, I take a cold shower to decompress. It's almost comical how this day soured so quickly. The downward trajectory of my life has to shift at some point. All hope can't be lost. After all, there's a very simple solution to this problem I'm having, and I know just who to go to.

Dad and Amy are at the dining table when I step out of the bathroom.

"Lynda, have some cheesecake!" Amy says. "I picked one up on the way back—thought we could all use a treat."

"No thanks," I say as she serves a slice to Josie, who's been sitting so quietly I almost didn't notice she was there.

"There'll be plenty in the fridge if you change your mind—and speaking of the fridge, I can tell Val was here. I wish she'd ask instead of dropping by unannounced," Amy says. And then under her breath, "I hope she behaved herself. . . ."

"About that . . ." I clap my hands together and recite the words I rehearsed in the shower. "Luke killed Henry, and I was wondering if you could speak to Val about paying me to replace him."

There, I said it. I planned to wait until Dad and Amy got a chance to rest, but now seemed like an appropriate time.

"Who's Henry?" Amy asks, her brows furrowing.

"Her drawing tablet," Dad clarifies, and she noticeably relaxes.

After I explain the incident, something passes between

them. It's the kind of look adults share when something bad happens, but neither of them wants to handle it.

Finally, Amy sighs. "I'm sorry Luke did that, really I am."

Dad clears his throat. "However, it would be discourteous of us to ask Val to compensate you, considering her . . . significant contribution toward our wedding."

Are you kidding me? So that's how they were able to afford the venue. Well, in that case, demanding money from Val would be hypocritical of them. But *they* chose to have an expensive wedding. I didn't.

"Okay . . ." I grind my teeth, chewing over my next words. "If not Val, then who? Who's getting me a new drawing tablet?"

As if on cue, Josie makes her exit while Amy slinks into the kitchen.

"Don't you have money saved from your art commissions?" Dad asks.

I don't like where this is going. "I do . . . but why should I pay for someone else's mistake?"

"It's not fair, but sometimes we have to let things go."

"I am. That's why I'm not pushing you to call Val. Why can't *you* front the cost?"

Dad lifts his glasses and rubs the bridge of his nose. "Amy and I . . . We're tired. It's been a long day, and we have an early flight to catch tomorrow. Let's talk about this after our trip."

I cross my arms, fully aware that there's no point in fighting. "Fine."

4

SO MUCH FOR a housewarming.

The newlyweds flew out to Singapore this morning. They're visiting Amy's family, the ones who couldn't make it to the wedding, before staying at a beach resort.

I'm jealous. I've never been to Asia, let alone left the country. While Dad's having the time of his life, I'm mourning the death of Henry. Josie tried to make things right by offering me her iPad. But I passed. Her late grandfather gifted her that iPad. I'm not taking a sentimental item from her to make things even. As for my dad, well, he didn't even try. I can't believe he left for vacation one day after I uprooted my life—for *him*.

I didn't choose this. He did.

It's so like him to never be around.

At least I have Bora.

Baa Bing, the shaved ice shop where Bora works, has a line out the door by the time I arrive. Even in shorts and a tank top, biking in this heat was a bad idea. Breathless and sweaty, I secure my bike at a nearby rack and hop in line. Up ahead I spot familiar faces: Tyler Louis, running back of our football team; Gemma Stone, my occasional language partner during sophomore year Mandarin; and right in front of me is Angela Wu, top student at Fallbank High. Angela and I have been in a couple classes together, though neither of us has made any effort to be anything more than acquaintances.

Angela is an odd story. We attended different middle schools, so I'm not sure how true this is, but she was supposedly a nobody in eighth grade. Just a bookworm with braces and no fashion sense until that one summer she turned pretty. She ditched the braces, overhauled her wardrobe, and became the Cool Girl freshman year. The cheer team welcomed her with open arms, she got invited to every party, and guys asked her out left and right.

But then spring break happened, and without warning, she quit cheerleading, erased all her newly acquired contacts, and went back to hitting the books harder than ever. It was surreal watching it unfold. Now she's known as the "pretty nerd with an ego the size of Jupiter." Don't ever disagree with her in class. She will tear you down from the pedestal that is your opinion (curse every book discussion we had in Honors English).

"Can you stop breathing on me?"

It takes a moment for Angela's voice to register.

Cool as snow, sharp as icicles.

Each word needling me.

Before I can conceive a comeback, she does that calculated head turn of hers, where she pivots herself just enough to lend me a clear view of her temple and the slope of her nose while deliberately avoiding eye contact, leaving the scowl on her face to my imagination. I sat behind her long enough in Honors English to know that's a sign she's about to get confrontational if I don't comply. So I back up.

Angela keeps her gaze ahead, saving whatever comment she was about to make to herself. I wipe away the sweat pooling at my brow, unsure if it's from the heat or Angela's attitude. Out of nowhere, a loud smooching sound disrupts the peace. Angela startles and drops her phone on the concrete. I bend over to pick it up, my fingers barely grazing it when she snatches it off the ground.

Our eyes finally meet.

"Only trying to help," I say, hands up, palms out.

"Do I look like I need it?" she says, holding her phone close to her chest.

I know a rhetorical question when I hear one.

Angela stares me down for an uncomfortably long moment and then leaves the line.

Like I said, an ego the size of Jupiter. I don't understand the hostility, but that's one fewer person in front of me.

When I'm finally up to order, Bora lunges across the counter to hug me. "Salvation! Give me a sec while I find someone to cover me." After more than a second, she hands me a bowl of shaved ice topped with red bean and matcha ice cream, finished off with a drizzle of condensed milk. She swipes two spoons from behind the counter and then we're out the door.

"You're angry," Bora says as soon as we park ourselves on a bench.

"Is it that obvious?" I ask before taking a bite of shaved ice.

"You're scowling. So. What happened?"

I tell her everything. Henry is beyond repair, and I'm pretty sure Dad's holding out until I buy myself a new iPad. The money I've been saving is earmarked for my future. A car, first and foremost, then tuition. I can't go out of state for college if I don't have my own ride. Dipping into my savings will set me back—again. Last month I had to buy a new phone because my old one was so ancient it couldn't support the latest security update.

I know the sooner I reopen commissions, the sooner I can earn back the money.

But I'm petty.

"What now?" Bora asks. "You can't be Henryless forever."

"You think I should drop the whole thing and take the loss?"

"Sort of? I mean, pride never won me any arguments with my parents."

In the five years we've been friends, I've only met Bora's parents a handful of times. Their entire personality is *it's my way or the highway,* as evidenced by their double standards when parenting Bora and her younger brother. She once locked her bedroom and refused to let him in while she was studying. He threw a tantrum that ended with Bora getting grounded and having her bedroom door temporarily taken away—all because she wanted to study in peace.

At least my dad leaves me alone when I want to be.

Since then, Bora's been staying with her grandma. She

also started working part-time to achieve some independence since she can't depend on her parents for anything. In fact, now that she's making money, her parents use it as an excuse to not buy her birthday gifts. I make sure to compensate for them, but still, it stings knowing your parents don't care.

"Can't wait until we graduate," Bora mutters to herself. She's gunning for UVA's nursing program. "Maybe once I'm rich and successful, my parents will realize who the real golden child is."

I don't know how she copes. My problems seem so minuscule compared to hers. If she can keep her chin up, I can too.

"I'll replace Henry once school starts," I tell her. "Maybe there'll be discounts."

Bora gives me an encouraging pat on the back. "On a lighter note, I know just the thing to distract you from your woes." She whips out her phone and enters the passcode. "Check out this new otome game."

I scoot over so we're sitting shoulder to shoulder with her phone between us.

Otome games are narrative-based games told through the perspective of the player, the main character (MC). They usually contain romantic subplots for various nonplayable characters (NPCs)—suitors, as I like to call them. Each suitor has their own route, and the choices you make throughout their story will affect its ending.

A choose-your-own-adventure dating simulation, basically.

Bora taps her phone, and an opening animation commences with a dramatic violin track. The first suitor to be introduced is a man in a navy pinstripe suit with eyes as bright as gold. His name: Theodore Tudor of the Emperor Moon. The camera zooms in on the monocle adorning his right eye before panning out to reveal the second suitor: a sinewy man with long white hair, his body shrouded in a ruby-red cloak. His name: Marlo Montgomery of the Wretched Moon.

Bora waggles her brows. "Sexy, no?"

"If you mean the art, then yes, very sexy." I admire the bold line art and color blocking in the character design.

"The game's called *Romancing the New Moon*. It's set in an alternate twentieth-century England with vampires that rule London."

"Let me guess, the MC is a human who gets kidnapped by vampires."

"MC's a *vampire hunter* who gets kidnapped by vampires."

"An incompetent vampire hunter. Even better."

Bora bumps shoulders with me. "Don't act like you don't have your dumb moments."

After introducing more attractive men of various archetypes, the opening concludes with all five suitors grouped together in one image, followed by a smooching sound as a red lipstick stain stamps the screen and the title of the game appears in lush gothic letters.

Bora clutches her chest and moans. "I read up to chapter four of Theodore's route. I'm at war with myself, Lynda. I want to keep seeing Theodore, but I don't want to use the birthday money you gave me to buy chapter tickets."

Otome games are usually broken into chapters. Each day, you're allotted tickets to read one chapter for free. If you don't have the patience to read one chapter a day, you can buy tickets.

"That money is yours," I say. "Buy whatever you want."

"What if I gave it back so you could—"

"Don't. I'll figure something out."

She gives me a reassuring smile. "You always do."

• • •

After Bora returns to her shift, I linger outside in the shade and enjoy the intermittent breeze. I don't want to go home, not where it's so tempting to sulk and rage. Lately, my mood has been anything but good, and honestly, it's draining. The shaved ice and matcha ice cream helped a little, but what I really need is to draw.

I grab my sketchbook from my backpack and continue the Buncleaver drawing I started the other day. As I furiously scribble away at the page, a shadow creeps over the edges of my sketchbook before engulfing me entirely. I glance up and startle at the sight of Angela hovering over me, blocking my light.

"Mind if we talk?" she asks, her expression unreadable.

Our earlier encounter left a bitter taste in my mouth. Whatever she has to say, I don't want to hear it. I resume my drawing and pretend I didn't hear her.

She clears her throat.

"I'm busy," I finally say.

"I heard you need a new drawing tablet. I can help."

The tip of my pencil snaps, and my hand freezes mid-stroke. "You were eavesdropping?"

"You and your friend weren't exactly quiet."

"I'm listening. . . ." Sheesh, it's only been a few seconds and already I'm eating my words. She motions for me to scoot over on the bench, and I give her my undivided attention.

"This is between you and me," she says, crossing one leg over the other. "Understood?"

"Sure, whatever you say." I wave my hand, signaling her to get on with it.

"My friends and I are developing a mobile game, and we're on the hunt for a character designer. I've seen your portfolio and your style suits the aesthetics we're aiming for." Angela scrutinizes me with an ambiguous look. "What I'm proposing is a trial run. I buy you an iPad, you draw up some concept art, and if I like what you produce, I'll commission you for the official art. If I don't, the iPad is still yours to keep."

She had me at character designer.

"What kind of game is this?" I ask.

Angela leans in to whisper. "An otome game."

I instinctively clap a hand over my mouth.

"No need to act shocked," she says.

"It's just . . ."

Angela Wu—former Cool Girl, shoo-in for valedictorian, secretary-general of Model UN, bearer of more titles than I can recall—plays otome games? It's not a bad thing. I just never expected it, not from her.

I sweep over her with my eyes, taking in her thick black hair wrangled into a bun, the tortoiseshell glasses that are too big for her face, and the oversize button-up she wears as a dress.

"Quit staring." She snaps her fingers in my face before crossing her arms as if to shield herself. "Preconceived notions aside, are you up for this or not?"

"You haven't given me much information. How many characters are we talking here? How detailed do you want the concept art to be?"

A mobile game is a big undertaking. I want to know exactly what I'm signing up for—even though I already know I'll say yes.

"I'll email you the details. For the price of an iPad, I believe you'll find this arrangement more than fair," she says. "As for the game itself, I'll answer any questions you have if I decide to hire you for the official art. How does that sound?"

I make a show of contemplating my answer to avoid coming across as overly eager—and to test her patience. Then I jot down my contact information.

"Sounds like a plan."

• • •

Angela emails me that evening.

Her otome game, *Love Takes Root,* is set in Lianhua Po, a fictional country that operates under a feudal system ruled by Emperor Feng Wei. The year is 1639. The country is split into feudal states governed by nobles and protected by warriors. Farmers and peasants toil the land; goods are produced by artisans and craftsmen. Ancient China, basically.

As promised, Angela's offer is more than fair. For the price of a new iPad Pro, she wants two full-body character sketches, front angle only, accompanied by an expression sheet depicting three emotions: happy, annoyed, and surprised. So long as I fulfill those requirements and keep the East Asian–inspired setting in mind, I have creative liberty.

The characters I've been assigned are the MC's love interests.

Sun Hong is a twenty-year-old thief. Orphaned at a young age after a hurricane destroyed his village, he joined a team of bandits who taught him how to hunt and steal. When their leader orders the attack and slaughter of a family caravan, Sun Hong intercepts his comrades and saves the family from a gruesome fate. He now operates alone.

Meng Li is a nineteen-year-old acrobat raised in a family of traveling performers. She's hustled all her life and yearns for the day when she can reunite with her childhood friend (MC) and they can open a teahouse together. But with ailing siblings, a dead mother, and an absent father, Meng Li has a long way to go before she can achieve her dream.

Envisioning these characters will require research. Freshman-year world history only scratched the surface of Chinese civilization. Although my goal isn't to be historically accurate, if I'm going to draw inspiration from another country, I want to be respectful.

Most of all, I'm ready to get started.

I accept Angela's terms.

5

ANGELA WASTES NO time and has a factory-sealed iPad delivered to my address in two days. She is the blessing I didn't see coming. I can expect her to insult my intelligence during a debate, but to commission me for an otome game?

I never would've imagined it. Not in a million years.

Opportunities like this don't just fall into your lap. It's too good to be true.

But my happiness wins over my skepticism.

Now that Henry's reborn, I finally get to work. Without school to slow me down, for the next couple days, I brainstorm and rework my vision for Sun Hong and Meng Li. These characters must tug at the heartstrings. It's not enough to make them beautiful. Anyone can fall in love with a pretty face, but it takes personality for people to fall so deeply they can't find their way back—which is ironic coming from me.

I haven't had a burning crush in forever.

But think of it this way: You're in a museum, surrounded by paintings. You visit each one, stopping long enough to read the placard before moving on without a second glance. Then you stumble upon a painting that makes you linger longer than the rest, and as you observe its beauty, something in you begins to stir. Something about this stationary image has moved you.

That's what I want.

I want these characters to spring to life. I can't achieve that with the first idea that jumps to mind, nor the second or third. It's frustrating yet thrilling, because I know if I keep at it, I'll eventually arrive at my destination.

...

"When did you get a new iPad?" Josie asks while we're out grocery shopping.

Our parents are due back tomorrow, and she didn't want them coming home to an empty fridge.

"Like two weeks ago," I say as we peruse the produce section.

The otome game has been a welcomed distraction. It's taken my mind off everything I miss about my old apartment. I still don't like sharing a bedroom, but at least Josie's a decent roommate. She's tidy, quiet, and respectful of my (limited) space. While things could be better—much better—they're not awful. I'm not Cinderella with an evil stepsister.

I toss a bundle of bok choy into our cart. "How do you feel about stir-fried udon?"

Tonight, I'm on cooking duty while Josie's responsible

for the dishes. We've been taking turns, making good use of the groceries Val bought for us. Except for the meals we eat together, Josie and I have been doing our own thing. Whatever sisterly bonding our parents thought would occur during their absence hasn't materialized—which suits me just fine, but I noticed Josie's been out of the house for hours on end, sometimes coming back as late as midnight. She's also been glued to her phone. Even now, she's texting someone.

"How do you feel about stir-fried udon?" I ask again.

My question finally registers, and she hastily tucks her phone away.

"Sorry! You can eat without me," she says. "Tonight I'm meeting a friend."

"Oh, okay."

"I—I can cancel my plans if you want."

"You don't have to do that." That is the last thing I want.

"Are you sure?"

"You don't need my permission to hang out with your friends."

"Force of habit, I guess . . ."

"Well, whatever you're doing, just be safe about it."

Josie tucks a strand of hair behind her ear. "You can come too . . . if you want."

I give her a sidelong look before turning the other way. "I'm checking out the instant noodle aisle. Meet you at the register."

• • •

Dad and Amy return from the airport around noon the next day, sporting deep tans and a touch of pink on their cheekbones and shoulder blades. Josie and I help them haul in their luggage. They left with two bags and came back with four.

"How was your trip?" Josie asks after they settle in.

"Fantastic!" Amy pecks Josie on the forehead before opening her arms to me.

I hesitantly lean into her, my arms pinned to my sides as she gives me a brief hug.

"But too much durian and nasi lemak. You think your aunties worship food?" She pats her stomach for emphasis. "My aunties made me regain all the weight I lost for the wedding."

"Wait till you see all the photos we took." Dad starts arranging miscellaneous items on the dining table: pandan cakes, pineapple tarts, durian candy, and kaya jam. "Let's put on a pot of coffee and have some kaya toast. Lynda, do you mind getting—"

"I'm heading out in ten minutes," I say.

I finally finished the character sheets and emailed the files to Angela early this morning. We're meeting at Baa Bing to discuss.

"Will you be back for dinner?" Dad asks. "I was thinking we could do a movie night."

"Uh . . . you can start without me if I'm not back by five." My meetup with Angela shouldn't take that long, but maybe I should find another reason to be out of the house.

"Just text me if you plan to stay out." Dad looks back and

forth between me and Josie. "So, what kind of mischief did you girls get into while we were away?"

I resist the urge to snort. Dad and Amy might've had their own adventure, but that doesn't mean Josie and I embarked on one together.

"I was busy drawing," I say. "On my *new* iPad."

Dad spots Henry on the coffee table. A look of recognition flashes across his face, as if recalling the incident with Luke and Val, and my stomach clenches.

Is he going to say something? Maybe apologize for flying off to another country while leaving me to solve a problem that wasn't of my own making? Will he at least own up to the fact that I had to, once again, rely on myself because he wasn't around?

There are so many things he could say, yet the silence he settles into says everything.

• • •

I'm not sure what to expect when I get to Baa Bing. Although I'm pleased with my work, that doesn't mean Angela will be. Sometimes clients don't know what they want until they see an example of what they *don't* want.

"You're right on time," Angela says as I approach her table and drop into the chair across from her. Two paper cups occupy the space between us. She slides one toward me. "A little pick-me-up from the shop across the street. Your friend"—Bora waves at me from the front counter—"said you like matcha latte."

"Thanks, you didn't have to," I tell Angela.

She shrugs. "What's done is done."

"You're welcome" is a perfectly fine response, I want to say. Instead, I motion toward Bora. "Is it okay if she overhears us?"

"I briefed her before you arrived." Angela reaches for her messenger bag. "Fellow otome gamers need to keep each other in the loop. After all, spreading the word is spreading the love, and we could all use more of it."

Wow. I've never heard her talk like this before. She sounds so sincere. It's . . . disarming. She's usually all about facts and logic, not love and peace. To think she might be a romantic . . .

"Now then . . ." She produces a folder containing printouts of the files I emailed her. "Where do I start?"

Judgment time.

I take a premature sip of my latte, the liquid scorching my tongue.

Angela spreads the printouts across the table. "I knew the quality I was getting when I commissioned you, but this . . ."

Suddenly, my mouth feels dry. I straighten up, my muscles tensing, nerves tingling as Angela continues mulling over her words. What will the verdict be? Is it back to the drawing board or—

"This is . . . incredible."

I release a quiet breath.

"I was expecting flat base colors, not full rendering."

"Is that . . . bad?" I ask.

"No, but I expected the concept art to be more rough-and-ready. What you produced is on par with what I'm seeking for the official art."

Right . . . somehow the word "concept" flew over my head. Maybe I was too intent on proving myself.

Angela points to Sun Hong's character sheet. "His design is typical of a swordsman, but the details are excellent. His inky robes are befitting of a thief. The blue highlights in his hair are a nice touch, and I like how a few strands are peeking through his cowl. The scar above his left brow also conveys a ruggedness that isn't visible through his physique."

Angela speaks in one long run-on sentence. I'm listening without comprehending. Before I can process it all, Angela moves on to Meng Li.

"At first, I was taken aback by her height, all six foot one of her, but it's growing on me. She has the limbs of an acrobat and the grace of a dancer. Her crimson lips, bold eyeliner, and loose indigo tunic . . . Everything about her is vibrant. Like a true performer, she's screaming at the world to pay attention. To see her."

I'm feeling seen right now.

I did not expect such eloquent feedback. Angela certainly took the time to appreciate the details. It means a lot coming from her, although I would never admit that out loud. No need to give her something else to be smug about.

"Does that mean you'll hire me for the official art?" I ask, trying to keep my tone light and casual.

"You've more than earned the job," Angela says, self-assured as always. "Now that I've said my piece, do you have any questions for me?"

Loads. I suppose I could start by asking—

"You said you're developing this game with friends. What's their role in all this?"

Angela traces her thumb along the lid of her drink.

"About that . . . I sort of"—she presses too hard and pops the lid off—"lied."

"You lied about having friends?"

"No, I lied about the people involved," she says, slightly agitated. "They're not exactly my *friends*. My brother's programming the game, his girlfriend's handling the background art, and a mutual friend of theirs is writing the script."

I have no idea why she felt the need to obscure these details, but I don't dwell on it.

"Will I be meeting them?" I ask.

"Unlikely. They're in California at college. As creative director, I oversee every stage of the project, so if you need guidance on anything, you can consult me."

"No music or sound effects?"

"This game is a big enough beast to slay without worrying about BGM."

True. We are a bunch of amateurs.

"Why are you making an otome game?" I ask without judgment.

Angela blushes and sips her drink, only to realize her cup is empty. "My brother knows I like them. I asked if he could make me one . . . as a graduation gift."

"That's one time-consuming gift. Your brother must love you."

"You make that sound like a bad thing."

"Wasn't my intention." I clear my throat. "Do you, uh, have a deadline for all this?"

"The script is in its second round of editing. Our goal is to finalize the art by midsummer. Once the creative work is done, we'll tackle the tech. My brother interned at the same studio that published *Romancing the New Moon*. He knows what he's doing."

From behind the counter, Bora fist-pumps the air and cheers. I shoot her a look over my shoulder.

"Barring any unforeseen delays, *Love Takes Root* should be complete by spring of our senior year. My brother might make the game available for purchase across all mobile platforms. You'll be properly credited and compensated, of course. Just remember this game is first and foremost for *my* personal use."

Too bad the game can't be finished sooner. If the game were to become commercially available, it would certainly boost my college applications.

"Are Sun Hong and Meng Li the only suitors in the game?" I ask.

"Correct. They will each get their own route, and each route will have two endings. If players don't make the correct choices and earn enough love points, they get the bad ending."

"What about the MC? Will players know what she looks like?"

"No, the MC's gender identity will be neutral. That way, anyone can play and fall in love with Sun Hong and Meng Li."

"Love is love." I scoot forward in my chair. "Let's get to the nitty-gritty. The official art, what does it entail?"

"I'm finalizing a few details. We'll touch base again sometime during the first week of school."

Damn, I was hoping to get a head start before then.

"Don't look too disappointed," Angela says with a meaningful smile that manages to be both gentle and haughty. "I'll make this worth your while."

6

"DID ANGELA GET back to you yet?" Bora asks.

We're at the mall for some back-to-school shopping. There's nothing I need to buy, but I thought I'd keep her company.

"No, she's keeping me in suspense," I say.

Bora plucks a frilly pink blouse from the rack and checks the price tag.

"The game she's making sounds right up your alley," I say. "You like historical fantasy romances, right?"

Bora snorts. "I *love* historical fantasy romances. The steamier the better." She returns the blouse to the rack and exits the store. "If Angela ever needs a beta tester, she can count on me. I'll be wet and ready."

I make a face. "I don't think it's that kind of game."

"Will you be reading the script?"

"I assume so...." I join Bora on the escalator, and it spits us out near the food court. "Mind if I grab some curly fries? I haven't eaten all day."

"Only if you share."

"I was going to from the start."

Bora elbows her way through the hungry crowd as I follow closely behind her. We're halfway across the food court when she stops abruptly in her tracks. I walk straight into her and nearly fall backward on my butt.

"Who's that guy over there?" she asks as I regain my footing. "He looks familiar . . ."

"What guy?" I peer over Bora's shoulder and spot Josie a few yards away, sitting with some guy around our age. An ice cream sundae languishes between them, melting away as they talk with their heads dipped low.

"Looks like a lovers' quarrel."

"Oh, please." I hook my arm through Bora's and drag her away as my stomach growls. "Come on. I need some food before I get hangry."

Once our curly fries and sodas are paid for, we snag the last available table, which happens to be a short trek from where Josie's seated.

"Now I remember. That's Calvin Park," Bora says. "He's a junior at Bay Peak. My coworker goes to school with him." Then, after a pause, "He's hot."

"If you say so." I shrug.

"You think they're dating? Josie and Calvin?"

"I don't know when she'd find the time. She's practically married to her violin." I watch as Josie leaves the table, giving me an unobstructed view of Calvin's distressed face. He rakes a hand through his hair and mouths something under his breath. "Come to think of it, she *was* leaving the house a lot while our parents were on their honeymoon. . . ."

"Maybe their relationship is a secret." Bora whips around to see what I'm seeing. "Oh crap, he's coming over." She looks away, slurps her soda, and tries to act natural. "Lynda!" she hisses. "Quit staring."

I twirl a fry between my fingers as my eyes find Calvin's.

"Too late," I whisper. "Prepare for impact."

Bora latches on to my wrist and braces herself. She hates confrontation, and Calvin looks far from happy. Something is clearly on his mind, but I can't imagine why he'd be angry at *us*.

Calvin stops at our table. "Hey, don't mean to interrupt. . . ." He scratches the back of his head. "You're Josie's sister, right?"

"Stepsister," I correct him. "Who are you? Her boyfriend?"

"*Ex*-boyfriend," he says, a quaver underlining each word that passes his lips.

I suppress my shock while Bora releases a gasp.

Calvin shifts his weight from one foot to the other. "I was just wondering . . . did something happen? Like, at home?"

"Not that I know of." I scour my brain over everything that has happened in the past week. "We're not super close, though. I don't know what to tell you. Sorry."

"Okay . . ." Calvin scratches his nose, his forehead creasing as he tries not to blink. My eyes flick down to his shoes, and he takes that second to collect himself. When he finally finds his voice again, he says "Thanks anyway" before sulking off.

"Poor boy." Bora shakes her head. "I have this whole

forbidden romance written in my head about two people from rival schools falling in love, and now they aren't together anymore."

I throw a fry at her. "You've been playing too many otome games."

•••

Hours later, I see Josie again at dinner, and she isn't behaving like someone who just broke up with her boyfriend. She's not sad, mopey, or gloomy. She doesn't seem to be feeling anything except hungry as she serves herself more mapo tofu.

Maybe she wasn't into Calvin as much as he was into her. From the way he acted, though, something must've given him the impression that she was forced to end things. But I don't sense any animosity between her and Amy. They're trading boring tales about their day as usual.

Calvin Park doesn't seem to be on anyone's mind but mine.

And then dessert is served.

Amy pours everyone a glass of iced tea to go with the pandan cake before retaking her seat beside Dad. "I can't believe it's almost been two months since the wedding! How are you holding up, Lynda? I know it's not your apartment, but I hope you're starting to feel at home here."

I respond with a shrug. Is she really looking for an honest answer? Because I don't think she'll like it, and neither will my dad. Living here is simply routine at this point. I'm apathetic at best.

After everyone satiates their sweet tooth, Dad folds his

hands on the table and looks from me to Josie. "A few more days before school," he says with cheerful anticipation. "You know what they say about junior year."

I inwardly groan.

"Lynda, I looked over your classes," Amy chimes in. Our schedules were recently uploaded to the student portal. It's a little weird how she now has access to my student records. Although Amy's never pressured me into calling her Mom, I'm not keen about her parenting me. Aunt Mindy will always be like a mother to me. "AP Lang Comp, AP Government, and Honors Chemistry—impressive."

I'm not particularly interested in history or science. I enroll in honors and AP classes because a weighted GPA makes you more appealing to colleges.

Art is my passion. Everything else is a means to an end.

"Are you leading Art Club again this year?" she asks.

"I'm not sure." I rest my elbow on the table, cradling my face in one hand while moving crumbs around my plate with the other.

Fallbank's Art Club is a joke. Last year I was elected president. Having joined the club as a freshman, I knew the vote was more about ousting the incumbent and not about what I could personally do. Soon after my "win," it became clear that club members didn't want anyone to lead them. My ideas for fundraisers and charity auctions were met with resistance. People didn't want to make the effort. They wanted to doodle and socialize, and I was apparently "a black hole that sucked the fun out of everything."

That said, Art Club is my only chance outside of school

hours to work with traditional art mediums. After drawing and painting digitally for so long, I sometimes forget that paint doesn't dry instantly, nor does it erase easily.

"Colleges always look for extracurriculars," Amy continues, "but if Art Club's not for you, maybe you can get a part-time job. Rumor has it that Tom's going to need a new assistant around Halloween."

Tom lives three houses down from us. The small business he runs involves scalping all the toys he thinks will be popular for the season and reselling them to desperate parents.

"More importantly . . ." Amy pauses. It's the pause adults make when they're about to dive deep into their lecture. "Now's the time to be thinking about college. Reflect on what you want and why you want it. Ask yourself, *Why this school? Why this major? What does success look like in this field?*"

Yes, yes, I've heard all this before.

"Amy and I"—Dad wraps an arm around her—"we won't tell you what you can and can't pursue. We want you girls to be happy, but we also want you to be realistic." I start to nod along. "If you want to pursue a passion, then give it your all. Sometimes that means making sacrifices, like turning down your friends when they invite you to parties or waiting until college to start dating."

Dad and Amy glance not so subtly in Josie's direction.

So something *did* happen.

To cover up their indiscretion, Dad follows up with, "Now, Lynda, even though you're not interested in dating, this advice applies to you, too."

I'm asexual. Not dead.

Amy interjects before I can respond with a snarky remark. "I understand it's tempting to neglect your studies when your peers are out partying and dating, but let's do our best not to get distracted this year, okay?"

"Okaaay," Josie and I say in unison.

...

Josie and I are in bed. Although it's been a while since the lights went out, I sense she might still be awake, so I bite the bullet and take a shot in the dark.

"How long were you and Calvin together?"

A moment passes, and I start to think Josie might be fast asleep until—

"Six months," she says, her voice clipped. If she's surprised to hear I know about Calvin, she gives no indication of it. "He was walking his dog in the park, a fluffy corgi called Taro." She tacks on that detail with a hint of affection. "I thought they were cute and asked for his number."

That's a bold move. She's never struck me as the type to be so forward.

I maneuver myself onto my side to better look at her in the dark.

"We started texting right away," she continues. "Two weeks in, he asked to be official. Can I . . . tell you how he did it?"

"I'm all ears," I say, partly because I'm curious, but more because it sounds like she really wants to tell me.

"He asked me to meet him at the park where we first

met. When I got there, Taro ran up to me with a note tucked into her collar, and I'm sure you can guess what it said." Josie sounds so elated right now. All I feel for her is pity. "We managed to keep our relationship a secret until one of Mom's friends caught us holding hands outside his house and, well, you know the rest. . . ."

How unlucky.

Does this mean Amy forced her to break up with Calvin? I want to ask, but I've poked my nose far enough into her business. Josie and I don't talk often, and when we do, our conversations aren't exactly meaningful. To suddenly express an interest in her love life seems disingenuous, like I'm only digging for drama to keep myself entertained.

"I'm sorry your relationship had to end that way," I say instead.

"I'm sorry, too. I hope Calvin isn't taking it too hard." If the look on his face at the mall today is any indication, he is, but she doesn't need to know that. "Mom called Calvin a distraction even though I've been keeping up with my violin lessons. Once school starts, she wants me practicing at least three hours a day."

"Three hours a day, *every* day?"

"Ideally. She'll compromise at five days a week."

Talk about living and breathing music. Who wants Curtis more: Josie or Amy?

Art takes practice and practice takes discipline. I try to draw every day, even if it's just a simple doodle, but I don't adhere to strict schedules for the sake of hitting an arbitrary number.

"Why is your mom so militant about this?" I ask.

"Because now is the time to be thinking about college," Josie says, mimicking Amy. "Practicing five days a week isn't much of a compromise in my opinion." It's kind of refreshing to hear her express herself so candidly.

"Three or four would be meeting you halfway."

"Halfway isn't good enough. Mom spoke to a Curtis graduate who convinced her I need to follow this regimen if I have any hope of getting in. She even fired Ms. Chen."

Ms. Chen runs her own music school and has been Josie's violin teacher since second grade. I met her a handful of times—nice lady.

"How does firing her help you get into Curtis?" I ask, perplexed.

"Mom replaced her with some guy who graduated from Juilliard. He charges thirty dollars per *half* hour for private lessons. Can you believe it?"

Cue the violin screech—$30 per half hour for three hours is $180. Multiply that by five and you're paying $900 a week. It doesn't take a genius to know that's more than an iPad.

"When did your mom hire this guy?"

"Yesterday, I think?"

So *after* Henry died, and Dad refused to help replace him.

"Are you . . . okay?" Josie asks as I repeat the calculations in my head.

"No, I'm not." I pull my blanket up and turn my back to her. "Good night."

• • •

Early the next morning, I catch my dad while Amy and Josie are out. He's on the back deck preparing for tonight's barbecue. One last hurrah before school starts.

Despite my grievances over sharing a bedroom, the house is spacious, and I have more freedom than I did before. Our apartment didn't have a courtyard or garden. Here, we have a private backyard. The deck is raised about two feet off the ground with steps leading to the grass and flower beds. A lounge area made up of wicker furniture and decorative cushions occupies most of the deck, but everything's been moved onto the lawn so Dad can hose down the surface.

I grab a broom and sweep off the excess water. Lending him a hand might put him in a better mood to listen to me. It also gives me more time to mull over my approach. Last night I was tempted to barge into his room and demand an explanation as to why he and Amy could afford expensive private lessons but not a drawing tablet. Storming in guns blazing wouldn't have gotten me anywhere, though.

"Weather sure is perfect," Dad says, adjusting the hose, the stream of water tapering into a mist as he waters some potted flowers. "Hope it'll be like this all day."

I check my weather app. "Forecast says it'll be sunny and in the low eighties by four."

"Good news is what I like to hear!" Dad high-fives the air. The act is so cringey, I can't even fake a laugh. This is becoming a chore. It's impossible for us to have a conversation. "Why don't you and I finish up here and—"

"I heard about Josie's new violin teacher," I blurt out.

Dad turns off the hose. Now it's nothing but metaphorical crickets. Irritation gnaws at me the longer he stays quiet. It shouldn't take this long for him to respond unless he has something to feel guilty about. I mean, he *should* feel guilty.

"Did Josie tell you?" is all he says.

"Yeah." Was she not supposed to? Were they planning to leave me in the dark?

As I take in the backyard with its vibrant landscaping and pristine furniture, confusion clouds my mind. This house is beautiful. I'm grateful for it, really, I am. And yet . . .

"If I didn't know any better, I would've thought we were rich," I say. This is not the diplomatic approach I intended, but alas, here we are.

Dad winds the length of the hose, hooks it into place on the side of the house, and does everything except look at me.

"Amy and I agreed Josie needed a new teacher. We made the decision months ago," he says. "I know you're upset about . . . Henry, but you have a new one now. No need to hold a grudge."

I tighten my grip on the broom handle and dig the bristles into the deck. "Is there anything else I should know now that all your money is going to Josie and not your *biological* daughter?"

"Lynda, don't. Josie *is* my daughter. Amy also sees you as her own."

"Doesn't mean you two don't play favorites." I try to tamp down my temper, but every word that leaves his mouth is like drops of water on a grease fire. "Last I checked, I'm the one who had to give up their bedroom."

A few months ago, I was an only child. Now I not only

have a sister, but I have a sister who seems to get everything while I have to settle for scraps.

"We're not doing this because we favor Josie," Dad says, exasperated. "We're doing this to improve her chances of getting into Curtis. She needs the help."

"And I don't need help?" I shout over the birds, the crickets, and the blood roaring in my ears as the injustice of it all consumes me. "I've kept my grades up, I save as much of my money as I can, and when the time comes, I'll apply for scholarships. But I can't do it all on my own! So let me ask you: Where are you in this?"

I sound like a brat for wanting to go to a pricey art school while expecting my dad to foot the bill, but we had a deal. You can't support one daughter's dream over the other's and then act surprised when they confront you about it. I could *maybe* understand if Dad and Amy wanted to prioritize a doctor over an artist—but Josie's a musician!

Is her artistry more important than mine?

Or maybe . . . they think she has a better shot at succeeding. Is that it?

Dad removes his glasses and screws his eyes shut.

He's thinking. That's good. That means he hears me.

Then he takes a deep breath and says, "There are other schools, Lynda."

I fling the broom over the banister, into Amy's rosebushes, and walk away.

7

FALLBANK HIGH IS bustling with cars, buses, and bright-eyed freshmen. People are scattered across the quad and loitering in the senior parking lot, elated at the prospect of a new school year while mourning the end of summer vacation.

I miss the days when school started after Labor Day.

Once the main doors open and you walk the familiar hallways interspersed with colorful banners spouting positive affirmations, a small wave of nostalgia mixed with acceptance rolls over you—before roiling into a tidal wave when you remember you'll be confined to this place for another 179 days.

Junior year kicks off with PE first thing in the morning. Having Bora with me is my only consolation. She bumps hips with me as I enter the gymnasium.

"Be proud, Lynda. Instead of chapter tickets, I bought myself a new outfit." She does a little twirl in her pink bomber jacket covered in anime pins before bending over to show off the heart patches sewn into the back pocket of her denim shorts. "Don't I look sweet?"

"Like bubble gum," I drawl, tapping her jokingly on the butt. We hook arms, find a spot on the bleachers, and wait for our teacher to give us the same spiel as last year.

The day unfolds with AP Lang Comp, followed by lunch, and then study hall in the music room. Just a short trek from the art wing, the music room has the biggest windows in the school, nearly taking up an entire wall. Daylight floods through with blinding clarity, instilling life in this sterile place.

I spot Angela at the front of the room. We haven't talked since she approved my concept art. I'm curious as to when she'll get back to me, but I don't want to approach her and seem desperate for work. I give her a wide berth as I make my way toward the last row of chairs.

Owen King flags me over before I can sit.

"Fanny!" He gives me a low five. "What's the deal with Buncleaver? I got all hyped when you posted the chunky fella chopping onions, but I haven't seen a new post from you in a week. This better not be a case of artist's block."

Owen's my most vocal Buncleaver fan. He buys my stickers, likes every Instagram post, and always leaves a comment. Just hearts. Lots of them. To think a cartoon beaver can bring so much joy to people is another reason to keep doing what I do.

"I'm going through some things at home," I explain.

"Say no more. Not unless you want to talk about it."

"I'm good. Thanks."

"Hang in there, Fanny. Hit me up when you release a new sticker sheet."

"Will do." As I turn to finally take a seat, I sense someone watching me. My eyes gravitate toward the front of the room and land on Angela. But I'm met with the back of her head. She does that subtle head turn again, and I immediately look away.

• • •

My day concludes with Honors Chem. Gemma is assigned as my lab partner, and she acknowledges me with a courteous smile. We worked well together last year in Mandarin, so I have little doubt either of us will be deadweight. I for one am not someone who likes to do all the work in a group project, even if I am capable of it. Tomorrow, I'll have the pleasure of attending the rest of my classes. Honestly, Art & Design is the only one I'm keen on.

After the dismissal bell, I meet up with Josie outside. We meander through the crowd and cut the corner at the end of the street to where Amy's car is parked, isolated from the congestion. Amy reports to the hospital twice a week and works from home the rest of the time, so she's available most afternoons to shepherd us around.

Josie takes the front passenger seat; I take the back.

"You survived your first day!" Amy exclaims like we're a bunch of kindergarteners. "Did you two find each other at lunch?"

"Uh, yeah" is all I offer while Josie nods along.

Josie and I are in the same lunch period. I sat with Bora while Josie sat with her own friends. Our schedules drastically differ. It's unlikely we'll cross paths often.

A young man with a violin case is staked out on the front porch when we pull into the driveway. Amy hurries to greet him after a sloppy parking job.

"Your new teacher?" I ask Josie as we dawdle by the car.

She looks on warily. "Yeah," she more or less sighs. "His name's Nick Liu. He used to play for the Chicago Symphony Orchestra."

That means nothing to me. I assume he's considered a hotshot in the violin world. How else could he justify his hourly—half-hourly—rates?

Amy waves Josie over with an urgent flap of her hand while Nick's back is turned. Josie obliges, and the three of them head into the house while I linger outside to disassemble the collage of thoughts messing with my head.

• • •

A little before seven, shortly after Nick leaves, Dad texts me to announce he's home. I find his car idling in the driveway, headlights engulfing me as I approach.

"Still up for Dee Dees?" he asks, stepping out of the driver's seat.

"I guess so," I say.

Dee Dees is an ice cream shop on the south edge of town. Grabbing sundaes on the first day of school is a tradition we started when I entered kindergarten.

Dad grew up in Fallbank, while Mom hailed from New Jersey. They both attended UVA but didn't meet until after freshman year. He was home for the summer while Mom stayed in town with a friend. One night, they were in line at Dee Dees and Dad realized he'd forgotten his wallet. Mom paid for him and said he could repay her by taking her out on a date. Naturally, Dee Dees became their go-to spot. Mom would meet him at the diner where he worked and wait for his shift to end. Then they'd grab sundaes and eat them at the drive-in theater across the street. Even though Mom's long gone and the theater is now a shopping plaza, Dad likes to sit in the parking lot with me and reminisce.

I take the wheel while Dad switches to the passenger seat. After he buckles in, I look over my shoulder and reverse onto the road, driving carefully so Dad doesn't panic like he did the first time I took him somewhere.

At Dee Dees, we order via the drive-through and pull into the shopping plaza. Dad hands me a bowl filled with two scoops of coconut ice cream and one scoop of green tea ice cream.

"Cheers!" He knocks his bowl against mine before digging into his usual: vanilla bean with rainbow sprinkles. "How'd your first day go?"

"Not bad." I pop a spoonful of creamy coconut ice cream into my mouth. "My chem teacher rapped about the periodic table."

Dad rubs his chin. "Back in my day, if a teacher wanted students to think they were cool, they'd never assign homework on Fridays."

I don't know what to say, so I take another bite, then another. Finally, I settle on "Times sure change."

"Except you, me, and Dee Dees."

He sounds so sincere. I hate it. It's nice that my dad dedicates an hour every year to get ice cream with me, but he gets so caught up in this silly tradition that he forgets there are 365 days in a year, a majority of which he spends at work and I spend at school.

"I'm not so sure," I say, trying to keep my tone light and conversational. "Next year might be different."

Dad scrapes his spoon against the bottom of his bowl. "Regarding the other day, Amy and I . . . We acknowledge how our arrangement with Josie makes us look."

I stare at my ice cream as it slowly turns to soup.

"If we had the funds, we'd invest in both your dreams equally," he continues, deliberately spacing out each word to give them time to sink in. "You're both dedicated and no less deserving than the other." I brace myself. "But equal isn't always fair."

Their decision doesn't make anything equal or fair.

I'm a self-taught artist. Middle-school art classes can only teach you so much, after all. Meanwhile, Josie's been to music camp and has one-on-one violin lessons. In her defense, Josie had those things before I came along. But our parents are married now. Shouldn't both sides of the family benefit?

What am I getting out of this *family*?

I'm tempted to remind him about all my nonexistent

private tutors. Instead, I swallow my pride and keep my unproductive comments to myself.

"Josie needs guidance, and Amy felt that Ms. Chen wasn't pushing Josie to where she needs to be." Dad fiddles with his spoon. "And what I said about there being other schools . . . it's not that I don't want you to go to RISD. I'll help you, but I need you to understand that I can't help *as much* as you want me to."

Keep my options open, basically.

This is the same bullshit he fed me the other day, just with a pinch of kindness. This time, I won't argue. There's no point in talking in circles.

If getting into my dream school means I'm on my own, so be it.

8

BORA SHAKES HER head at me.

We're having lunch on the quad. It's sunny and breezy out, a good time to get some fresh air. People mill about with their lunch in hand, searching for a place to sit now that all the tables and benches have been claimed. Bora and I are perched on the edge of an elevated brick planter, home to a tangle of wilting flowers.

"Your parents need to get their spending habits together," she says.

"Whatever," I grouse, balling up a napkin and shooting it into the garbage bin. "Josie can have her fancy tutor, and I'll stop making a stink over it. Problem solved."

"Your solution is to stew in your own resentment?" Bora throws her head back and releases a belabored sigh. "You still have to live with these people, Lynda."

"Not after I get into RISD. And I will get in—without their help."

Bora eyes me skeptically as I punch my straw into a carton of soy milk.

"You believe in me, right?" I ask.

"Of course I do," she says before trailing off with an antsy look on her face. "But in case you haven't heard, Claire's also applying to RISD."

. . .

Fallbank doesn't have a robust offering of art electives. This semester, I had a choice between Art & Design, Photography, and Ceramics. I'm not a sculptor or photographer, and neither is Claire Lipkin, which is how we ended up in the same class despite our low tolerance for each other. Luckily, I've been assigned to a table by the door while she's by the window.

Claire and I are equals in terms of drawing ability. My strength is human subjects. Hers is inanimate objects. Her gouache still lifes are breathtakingly beautiful, but her personality is trash. She worships traditional art, and that would be fine if she didn't harp so much on how little value there is in digital art. In her words, "No one would spend millions of dollars on a digital painting when anyone with half a brain can save a copy of it on their phone or replicate it with AI."

My Buncleaver stickers disagree. Then again, I'm not a millionaire.

I try to steer clear of Claire given how much she gets on my nerves. I don't need to prove myself to her, but I do want to confirm if the rumor about her applying to RISD is true. Last I heard, she wanted to attend NYU Tisch School of the Arts.

We're in the middle of a shading exercise when Ms. Friedman approaches my table to observe our progress. "Lynda, I haven't heard from you about Art Club," she says, hovering over me. "Shouldn't the first meeting be scheduled soon?"

Ms. Friedman is the club advisor, and I've been dreading this question.

"I'm not . . . interested in leading it anymore." I tap my pencil against my sketchbook. "I emailed the other officers last night to let them know."

Ms. Friedman makes a sound halfway between disappointment and disbelief. "You had some ambitious ideas last year. I know you couldn't get them up and running, but if you manage to this time, think of how promising that'll look to RISD."

Someone giggles from across the room.

Although my back's turned, I know that Claire's now nudging her friend as she loudly whispers, "RISD won't take two students from Fallbank. She better have a *fallback*."

I speak up before Ms. Friedman can interject. "I appreciate the concern, Claire, but there's no *you* in NYU if you don't pass remedial math."

That shuts her up.

. . .

I can't stop thinking about what Claire said.

The day's over. I'm in the school library trying to do homework, but Claire's annoying voice keeps breaking my concentration. She's right. It's statistically unlikely for RISD to accept two students from a small town like Fallbank. My grades are superior to hers (no contest there), and while I don't have anything to prove to her, I do have to prove *myself* to RISD.

I'm almost certain Claire is as incompetent a writer as she is a mathematician. There's no reason to worry about her college essay outshining mine. It's what she'll include in her senior portfolio that rattles me. Unlike her, I don't have a personal art studio that my dad rents for me every month. Also, unlike her, I appreciate traditional *and* digital art. While digital art might be undervalued because it's too accessible and replicable, that accessibility is what allowed me to become an artist. Not everyone has unlimited access to high-quality drawing pencils and paint.

"Ready for a confab?" Angela's voice wrests me from my thoughts. She's standing over me again, like the time she caught me outside Baa Bing.

"No one uses that word here," I say, leaning back into my chair. "How'd you know where to find me?"

"Intuition and perfect timing." She drops a binder on the table, and it lands with a resounding thud. "Here are the details you've been waiting on."

"First you gave me concept art to draw. Now you want me to complete some assigned reading?" I flip through the binder and quickly eyeball the pages.

"Nothing worthwhile is easily obtained." She winks at me, and the action throws me off. It's predictably smug, but also . . . charming? "Happy reading."

• • •

At home, I review the contents of the binder.

Angela outlined everything she needs for the official art, including details like file type, dimensions, and image resolution. She also provided a mood board and reference materials to help me visualize the final product.

Backgrounds: line art to be completed by the aforementioned friend in California. Interior scenes include commoner dwellings, a bandit hideout, a bustling teahouse, an apothecary, lavish living quarters, and the throne room of the imperial palace. Exterior scenes include an outdoor market, an alleyway, a courtyard garden, a mountainside trail, a riverbank, and the front gates of the imperial palace.

Characters: line art to be completed by me. Both Sun Hong and Meng Li require a basic template where their pose remains the same but their clothing and expressions change. Each of their routes will need an event CG. With their concept art complete, their in-game files shouldn't take long to finalize. What *will* take long are the four non-romanceable NPCs.

All line art and color palettes must be approved before rendering can begin. For the sake of style and consistency, I will be rendering *everything*. All characters are to be completed by the end of April while all background art is to be completed by July.

True to her word, Angela's making this worth my while by offering me ten grand.

I repeat. Ten. Grand.

I'll receive additional payment for any major revisions she requests.

"What teenager has ten grand lying around?" Aunt Mindy balks after I call and fill her in on the latest development. "Does she deal drugs?"

I've never been to Angela's house, and now that I think about it, I don't know where she lives. If her family is crazy rich, they don't flaunt it.

"She takes too many AP classes to be selling drugs," I say.

"Yet she has time to be a project manager for a video game?" Aunt Mindy counters.

"Touché . . . And it's creative director, not project manager." I pinch the space between my brows. I'm not sure why I corrected her. "Anyway, Angela first paid me with an iPad. I doubt she's lying about the ten grand."

Angela wouldn't scam me. We go to the same school, and although I don't know where she lives, I can easily find out—if I must.

"Don't assume. Make her pay at least a third of that up front."

"I will, I will."

"Good." Aunt Mindy sighs. "What's holding you back, then?"

I purse my lips. "Until now, I've only done small projects. I've never been involved in something of this scale, and yet, here comes Angela, who not only wants me to fulfill her vision but believes I can. That's a lot to carry—all that trust."

Angela loves otome games so much, she asked her brother to code one for her. To then trust me—someone she hardly knows—to be a part of it?

It's flattering and daunting.

I have an inflated ego, but it hasn't ballooned to the point where I suffer from delusions of grandeur. As confident as I am in my ability, there's a nagging feeling that I might disappoint her. I would have to fail spectacularly for Angela to hate something I draw . . . but love and hate are a long way from each other, and I don't want my art to fall somewhere in between.

You don't get far in art because someone *likes* it.

I don't draw to be liked. I draw to be loved.

"People believe in your art, including me," Aunt Mindy says. "Shouldn't that be more uplifting than intimidating?"

I release a bitter laugh. "That says a lot, doesn't it? That some classmate believes in my art more than my dad." Aunt Mindy's aware of what's been going on between Dad and me. No offense to Uncle Ben, but she's pretty much the only family I can confide in. Despite the fact that they're siblings, I can trust Aunt Mindy not to report everything I say back to my dad.

"Lynda . . . I know Brian isn't the most expressive person, but he does care."

"He has a funny way of showing it. Anyway, this could be my first real break. If this takes off, there's no way RISD will reject me."

"You know I'm rooting for you, Lynda. Always." My throat tightens when I hear her say that. "While I wouldn't mind having you close by in Chicago, let your dreams take you where you want to be."

9

AFTER TAKING ANOTHER day to think things through, I email Angela to let her know I'll do the official art so long as she pays me in two installments: the first half to be paid up front and the second at the end, *before* I hand over any final artwork.

Angela doesn't take long to send me an amended contract detailing her terms and mine. I'm no lawyer, but I'm satisfied with what's been outlined. I'll bring her a signed copy when I see her after Labor Day.

Since I'll be tied up with this project for the foreseeable future, I use what free time I have now to build a repository of future Buncleaver content that I can post throughout the upcoming months. I don't want to let my fans down, but I also don't want to burn myself out. Self-care is important, which means I can't take on any more commissions.

"What's Buncleaver doing this time?" Josie asks, popping into our room while I'm glued to my desk, engaged in a staring contest with Henry, my hand flicking back and forth as I sketch a pair of rabbit ears.

"He's spreading marmalade on a toasted brioche bun," I respond.

"That's cute." Josie laughs. "What flavor?"

"Apricot peach."

"Buncleaver has good taste." Josie inches closer to get a better view of my screen. "Who was that ninja character you were working on a while back?"

Ninja? Oh, she means Sun Hong.

"Just an OC someone commissioned," I answer vaguely.

Only Bora and Aunt Mindy are in the loop about Angela's otome game. I don't see the point in sharing it with Dad or Amy. They didn't care enough to help me buy a drawing tablet, so why do they deserve to know about my art? As for Josie . . . she has her music, I have my art, and we should both mind our own business. I don't feel a need to hide what I'm doing from her, but I also don't feel the need to include her.

"Aren't you closed to commissions?" she asks.

"Sort of." I sigh, my way of telling her this conversation is growing tiresome.

"I see. . . ." Silence passes between us. "That guy was handsome. I could see him in an anime or otome game."

"Oh?" This conversation suddenly took an interesting turn. "You play otome games?"

"Occasionally." Josie blushes. "Now that I'm single, I have to scratch my romantic itch somehow."

I laugh despite myself. "Are you playing anything right now?"

"Yeah, I'm really into this one game called *Romancing the New Moon*."

Why does it feel like everyone I know is playing that game?

"You should talk to Bora. She's obsessed with—"

The doorbell rings, announcing Nick's arrival. Josie and I share a look.

"You should get that," I say, before turning back to my drawing.

I listen to Josie's footsteps as she pads down the hall. After a few more scribbles, I stop to rest my eyes and massage my temples, my concentration fraying as Nick's voice carries into the room. Time for a break.

Heading for the kitchen, I catch a glimpse of Nick as he unlaces his boots in the foyer while Josie patiently waits for him. Nick is somewhere in his midtwenties and seems quite accomplished for his age. Amy couldn't stop raving about him after the first day of lessons. "A prodigy," she called him.

I grab a can of Apple Sidra from the fridge and empty it into a glass, my throat tightening as the liquid fizzes. On my way back from the kitchen, I find Nick and Josie talking by the couch. Their conversation seems one-sided, with Nick prattling on about the free tickets he received to a ballet. Before I can hang a left, he steps into my path, his hand stretched toward me. I stop to stare at him.

"Can I . . . help you?" I ask, confused.

"That for me?" he says, pointing at the glass in my hand.

"No?" Why would he think that?

"The drive here was pretty stuffy." He fans himself for emphasis. "A drink would be appreciated."

Great, another Aunt Val.

Like me, Nick's an artist. He can charge whatever he wants for lessons, and judging by the designer bag at his hip and the smartwatch on his wrist, he does well for himself.

Finally, I say, "Get your own drink, Mr. Thirty Dollars per Half Hour."

Josie's hand flies to her mouth. I take a noisy sip of soda and watch as Nick's confusion transmutes into something akin to rage. It makes the experience all the more delicious as I walk away.

• • •

On Tuesday the contract is signed.

"Pleasure doing business with you," Angela says, stowing her copy in a plastic sleeve (totally on brand for her). "Looking forward to our partnership."

"Same," I say noncommittally.

We're tucked away at a table in the library stacks. Our study hall teacher wrote us a pass after we lied about needing reference materials for a research paper.

"While the deadline is April, I trust you'll check in with me as needed," Angela says.

I dismiss her poorly disguised concern with a wave of my hand. The ink hasn't dried and she's already doling out reminders.

"How did you get into otome games?" I ask as Angela leafs through a dog-eared book of essays. This question's been in the back of my mind.

Angela pointedly flicks her gaze toward me. "I started playing them when I was thirteen." She pauses long enough for me to think she's done talking, then elaborates. "I was an avid reader and loved visiting the public library. I devoured every romance book I could get my hands on—historical romances, urban fantasy, contemporary rom-coms—but then, for the first time ever, I forgot to return a book, and I was . . . too ashamed to go back."

"Uh . . . how overdue was this book?"

"Fifteen days late by the time I realized."

I can't decide if I want to laugh or scoff. "You think the library has you on a watch list because of an overdue book?"

"Let me finish," Angela says impatiently. "During the time I stopped visiting the library, I discovered otome games and was obsessed with one that required a ton of microtransactions." She winces at the memory. "After a while, common sense reigned. If I could spend an obscene amount of money on dating sims, then I could certainly return an overdue book."

"An inspiring tale of courage." I give her a round of applause, laughing as she glares at me. "Why are you into love stories so much?" And just to get a rise out of her, "Did someone hurt you and since then you've sworn off *real* people?"

Angela snaps her book shut.

Mission accomplished.

"Allow me to set the record straight," she begins. "I like the idea of other people falling in love and getting their happily ever after . . . more than the idea of me being with someone. When I play otome games, I don't impose myself on the MC and pretend I'm dating these 2D characters. I play as if I'm Cupid shooting my arrow."

"I get it. . . ." I tap my chin in thought. "It's like when your friend has a longtime crush and you're rooting for them to get together."

"Precisely. I'm glad we have an under—"

"Is that why you've rejected everyone who's asked you out?" Confusion floods her face, so I clarify. "Guys were throwing themselves at you freshman year, but you never dated any of them. That's what I heard, anyway."

A faint smile tugs at her lips. "You seem to know quite a bit about me."

I shrug. "You were all anyone ever talked about back then."

"Oh?" She arches a brow. "I caught your attention too?"

"That's not what I meant." I'm not sure why I want the backstory. I could chalk it up to being nosy, but it's . . . more than that. I guess when someone shatters your expectations of them, you go searching for answers.

"My days of superficial popularity are over." Angela tents her fingers and leans forward, her voice conspiratorial. "Now then, what's your reason?"

"For what?"

"For being perpetually single."

I choke on my spit, then start coughing uncontrollably. I try to smother the sound with my elbow, with little success. The librarian pokes her head around the corner and shushes me, as if choking is a choice.

"Didn't mean to startle you," Angela says, all innocence.

"What makes you think I'm single?" I croak.

"You strike me as someone who is."

I'm tempted to pull out a mirror to see what exactly is so striking about me. "I'm single by choice," I say. Making friends is challenging enough as it is. Finding someone you vibe with emotionally and romantically? Sometimes it feels impossible.

"No crush or anyone you've been eyeballing?"

"I haven't been remotely interested in anyone since middle school."

Cass was the class clown all the sixth-grade girls cooed over. What started as a crush soured into contempt after he went too far with a prank and made a classmate cry.

Melody was spunky and quick-witted. We had all our core classes together, and the more I got to know her, the more I liked her. We kissed on the merry-go-round during our eighth-grade field trip, but she moved away soon after, and any lingering feelings departed with her.

Since then, I haven't had the desire to kiss anyone else. My heart does flutter for others, and I do get butterflies if someone special happens to be nearby. That someone just hasn't existed in some time.

"Hmm . . ." Angela rests her chin in the palm of one hand and drums her fingers on the table. I try not to shrink from her probing gaze. "You've never been madly in love before?"

"No one in this school is worth going mad for." I shake my head. "Anyway, I don't know how we started talking about this, but I have a quiz to study for."

"You're missing out. Your fictional soulmate could be waiting for you"—she points at my phone—"right here."

• • •

Angela wastes no time transferring the first half of the payment. My phone vibrates during last period with a notification that I'm now five grand richer. Her condescending nature doesn't win her any personality contests, and in fairness, neither does mine, but I appreciate her no-bullshit approach to business.

There's a skip in my step when the bell rings. I leave through the main entrance, my good mood fizzling when I find Calvin hanging out by the bike rack. Bora and I are biking to my place for homework and egg tarts, and although I told her to meet me here, she's nowhere to be found. I'm about to turn back the way I came when Calvin calls out to me. "Sorry to bother you, but is Josie meeting you here?"

"Not that I know of," I say.

"Do you know where I can find her?"

Last I heard, Josie's catching a ride with a friend. If she wanted to see him, he'd know where to find her. I unlock my bike and roll it backward onto the sidewalk.

"I need to talk to her, but she isn't replying to my texts." Calvin does that thing again where he hops from one foot to the other, like he's in a perpetual state of fight or flight.

"What's there to talk about? You're her ex."

He flinches. "She broke up with me so suddenly . . . I

need closure, you know? Is there really nothing you can tell me? I mean, you're her sister."

Footsteps sound behind me. I glance back over my shoulder to find Bora walking in on Calvin's emotional plea. I'm baffled as to why Josie won't be up-front with him. She was openly resentful of the breakup on the night she confided in me. She has every right to pin the blame on Amy, and yet, she hasn't.

Well, if she won't put him out of his misery, I will.

"Did Josie tell you about wanting to go to Curtis?" I ask him.

"Many times. It's her dream school."

"Then you must know how much her mom worships that place." He nods. I mount my bike, keeping one foot on the ground, the other on the pedal. "She told Josie to end things with you because you're a distraction." I interpret Calvin's downcast eyes and slumped shoulders as acceptance. Then I'm off.

• • •

Bora releases a heavy sigh as we bike past perfectly manicured lawns and blooming flower beds, the landscape of bungalows and ranches interspersed with the occasional multistory statement house set far back from the road.

"No need to be so harsh, Lynda," Bora says, wind catching her hair as we accelerate down a hill. "It costs nothing to be kind."

"He was bordering creep territory. I don't get the desperation."

"Love makes people act in ways they normally wouldn't. Why do you think Romeo poisoned himself without checking if Juliet was truly dead? Because all he could think about was joining her in death."

We stop at a busy intersection and wait for the crossing guard.

"Josie isn't worth drinking poison for."

"Lynda!"

I shrink at her tone. "It's an opinion based on what I know about her."

"Do you know her, though?" Bora side-eyes me as traffic comes to a halt. "I take your silence as a no," she says before launching herself across the crosswalk.

A twinge of guilt jabs me in the chest. I pedal hard to catch up to her.

Bora's a bottomless pool of empathy while I'm a fountain that spouts unkind things until you feed me a shiny penny. Even now, as I tell her to "Please slap some sense into me if I ever act like Calvin." Just imagining myself all mopey churns my stomach.

"I suspect it'll take more than a slap." Bora releases the handlebars and punches the air.

"You wish!" I take this chance to outpace her, but my legs tire quickly, and I soon fall back in line with her.

Bora appraises me with a look. "I thought artists were romantic by nature."

"We're a practical bunch, too."

"Let's be real," she says. "You are *not* always sensible or logical." My mind instantly flashes back to throwing a broomstick into the bushes. "Lovestruck and dumbstruck are, like, statistically correlated."

"What scientific journal did you read that in?"

"Come on, Lynda. Haven't you encountered someone so stunning, you wanted to immortalize their beauty in a painting?"

"Romanticism and romance are not the same. I romanticize my subjects all the time. I love them as an act of creation, as something to admire, but I'm not *in* love with them."

Who needs romance when I have art?

If anything, my true love is art.

10

AMY INSISTS ON going out for dinner Friday night.

"We all had a busy week, and I doubt anyone wants to cook," Amy says as Josie and I pile into her car. "Besides, I feel like I barely see you, Lynda."

Ever since I signed the contract with Angela, I've been drafting hairstyles and outfits for an NPC. Once homework's done, all I do is draw until I'm satisfied.

"We need to coordinate a girls' night soon," Amy continues. "We could go to karaoke or maybe even a Korean spa."

"I don't know," Josie says, picking at her cuticles. "I'm a bad singer, and isn't mandatory nudity a thing at Korean spas?"

"Where exactly are we eating?" I ask, changing the subject.

"Why don't you pick a place?" says Amy.

"How about Han Seoul-oh?" The Korean barbecue place where Bora and I celebrated her sixteenth birthday. I haven't been back since. Thinking about their banchan and marinated kalbi triggers my salivary glands, and it seems to have the same effect on Josie, as she perks up at my suggestion.

"Korean it is!" Amy exclaims, and then we're reversing out of the driveway. "Josie, can you text Brian to tell him to meet us at the restaurant?"

I don't know what Dad's up to these days. He came home at a decent time the night we went to Dee Dee's. Since then, he's been returning at odd hours. Yesterday I heard him fumbling through the front door at midnight.

By the time we arrive at Han Seoul-oh, the place is swarming with people. The restaurant requires all members of our party to be present before they'll add us to the wait list. With my dad stuck in traffic, the situation doesn't look promising as more and more people line up. Twenty minutes later, Dad finally shoves his way through the crowd.

"I got here as fast as I could," he says, unfastening his necktie to better catch his breath.

Now that we're all here, the hostess informs us it'll be an hour wait. My stomach roars at the disappointing but not entirely unexpected news.

"Should we go somewhere else?" Amy asks, surveying the restaurants across the street. "Anyone in the mood for Malaysian? Greek? Tex-Mex?"

"Tacos and queso work for me," Dad says.

"Hold on, that place gave me food—" Before I can interject, Josie crosses the street, barely looking both ways before Dad and Amy follow.

So much for letting me choose.

"Lynda?" I turn in the direction of the voice and find Angela standing outside Han Seoul-oh, propping the door open with her foot for two older folks. I almost don't recognize her. She's like a different person with her hair down and glasses off, more like Angela from freshman year. Except, the oversize sweater with our school mascot emblazoned on it isn't something that Angela would've worn.

"Are you coming in?" she asks, making me too aware that I'm gawking.

I shake my head. "Wait's too long."

"My mom made a reservation," she says before looking around. "Are you by yourself? We can fit you in if you want." I'm taken aback by her invitation. It must be evident on my face because Angela then says, "On the condition you don't mention our agreement to my parents, of course."

The polite part of me wants to decline, but as the aroma of roasted garlic and charred meat wafts through the door, my hunger prevails.

"If you insist," I say, like I'm doing her a favor.

I shoot Dad a quick text telling him to eat without me. Seconds later, I'm settling into a booth tucked into an alcove along the back wall of Han Seoul-oh. As soon as my butt hits the cushion, Angela launches into introductions.

"This is Lynda from school," she says before turning to face me. "And these lovely people are my parents, Alvin and Grace. They prefer to be addressed by their first names, so you can skip the formalities."

Angela's S-shaped brows are identical to her mom's.

They also share the same courtly demeanor. Meanwhile, Angela inherited her dad's roundish face and catlike eyes, which I'm now noticing are more hazel than brown.

Her dad hands me a menu. "Nice to meet you, Lynda."

"Likewise," I say. "Thank you for having me on such short notice."

"Food always tastes better with more people," Grace says. "Order whatever you like."

As much as I'd like to accept her offer, I let them take the lead.

After our waiter jots down our order, another one swoops in and unloads a heaping tray of banchan, the available surface area of our tabletop dwindling with the addition of kimchi, pickled bean sprouts, braised potatoes, spicy cucumber salad, fish cakes, and stewed tofu.

This beats tacos any day.

It did cross my mind that dinner with Angela's family might be awkward, more so than with mine. But as we settle into easy conversation, I learn that Alvin is a freelance web developer who runs D&D campaigns on weekends, while Grace is a packaging engineer, a hobby baker, and the president of an online book club. Like Angela, they're ambitious and seem to operate more than twenty-four hours a day. They're funny, too, and full of interesting stories. Alvin brings me to tears with his story about a self-published author who wanted a website for their dinosaur erotica.

"Don't knock it till you try it," Angela says as I take a sip of water. "We could be missing out on an entire subgenre. I keep asking my mom to feature *T-Ex: A Roaring New Year's Special* as a book club pick, but does she listen? No."

Laughter bubbles in the back of my throat. I clap a hand over my mouth to stop myself from spitting, failing stupendously when water shoots out of my nose. Alvin hands me a tissue. I take it and wipe my face, only to realize it's a leaf of lettuce.

The whole table erupts.

With parents like Angela's, I'm not sure why she's keeping her otome game a secret. They seem so likeable. I hate to admit it, but it makes me jealous.

• • •

When Grace asks for the check, I finally sneak a peek at my phone. I have one missed call and a bunch of unread messages from my dad.

> 6:15 PM:
> **Where are you?**
> 6:20 PM:
> **Are you with Bora?**
> 7:00 PM:
> **Do you need me to pick you up?**
> 7:30 PM:
> **Let me know when you're on your way home.**

I send him a brief text to let him know I got dinner elsewhere and don't think much of it until after the Wus drop me off at home and I find Dad pacing in the living room. He points to the couch. "Sit."

There's no talking myself out of this one, so I do as I'm told.

"You're not going to ask me how my night went?" I ask dryly, though it's more a statement than a question.

"I hope you had a good time, Lynda, because what you did tonight—ditching us like that—was rude," he says, standing over me.

"I thought it was *rude* of Amy to ask me where I wanted to eat," I say without looking at him, "only to pick the same Tex-Mex place that gave me food poisoning."

The first and last time I went there, at Amy's suggestion, the enchiladas had me curled up by the toilet, puking my guts out. Never again.

Dad smacks his forehead. "Then you could've recommended something else! You're not a baby, Lynda. Use your words!" He gestures wildly at the air, miming gibberish. "Amy was trying to do something nice. Is sitting down with your family and enjoying a meal together after a busy week too much to ask of you?"

"Oh, because you haven't asked enough of me already?" I didn't want to yell, but now I'm yelling. "You think I wanted to move into this house?"

"I understand there've been a lot of changes, but, Lynda . . ." He takes a deep breath, holds it for a moment, and exhales. "You're not an only child anymore. Please think about the people around you. We're a family, and family sticks together."

What the hell. I ditch them once because I didn't want food poisoning and now my dad's acting like a mafia boss who's been betrayed by his one and only daughter.

"Sticking four people in a house doesn't make us family."

"Lynda." This is the fourth time he's said my name in the last five minutes.

Has it only been five minutes?

It feels like forever.

"Amy and Josie were gracious enough to take our last name. They're trying. Why aren't you?" Dad runs his hand through his hair. "I thought I raised you better."

I leap up from the couch, and he instinctively takes a step back. "That's the problem, isn't it?" I throw my hands up as if in surrender, when really, I'm just getting started. "You didn't raise me."

11

DESPITE LOSING MY mom, growing up, I still had a maternal figure to rely on.

Aunt Mindy attended all the school functions my dad couldn't make and signed every permission slip he forgot to sign. For years I started my mornings with her smiling face as she handed me my lunch and dropped me off at school. Uncle Ben had pickup and homework duty after school. Dad did what he could, which wasn't much, due to his demanding job.

After Aunt Mindy and Uncle Ben moved away during seventh grade, my dad promised to be home more, but his presence couldn't make up for their absence. Getting sundaes on the first day of school every year doesn't mean he isn't forgetful. Letting me go on field trips doesn't make him fun, and eating dinner together in silence isn't bonding. Just because he cut back on the overtime didn't mean he was *there*.

I didn't need him the way I needed Aunt Mindy, and I

didn't miss him in the same way I didn't miss my mom. How do you miss someone you never knew?

Tension hangs in the air as everyone in the house avoids me, and I avoid them. Amy and Josie overheard everything I said. (I wasn't exactly quiet.) I'm one pixel away from biting someone's head off, so I take my meals in my room, finding solace in digital color palettes and textured brushes. Funny how I feel more at home with Henry than with the people in this house.

. . .

Once I fine-tune the character sheet I've been working on and revisit it a week later, I submit it to Angela for review. She'll definitely have positive things to say.

"This is underwhelming." Angela's tone carries even less fervor than her words. "Your interpretation is off."

We're back at the library, hidden in the stacks with my character sheet pulled up on her laptop. She's critiquing Li Fang, a merchant who deals in both legitimate goods and stolen ones procured by Sun Hong. She described him as charming, persuasive, and pragmatic. The only thing he values more than money is loyalty. How off could I have been by dressing him in flashy robes, gold jewelry, and a sleazy grin?

"Care to elaborate?" I ask.

"Li Fang loves money but doesn't flaunt his wealth. That's a sure way to get his throat slit in his sleep"—*Excuse me for not thinking like a merchant in a fictional country*—"and flamboyant is not synonymous with charming."

"You should've said so," I say, flipping through the character notes she provided me.

"I assumed the bit about him valuing loyalty would steer you away from characterizing him as a typical greedy merchant."

I bristle at her comment.

She's right. I somehow overlooked that detail. Rookie mistake.

"I also instructed you to use Varrick from *Legend of Korra* as a reference. Have you watched the show? Varrick starts off as an antagonist but redeems himself in the last season by setting aside his inventive genius for the good of humanity."

"Thanks for the spoiler." Bora and I were supposed to binge-watch season four until wedding plans consumed my life.

"Please edit Li Fang. I'm here if you have questions." Then, as an afterthought, she says, "Don't worry. I'll pay you for the changes."

"That isn't necessary." Eyes trained on my lap, I massage my wrist as if it'll assuage my wounded ego. (It doesn't, but it eases the carpal tunnel.) "It's my fault. I should've paid closer attention to his profile."

For the first time today, Angela seems impressed. "See? Just like Li Fang, you don't sacrifice your principles for money. If we were living in an otome game, I'd award you max love points for that answer."

"That's a backhanded compliment if I ever heard one, though I have one of my own." That elicits a smile from her. "Your parents aren't what I expected them to be."

"You're not the first to make such a comment," Angela says. "Being the overachiever that I am, people often assume my parents are classic tiger parents. They support my dreams and hobbies, but they also believe in security, which is why my dad never became a dungeon master for hire, though he has entertained the idea."

"Are otome games something you want to pursue professionally?"

"Like I said, *Love Takes Root* is for my personal use." Angela turns off her laptop and nonchalantly adds, "Going commercial is more my brother's dream."

"How come you don't want your parents knowing?" I press further.

"I want this to be . . . for me." Angela meets my gaze head-on. There's a softness to her determination that I can't quite explain. "Don't you ever draw something, take pride in it, and let it be?"

All the time. I have countless doodles, sketches, and polished pieces that only my eyes have seen. Each piece sparks a happiness that I keep to myself, a kind of happiness that doesn't need to be shared with the world because what I've created is enough, and I'm enough.

Even though I haven't answered her question, Angela smiles in that all-knowing way many have come to hate, but it lacks her usual smugness and instead radiates warmth.

"I feel like you know me more than I know you." The words leave my lips before I can stop them. But once they're out there, I don't shy away from them.

"There are a lot of things we don't know about each

other," Angela says, flipping her hair. "You probably feel that way because your initial impression of me was far more negative than the one I had of you."

• • •

"Hey, Bora, what was your impression of me when we first met?"

A noodle dangles from Bora's mouth as she contemplates her answer. Her grandma just left for a beach trip, leaving Bora by herself for the week. As soon as she called me for a sleepover, I came running, armed with shrimp crackers and fire noodles.

Of course, no sleepover is complete without a blanket fort.

Bora wipes away the flaming red sauce coating her lips. "I thought you were smart, if not a bit conceited," she says, twirling her chopsticks around in her bowl.

"Come on." I bump shoulders with her before tipping my head back and scraping the last bits of fire noodles into my mouth. My nostrils flare as delicious pain ignites every nerve on my tongue. Bora passes me a carton of peach juice to neutralize the heat. "How cocky could I have been as a sixth grader?"

"We sat next to each other in math class," she starts to recount. "When I told you I didn't know what PEMDAS meant, you had this look of disbelief on your face, like *Oh, you sweet summer child.* I wanted to punch it off."

Oh. I don't remember that.

Bora grabs our empty bowls and deposits them in the kitchen sink.

I linger behind her as she washes the dishes. "Do you still think I'm . . . full of it?"

She hesitates. "Yeah? I mean, you know what you want and don't let people drag you down. I love that about you—really, I do—but sometimes you get carried away." She dries her hands before throwing a bag of popcorn into the microwave. "Anyway, what's with the sudden self-reflection? Did someone call you out and now you're insecure about who you are?"

"What? No!" I release a hollow laugh that quickly dies in my throat.

Damn it, Bora! Stop being right!

She stares at me, unconvinced.

"Okay, fine." I give in. "Angela and I have been meeting at the school library, and she said something that got me . . . thinking."

Bora gasps, scandalized. "You two have been secretly meeting?"

"Save the wild assumptions. We only met to talk about her otome game." I recap her on the details, going back to the night at Han Seoul-oh.

"Anyone who plays *Romancing the New Moon* can't be a bad person. I knew Angela had redeeming qualities." Bora flings open the microwave and empties the popcorn into a bowl. "Your ego is the size of Montana, hers Alaska."

I groan but don't object. "Can we stop talking about me now?"

"But you love talking about yourself." Bora gauges my reaction before bursting into laughter. "Sorry, yes, let's talk about me."

I snatch the popcorn from her, and she chases me back into our blanket fort.

"How's your grandma doing?" I ask.

"You know Halmoni. She's eighty years old but thinks she's in her fifties. I told her not to go on this trip because her knees have been bothering her. Does she listen, though?"

"And your parents? Have you gone back home to see them?"

"I dropped by recently to ask them to sign some forms." Bora shrugs. "Must've caught them in a good mood, because they asked me about school and even gave me lunch money."

"Signing forms and asking their daughter about her education. The bare minimum a parent can do."

Bora shoots me a meaningful look, and I resist the urge to say more. I know she doesn't want my pity or my fury, but she deserves better. So much better. Even if I did give her parents a piece of my mind, they wouldn't see the error of their ways. That's the kind of people they are, and this is the family she was born into. You can either accept them or leave them, but you can't change them.

• • •

Josie's doing homework in the dining room when I return Sunday. I place the tray of crumb cake Bora and I baked at the opposite end of the table, away from discarded scrap paper and eraser peels that continue to pile up as Josie powers through some equations.

"Welcome back," she says, gnawing on her pencil while clutching a fistful of her hair.

It's rare to see her out here and not in her practice room. We haven't talked since my argument with Dad. Despite how I feel about living here, I have no bone to pick with Josie. Now that my anger has subsided, things are just . . . awkward between us.

"Help yourself to some cake," I say before putting on a pot of coffee in the kitchen. Once I'm caffeinated, I'll be back to the drawing board.

Josie sidles up to me as I'm spooning sugar into my mug. "Mind if I have some?"

"Knock yourself out," I say, motioning toward the steaming carafe. "Need the boost?"

"I've been tackling this math problem for twenty minutes." Josie screws her eyes shut and sighs. "I don't know what I'm doing wrong. Mom's checking my answers when she gets back from the gynecologist, and if I'm still not done . . ."

Josie's a junior, and Amy still looks over her homework? That's rough.

"Do you want me to take a stab at it?" I think back to what Bora said and make a note to myself not to sound like a know-it-all. "Sometimes you need a fresh pair of eyes, you know?"

"Sure, if you don't mind." Josie nurses a cup of coffee while I work out the equation. I try to explain where she went wrong in her calculations as politely as I can, and just as I'm wrapping up, she smacks herself in the face.

"Sorry, I'm not . . . patronizing you, am I?" I ask.

"No, no. Your explanation makes sense. I get it now," she says, relieved yet exasperated. "The answer was right there, in my face."

"Don't sweat it. Like I said, sometimes you just need a fresh pair of eyes."

"And coffee."

I offer her a small smile. "Of course."

12

FALL COLORS ARE full-on rioting by mid-October, and there's a familiar nip in the air that many people chase away with cinnamon and pumpkin spice.

Angela approved my changes to Li Fang and greenlighted the fully rendered version. Since completing my first NPC, I haven't had the mental fortitude to draw. Deadlines are closing in. Chem requires endless index cards and memorization, while Lang Comp is criminally time-consuming. All this reading, writing, and studying doesn't leave me with much willpower. At the end of the day, all I want to do is turn off my brain.

I don't know how Angela manages her course load, extracurriculars, and personal side projects. She's academically gifted, sure, but even she must have a limit. The next time I see her in study hall, I ask her. How *does* she balance everything?

"Aptitude," she says as she types up an essay. I look on, unamused. "My grandparents were accomplished academics in Taiwan. Although my parents found careers outside of higher ed, they're bright and successful in their own way. Naturally, I inherited my intelligence and drive from them."

I'd usually roll my eyes, but I know she isn't gloating (although she sounds like she is and maybe she should work on that). There's no denying that she *is* smart. She knows it in the same way I know my art is good, and we're unapologetic about it.

"Are those born from low-achieving parents destined to be dumb and unmotivated?" I counter.

"Of course not, but your odds of success are greater if you win the genetic lottery. How else do you get people like Mozart composing symphonies at the age of eight?"

"Are we debating natural talent versus effort?"

"Let's not." Angela sighs in a defeated sort of way, her fingers retreating from her laptop. "The last thing I'll say is that people can be successful without working hard or possessing any talent. Luck, wealth, and institutional prejudice make a hell of an impact."

"Oh, to be born into privilege," I half-jokingly lament.

"So." Angela continues typing her essay. "Care to tell me about your parents? I heard your dad remarried."

"He married Josie Koh's mom. Their wedding was in July."

"Josie Koh." Angela says her name like she's trying to attach a face to it. "I tutored her in math freshman year." That's news to me. "What's it like now that you're sisters?"

"Not much to say." I shrug. "We're complete opposites."

"Really? You two *look* like sisters."

"Not all Asians look alike, Angela."

"But you two do! You and I couldn't pass as relatives."

I inwardly gag at the thought before ejecting it from my mind. "What I mean is, we're complete opposites personality-wise."

"You are rough around the edges. Loquacious, too. During my five months tutoring Josie, I don't recall hearing her talk as much as you do."

I roll my eyes. "So smooth of you to slip in an SAT word."

Angela completes the last line of a paragraph and taps the period key a little too hard. "What about your bio mom? Did she remarry?"

"No, cancer took her." As sympathy begins to rearrange the self-assured look on Angela's face, I tell her, "It happened a long time ago, before I got to know her."

"Was she an artist like you?"

"I don't think so."

"Is anyone in your family an artist?"

"Sort of? Josie's a violinist."

"That makes her an artist, then." Angela pauses for a moment. "Oh. 'Sort of family' is what you meant. Well, I won't pry if you don't want me to." I let my silence speak for me. "Let me try again. What got you into art?"

"I was always good at it. My dad said I was coloring within the lines and drawing shapes before other kids my age. Then I started watching anime in fifth grade, which is what inspired me to learn how to draw people."

"I assumed as much with Instagram and all. You draw a lot of anime characters and kawaii stuff." Angela chuckles to herself. "Your latest post was a hit, and judging by all the hearts Owen left you, he thought so, too." She's referring to the drawing I uploaded yesterday, the one where Buncleaver goes trick-or-treating in a purple dinosaur costume.

"Why didn't you leave me any hearts?"

"I did," Angela says defensively, missing the fact that I was only teasing. "Haven't you noticed? I heart all your posts."

"Oh . . ." Well, color me flattered.

"Anyway, Owen's hosting a party on Halloween weekend. Will I see you there?"

"Since when do you go to house parties?"

"I used to go all the time," she reminds me.

"Right . . . but then you stopped after dumping all your friends."

"My *actual* friends want to release some steam before our next Model UN event. Diplomacy can be exhausting when all you want to do is invade another country."

"Better to get wasted than sever foreign alliances."

"Are you going or not?" she huffs impatiently. Then, before I can tell her no, "I'll go if you go."

My phone slips from my hand and clatters to the floor. I bend over to pick it up and accidentally bang my head against the edge of her desk. "Ow!"

Angela stifles a laugh. The bell rings, and she packs up her things while I nurse the bump on my head. "Well, the party isn't for another week. Think about it, and text me if you need a ride," she says, hugging her books to her chest. "Party starts at seven. If you're going to be late, at least be fashionably late."

· · ·

The night of Owen's party, I don't text Angela, even though I've decided to go. I want to surprise her and see if she recognizes me. Bora wanted us to cosplay as characters from *Romancing the New Moon*. Since I decided to attend last minute, neither of us could order a costume in time, so the best we could do was improvise with clothing that suited the game's aesthetics.

We arrive at Owen's house in complementary black dresses. Bora's is reminiscent of a 1920s flapper girl: beaded tassels, a straight silhouette, and sequins—everywhere. My dress is more 1950s: an A-line with cap sleeves, a cinched waist, and gold mesh overlaying the skirt. What really completes our look are the butterfly masks I made. In *Romancing the New Moon,* Marlo Montgomery leads a secret society where all the members wear these sleek onyx masks accented in gold. I re-created those masks with some cardstock, tissue paper, and paint.

"Welcome, ladies," Owen says, sweeping an arm toward the open doorway. "Noms in the kitchen, boogie in the basement, games in the living room, and upstairs is open if you need to get away from the crowd—no naughty time!"

"Sorry, friend, no fornication for us tonight," I say to Bora, feigning disappointment as we enter a field of fog while music assaults our ears.

Nearly every surface of the house is strewn with orange string lights, shedding a warm yet eerie glow throughout. The farther I walk, the more faces I encounter—uglier, too. Claire and Calvin are huddled around the kitchen island, chatting with a trio of chipmunks sucking helium out of a balloon. They're both dressed as bananas, and judging by his arm around her waist, they arrived together.

Whatever happened to that heartbroken boy desperate for closure? Also, how do you go from dating Josie to dating someone like Claire?

"Pardon me, coming through!" I squeeze myself between Calvin and Claire to reach the bowl of punch on the center of the island. I ladle up two servings of "alcohol-free blood type B," making sure to drop a candy eyeball into Bora's cup.

"What was that about?" Bora asks after I hand her a drink and we retreat into the dining room so that I no longer have to bear witness to Claire and Calvin's PDA.

"Just being petty," I say.

"No surprise there." She pops the candy eyeball into her mouth. "Mmm, veiny."

We have our fill of pizza, sugar, and gossip. As Claire *loudly* shares a story about an antique auction her dad recently attended, boredom sets in, and my mind begins to wander.

Owen assured me that Angela was coming tonight. She has to be here somewhere.

Don't get me wrong. The world isn't going to end if she isn't here. I didn't go through all this effort just to surprise Angela. I mean . . . it would be nice if she *did* see my costume, but that's just icing on the cake. Nothing more.

Cup in hand, I excuse myself to the bathroom, only to bypass it and take the stairs to the second floor, the bass pounding beneath my feet. I expect to find people making out, but there's not a single soul in sight . . . until I hear muffled voices behind the door at the end of the hall.

Before I can press my ear to the door, it flings open and whacks my mask clean off my face, the contents of my cup splashing over me. "Screw you, Angela!"

Arun Kapoor storms out of the room and down the hall as I lie slumped against the wall, clutching the left side of my face.

"Lynda?" I hear Angela before I see her. "Are you okay?" I groan as she brushes my hand aside, gently takes me by the chin, and examines my face. "Looks like the door nicked you in the temple. . . . Do you know where you are?"

"I'm at Owen's house, my name is Lynda Fan"—I squeeze my eyes shut and rub my forehead, begging for clarity— "and I smell like pomegranate." The blurred edges of my vision begin to recede as I sit upright, my arms wet and sticky with vampire punch.

Taking a door to the face is one way to find someone.

"You were looking for me?" Angela asks, flabbergasted.

Damn it, did I say that out loud? My vision clears, and I startle at the sight of her. Hair in braids, eyes rimmed with rouge, a touch of gloss on her lips, body swathed in indigo chiffon—she's dressed as Meng Li from *Love Takes Root!*

My idea has come to life, literally.

Angela laughs as I flounder. "Surprised? That was my intention, and we all know Angela Wu never fails when she sets her mind on something." She gets up to preen her hair in the mirror mounted on the hallway wall. "I would've felt rather silly if you hadn't shown up. You're the only one here who knows who I am."

I don't know you, Angela. You confuse me.

Oh, wait, you're talking about your costume.

Maybe I have a concussion and can't think straight. My fault for trying to eavesdrop. Considering how I immediately suffered the consequences of my actions, I think I deserve to know why Angela and Arun were alone upstairs.

"So . . . what pissed Arun off?" I ask, stumbling to my feet, mask in hand.

"Tyler Louis is throwing a party at his place. Arun wanted me to go with him."

That explains why Owen's house hasn't been mobbed and I can take three steps without crashing into someone. "Arun's poaching people for Tyler's party?" I ask, incredulous.

"You missed the key word. He wanted *me* to go with him. Someone must've tipped Arun off about me being all dolled up tonight, and he incorrectly assumed I was attempting to relive my so-called glory days. Laughable, really."

I vaguely recall Angela and Arun hanging with the same crowd freshman year.

Angela reapplies her lip gloss. "You put on a full face of makeup for one night and people think you're doing it for attention." Her eyes flick to the ceiling. "To be fair, I did do it for attention freshman year, but not today."

You did it to surprise me. I catch myself homing in on her lips and swiftly avert my gaze. "About that, what exactly happened between you and, uh, basically all the popular people in our grade? You were *the* girl until suddenly you decided not to be *that* girl."

Can I be any more articulate?

Angela beckons me to follow her. "I'll gladly spill the tea after you fetch me a drink. Pick something you think I'll like, then meet me in the backyard." I make a noise that's equal parts vexed and conflicted. "I'm not asking for much, Lynda."

"Sorry, I don't think I heard a question in there."

"Get me a drink, *please*?"

"I don't usually take orders." I pass her on the stairwell and stop once I reach the landing. "But just this once I will."

• • •

The din of the party penetrates the night as I step out into the backyard, becoming a dull murmur once I shut the door behind me. The patio is brimming with candlelight from the dozen or so jack-o'-lanterns paving the walkway. I do a little dance inside when I spot a Buncleaver carving.

I find Angela seated on a stone bench and hand her a plastic martini glass filled with a bright green concoction made from lime sherbet and ginger ale, the rim garnished with a sour gummy worm. "May I present you with a sample of witch's brew, Your Majesty?"

She takes a cautious sip, then nods in approval. "You chose wisely, peasant."

"You're ruining the role-play. Why would a peasant serve

royalty, let alone be within proximity? Calling me a lady's maid would be more accurate."

"Schooling me, are you?" she scoffs. "To the oubliette with you. Guards!" Her voice melts into the shadows, her command unanswered. She clicks her teeth. "These court fantasies always sound better in my head."

"Acting isn't your forte." I tuck the folds of my dress behind me and plop down next to her. "Now that your guards have failed you, time to spill the tea."

"It's not the buzzworthy story everyone thinks it is." Angela throws back the rest of her drink before staring into the bottom of her glass. "It's juvenile, really."

Then, after a small sigh, "When I first started playing otome games in eighth grade, there was a . . . steamy one that got adapted into a novel. I was so eager to read it that I brought it with me to sleepaway camp. One day, I accidentally left it outside. Arun and his friends found it and returned it to me—after scribbling a bunch of . . . male genitalia in it." I make a face. "Delightful, isn't it? Anyway . . . they made fun of me, said only ugly girls read romance books since no guy in real life will ever touch them."

"Wow. Screw them."

"That's exactly what I *didn't* do. Instead, I sought revenge." She plants one hand behind her on the bench and leans back to look at the sky. "I didn't care that they called me ugly, but vandalizing my book? Unforgivable. So I kicked off high school by becoming the 'pretty girl.' I joined cheer and wormed my way into their circle, and the same guys who ridiculed my reading preferences were suddenly fawning over me. I threw their desires back into their faces, told them girls like me didn't date guys like them."

I release a low whistle. "When you start something, you really see it through."

Angela chuckles. "I don't do anything half-heartedly. Eventually, I'd had enough and went back to being myself after spring break."

"I take back what I said about acting not being your forte. You pulled a long con." That takes dedication and skill. I can't help but admire her for that. "Wasn't it hard, though, dropping everyone like that? There wasn't anyone worth . . . keeping around?"

"Really, Lynda? You're giving those people the benefit of the doubt? Can you even name anyone on the cheer team?"

I can't. "All I'm saying is, after all that trouble, making an actual friend would've been, I don't know, nice?"

Not that I'm one to talk, considering Bora is my only friend.

"I did enjoy hanging out with some of Arun's friends, but that was temporary, just fleeting moments of fun. In hindsight, I shouldn't have wasted my time on a revenge fantasy that could've gone terribly wrong. I was lucky things worked in my favor." Angela doesn't sound too regretful. "But I wanted to make a point. Guys like Arun can't handle rejection. The idea that someone would spend time with a fictional character over them makes them feel inadequate—as if their ego has anything to do with what I find attractive."

"And what exactly do you find attractive?" I laugh. "Wait, let me guess, you like guys who could be the main love interest in an otome game."

"I prefer girls, actually."

"Of course," I say without really hearing her. Then I pause. "Wait. You like girls?"

"I do—and boys, too. I appreciate a handsome guy when I see one, but girls? We're magical."

"I . . . never would've guessed. Not that there's anything wrong with what you read, it's just . . . most otome games, at least the ones I know, follow a straight female MC and a straight male love interest."

Angela arches a brow. "Haven't you noticed the discrepancy between what media people consume and what they want in real life? Yes, I am limited in my pickings, as many otome games do take a heteronormative approach to storytelling, but sometimes . . . games and books are simply fantasies. We indulge in them for escapism, not to shape our own expectations."

"Like dinosaur erotica," I deadpan.

"Yes, until someone invents a time machine that can transport us back to the Mesozoic era, sexy times with dinosaurs will only ever be a fantasy."

I don't know who cracks first, but Angela and I are suddenly doubled over, laughing. I've learned more about Angela in these last few months than I ever did in the two years I've known her. Strange, how life works. You can know of someone and live your life happily without them until unpredictable forces suddenly bring you together—like a cosmic shift in the universe bridging two vastly different dimensions.

Instead of resenting Luke for killing Henry, perhaps I should be thanking him.

Once the cramp in my stomach subsides, I wipe the tears from my eyes and take a deep breath. "Dinosaurs aside, thanks for sharing something so personal with me."

"You're easy to talk to." Angela raises her empty glass and waves it around. "That, or perhaps the witch's brew has cast a spell over me and now I'm charmed."

She winks at me.

A shiver rushes down my spine, and instinctively, I hug myself.

"Cold?" Angela presses her knuckles against my neck, and I flinch, my breath hitching as heat prickles my skin. She lets her hand drop. "Let's head inside before we miss the party. I need to ask Bora if she finished Montgomery's route."

We get up at the same time. I let her go first, and she lifts her tunic in a brief curtsy. As we near the back door, she stops midstride and peers over her shoulder, a smirk playing on her lips as she says, "Nice costume, by the way. You make a superb NPC."

"Oh, yeah?" I laugh. "Do I earn any love points for it?"

Angela sizes me up and down. "Two out of four, if I'm being generous. Your line art on the mask is ever so slightly crooked." Then, before I can express my outrage, she adds, "But flaws do have their charm."

13

DAD IS FINALLY ready to make peace. He catches me while I'm rinsing my mug in the kitchen sink and asks about school—completely glossing over our argument.

Going a whole month without talking to your dad seems excessive, but I didn't have to go out of my way to avoid him. We've been too caught up in our own lives to make time for each other. Not unusual for us at all, and even if we did talk, stilted conversations aren't much better. I suppose with Thanksgiving coming up, he wants to call a truce.

"School's fine," I say, flipping my mug upside down to let it dry on the rack.

The teachers at Fallbank must've conspired, because I had a slew of assignments due yesterday. It takes a special kind of evil to schedule deadlines on Halloween. Any procrastinator who attended Owen's party must've been cramming. I feel bad for Josie. She wanted to go with me but flunked a math quiz, so Amy made her stay home.

"How's your art coming along? Amy tells me you're always in your room," Dad says good-naturedly.

"It's coming along."

Dad leans against the fridge and nods to himself, oblivious to the fact that this conversation is going nowhere. "Working on anything interesting?"

"I guess." *Everything I draw is interesting, at least to me.*

"Whatever you're working on, I'd love to see it."

"I'll think about it." *Yeah, no.*

I don't begrudge Josie for her private lessons—not anymore. Firing Ms. Chen in favor of Nick wasn't her decision. If Dad's prioritizing Josie's music over my art, then he doesn't deserve to see it. Don't use my art as a conversation starter to bond with me when you don't respect it as my lifelong passion. Don't tell me you support my choices and in the same breath say you can't help me achieve my dream because you're helping Josie achieve hers.

"A little help, Brian?" Amy shuffles into the kitchen, hunched over by the weight of the groceries in her hands. "Hi, Lynda," she says, brightening as she looks at me, then at Dad, all hope and unrealistic expectations. Whatever she thinks happened between us did not happen.

I scratch my neck and give her a lazy wave. "Hi."

"We're having cold sesame noodles and fan tuan tonight," she says. "Dinner will be ready by six-thirty if you'd like to join us."

"Sure . . ." I tug at the collar of my shirt and continue picking at my neck. "Thanks for letting me know."

While Dad and Amy unbag the groceries, I take the chance to slip out—but not before I hear Amy ask, "Do you know the Wus? They live on Keffer Drive."

I slip behind the wall and listen.

"The Wus?" Dad says. "No, don't think so."

"I dropped by the library earlier and overheard the front desk talking about how Grace and Alvin Wu donated three grand to revamp the library's collection."

I haven't borrowed a book from the public library since elementary school. Still, go Grace and Alvin for giving back to the community!

"They should've earmarked that money for replacing the carpet," Dad says. "Those rust stains on the second floor have been there since I was a kid."

Leave it to my dad to criticize how someone else spends their money. I doubt Alvin and Grace took out a loan for their honeymoon.

I sink into the living room couch and text Angela. *Heard about the donation your parents made. Hopefully the library spruces up their romance collection.*

Although I've had her number for a while, most of our communication outside of school has been via email. She said I could message her about anything, but I've held off. Until now.

Angela surprises me with an immediate response. *Can't wait for all the enemies to lovers, friends to lovers, and fake dating books!*

I write back right away. *I'm not a big reader myself, but when are you sharing the script for LTR? I want to learn more about Meng Li's route.*

No love for Sun Hong? Everybody loves a handsome thief with a tragic backstory.

He's cool, but Meng Li's childhood friends with the MC. I like that better than the bad boy trope.

Duly noted.

So . . . when can I read Meng Li's route?

Our contract didn't stipulate any conditions regarding the script. I'm only responsible for the art, but I'm sure reading the actual story would give me a stronger understanding of the characters. Angela did say the script was in its second round of editing.

Nine minutes go by without a response. Then twelve. Knowing Angela, she's probably in the middle of a chess tournament or completing an application to intern at NASA. Or, I don't know, taking a bathroom break. I don't see how anything I wrote could've put her off.

I wasn't that pushy . . . was I?

This is ridiculous. *I'm* ridiculous.

Why am I wasting away on the couch, overanalyzing our conversation? Not everything warrants a lightning-fast response. People have lives, and I should move on with mine.

I start to get up, but then my phone dings and Angela's name appears in my notifications. My heart stutters despite myself. After a deep breath, I read her message and frown.

Shouldn't you be drawing?

. . .

I channel all my energy into my next character sheet.

This time, I'm drawing Yu Xiaohua, a palace maid who closely serves the empress and is described as humble and efficient, unassuming yet observant. Because she's a servant, people pay her no mind when trading royal gossip. I want her to be doll-like and petite since people often associate small stature with submissiveness, but I can't pin down her personality. Is she observant in a cunning way? Is she unassuming because she's plain?

This is exactly why I need to read the script. It would eliminate all the guesswork. I could ask Angela for clarification, but I want to get the character right without her help. She's given me creative liberty because she trusts my vision, and I want to prove to her that her trust wasn't misplaced, especially since she hasn't expressed the same level of enthusiasm since I did the concept art for Sun Hong and Meng Li.

Her reaction that day at Baa Bing is all the motivation I need.

I roll up my sleeves and crack my knuckles.

I can do this.

I don't draw to be liked. I draw to be loved—not that I want Angela to love me. I want her to love Xiaohua as much as she loves Sun Hong and Meng Li.

That's all.

14

"LYNDA, WAKE UP."

I pry my eyes open and wince at the harsh fluorescent lights beaming down on me. It's only first period and already I want the day to be over.

Bora tosses a pair of yoga pants into my face, the impact nearly knocking me off the locker room bench. Slowly but surely, I change my clothes.

"Pulled an all-nighter?" Bora asks, crouching down to tie her sneakers.

"Yeah" is all I muster as we enter the gymnasium. We find our assigned spots and start stretching. I am not looking forward to running laps on the track. I'm not sure if I can even walk a straight line without succumbing to fatigue.

Last night I was so engrossed in Xiaohua, by the time I finished drawing, it was three a.m. I'll let her sit for a day or two before sending her to Angela. It feels wrong to deliver Xiaohua so soon when Li Fang's character sheet took me longer, but something about her lit a flame in me. I was hyperfocused. Transfixed, even. Like my hand was moving on its own. That said, something might seem perfect upon completion until you revisit it later.

Sleep deprivation doesn't help either.

I overslept and missed breakfast and the first bell.

Bora and I are planking when she says, "Ready for your quiz today?"

My arms give out and I collapse onto my stomach. "What quiz?"

She stares at me, mirroring my confusion. Then panic creeps in.

Oh crap. I have a chem quiz today.

After reviewing my planner and realizing I am completely unprepared, I skip lunch to cram in the library, which turns out to be a mistake because I'm starving by study hall. The first thing I do is ask Owen if he has food.

"Nah," he says, shaking his head, "not unless you want a mint."

"I'll take anything," I tell him.

Seconds later, I'm savoring a peppermint swirl while cramming concepts into my brain: covalent bonds, ionic bonds, cations, anions, polarity—

"Here." Angela hands me a bagel with cream cheese, bundled in plastic wrap. "I overheard you and Owen and decided to hit the cafeteria."

I swipe the bagel right out of her hand. "You're a lifesaver. Thank you!" For the sake of decorum, I take small bites, when really, I want to shove the whole thing down my throat.

Angela eyes my chem notes and lends me an encouraging smile. "Good luck."

• • •

Thanks to Angela, I didn't have to spend last period doubled over my desk, crippled with hunger, while racking my brain over chemical bonds.

"It's not like you to forget," Bora says after I tell her how the quiz went. We're in the lobby, waiting in line for a bake sale hosted by the Film Club.

"You know how I get when I draw." Then I ramble on about wanting to impress Angela and relive that day when she gushed over my art. "Since then, I haven't seen her light up like—like a firework on the Fourth of July! I want everyone to adore my art, but it's . . . more than that. I also don't want to disappoint Angela. Does that make sense?"

Bora gapes at me, speechless.

"What? Is there something on my face?" I feel my cheeks. My skin is warm and slick with oil. Nothing a tissue can't fix, and while my jawline is clearing up from a recent breakout, I don't understand Bora's reaction.

"Lynda." She claps a hand on my shoulder. "You're my best friend and I love you, but holy hot dog on a bun, are you dense sometimes."

I know I can be hotheaded and stubborn.

But dense? How?

Before I can ask Bora what she means (which I suppose proves her point), she steps forward to buy half a dozen snickerdoodles. She's here for the cookies, while I'm here for the cranberry scones. After I do my good deed for the day by helping the Film Club with their fundraiser, I hear Angela calling out to me.

"Look who it is," Bora says as Angela advances. "The source of all your motivation."

"I wouldn't word it like that," I mutter.

She shakes her head and laughs. "Anyway, I have somewhere I need to be." Then she darts for the exit.

"Where are you going? I thought we were—"

"Hey." Angela arrives before I can chase after Bora. I can feel the cold emanating off her clothes as she says, "You should try checking your phone after school. I was outside looking for you."

"I left it at home." One more thing I forgot in my mad dash to get to school this morning.

"Did you need something?"

"I wouldn't say *need*, but . . . would you be interested in coming over to my place?"

"Like right now?"

"Yes, my dad's outside. He's doing a seafood boil tonight and said I could invite you."

"Just me?" I ask. Angela nods. That's flattering. What makes me so special to receive this exclusive invitation? What about her friends from Model UN?

"Don't overthink it, Lynda," Angela says, reading my thoughts. "Priya is allergic to shellfish, Holly has cross-country, and Mason doesn't like to socialize if he doesn't have to. So that leaves you."

"Oh." I blush. *Am I that transparent?*

"Don't look so forlorn either. I need my lady's maid with me to crack open the crawfish and crab legs. You think these dainty fingers of mine can withstand such labor?" She twiddles her fingers for emphasis.

A sarcastic comment seems fitting right now, but I give in to her whims.

"Lead the way, Your Majesty."

• • •

Angela lives in a ritzy town house community on the northeast side of town. Dogs with majestic coats and elongated snouts roam about in a spacious fenced-in field. There's also a private tennis court, pool, and playground. The three-story housing units alternate between stucco and brick, flaunting more windows than I'd know what to do with. Every car in the driveway is a luxury brand, and I'm stepping out of one as we speak.

It's no mystery how Angela can afford to pay me ten grand.

Alvin unlocks the front door. After taking off our shoes, we traverse a narrow foyer and ascend a short flight of stairs to the main floor.

Everything here screams chic, from the cream-colored furniture and patterned rugs to the marble kitchen counter and stainless steel appliances. Above the digital fireplace hangs a giant painting of a little girl reading a book on a balcony that overlooks a garden—innocuous at first until you notice the macabre illustration in the girl's book and how the rosebushes seem to be weeping over a decaying finger protruding from the ground.

"My mom has unique taste," Angela says as I hunt for more grisly imagery hidden in the painting. "This is the tamest piece in her collection. She's a fan of surreal horror in the vein of Hieronymus Bosch and Jeff Lee Johnson."

"*Unique* is—" I start to say something, then think better of it.

"Is your mom an art enthusiast?" I ask instead. "She and I might have a lot to talk about." I'm not a walking encyclopedia of art facts. However, I know enough to sustain a conversation.

"She's not artsy per se," Angela says thoughtfully. "She appreciates certain aesthetics but isn't knowledgeable enough to speak on them. In other words, she likes shopping more than she likes art history."

I suppose that applies to most people.

"Dinner will be ready at six," Alvin says, donning an apron and a pair of kitchen gloves. "Until then, don't do anything I wouldn't do."

"Like homework?" Angela quips before bounding up a staircase tucked farther back in the house. There's a bounce to her step that I inexplicably find myself mimicking.

I'm baffled by Angela's willingness to let me see into her life—welcoming me into her house, inviting me to dinner with her family, and hiring me to work on a personal project with her. Home is an intimate place I rarely share with others. It's not what it used to be now that I live with Amy and Josie.

Still, it's where I am most candid—like an unfiltered photo. Everything is natural and imperfect. One visit to someone's house can reveal so much, and I've already gleaned some unsurprising yet interesting information today.

Angela sweeps in front of me once we reach the second floor, her hand pressed against a door as white as a freshly painted picket fence. "Welcome to my humble abode."

All at once I'm greeted by the color of her bedroom walls, my mind flashing back to July.

Dusty rose. We meet again.

"Is something wrong?" she asks. "You made a face just now."

"Sorry . . ." I shake my head to dispel the wedding memories. "The walls remind me of the bridesmaid dress my stepmom picked for me," I explain. "It was hideous."

"I hope you're not implying my room is ugly."

"Quite the opposite, actually." The birch furniture and sparing use of floral motifs lend a modest elegance to the room. "I'm an artist. I know good taste when I see it."

What I don't know is why I'm jumping to reassure her.

Angela smirks at me. "Way to stroke your own ego."

Oops. I did come across that way, didn't I?

"You're making a face again," she says, chuckling. I school my expression, which only seems to amuse her more. "Don't worry, no offense taken. I stroke my ego all the time. That is, when others aren't doing it for me."

She tosses her cardigan onto her bed, and my eyes dart across the quilted sheets to the bookcase nestled under the window, packed with manga and paperbacks.

"Don't go poking your nose into my stash," she says in a singsong voice, "not unless you want to be titillated."

"Are you trying to warn me or entice me?" I laugh.

Deep into the recesses of her room, there's a cozy study nook furnished with a long desk pushed up against the wall like a bar counter. Sleek shelving units run the entire length of the nook, holding knick-knacks, anime figurines, and books with their spines turned inward.

I would kill for a space like this.

Angela sits down and unzips her backpack. "Homework first? Fun later?"

I drop into the chair next to her. "Sounds like a plan."

"And save those bake sale goodies for later," she says. "Don't spoil your appetite before tonight's royal banquet."

"Of course, Your Majesty." I dip my head in a small bow.

We fall into an easy rhythm. Angela types up a report while I punch formulas into my graphing calculator and scribble numbers in my notebook. There is comfort to be found in the clicking of her laptop and the sound of graphite on paper. Occasionally I catch Angela glancing in my direction, and she catches me just the same. Like a game of tag—silly and childish yet lighthearted fun.

Despite my exhaustion this morning, I feel energized and giddy as I smile into my math homework. That is, until Angela slides a flyer my way.

"Are you participating in this?" she asks as I read over the details.

The Art Club, now led by Claire Lipkin, is hosting a charity auction during winter break. Various paintings and sculptures will be up for bidding, the proceeds to be donated to Art Is a Gift, a countywide nonprofit that hosts free art workshops for those with special needs. A lovely idea that I fully support—except I thought of it first.

"I have no affiliation with the Art Club," I mutter, returning to my homework while my mind dives into an abyss of violent fantasies. I want to grab every event flyer out there and use them to sculpt a paper-mache head that may or may not resemble Claire—and smash it.

"You mean you have no affiliation *anymore*."

Since there's no use hiding things from Angela, I fill her in on my history with Claire. Not only are we vying for the same school, but she's also now replaced me as Art Club president and is stealing my ideas. Not just stealing but executing them with the support of other club members, which I failed to do.

"That is infuriating," Angela says. "Shouldn't Ms. Friedman recognize it was your idea?"

"Probably—what's she going to do, though? It's not like I invented charity auctions." I release a heavy sigh. "What boggles my mind is the same people who rejected my ideas are now listening to *Claire*. Why? If I'm a stick in the mud, she's, I don't know, a sword in a rock."

"Maybe new people joined, and she rallied enough club members to make this work. Also, just because the auction is happening doesn't mean it'll succeed."

I would love for Claire to fail, but the auction is for a good cause. I came up with the idea because I wanted to help Art Is a Gift. A personal vendetta shouldn't change that. At the same time, though, I can't extinguish the spite roiling inside me. Life would be easier if I were the type of person who didn't hold grudges.

But I'm not.

"Honestly, I wouldn't care as much if Claire weren't applying to RISD," I say. If the Art Club were to catch the attention of the local paper, Claire could have me by the throat.

"What exactly do you want to study in art school?" asks Angela.

"Maybe 2D animation? I'm on the fence about 3D. If I ever got to do concept art for a film, that would be a dream come true," I muse. "I'm also interested in illustration and graphic design, so in short, I'm not married to any particular specialization."

The art world is competitive. From the industry discourse I follow online, animation is nearly impossible to break into, and those who do get in are usually overworked and underpaid. Still, I want to give it a shot. There's much to learn and plenty to explore. I'd like to create my own storyboards and shorts someday—among many other things that Fallbank can't offer. RISD isn't number one when it comes to their animation program, but some people say you don't even need a four-year degree to work in animation, just a strong portfolio and excellent people skills. . . .

"Why RISD?" Angela clicks the trackpad on her laptop and scrolls through their admissions requirements. "Did you visit their campus and fall in love?"

"I've never been. Bora and I are planning to visit during spring break, though. As for why . . . Well, they're a top-rated school. Getting in would be proof that I'm an exceptional artist."

"Do you need a school to tell you that? People pay for your art now."

"But RISD is *the* art school. Think of all the connections I could make. A lot of artists I follow graduated from there and they all speak highly of their experience. One's a 3D modeler for Disney, and then there's that lady with the funny pen name whose webtoon is getting a movie adaptation."

Angela purses her lips. "I see where you're coming from. It's just . . ." She sighs. "It just seems like a shallow reason for something you consider your dream school."

Excuse me? Nothing about my dreams or motivations is *shallow.*

Why is she even questioning me? Is it because she doesn't think I have what it takes to get into RISD? Have I not . . . done enough to show her what I'm capable of?

It has been a while since I last wowed her. . . .

Everything around me dulls to gray as my thoughts slowly come to a standstill. In that moment of quiet, all I hear is my dad.

There are other schools, Lynda.

And then I snap.

"Well, Ms. Know-It-All, since my reasons aren't good enough for you, why don't *you* tell me about your dream school? Should I even bother asking? After all, whatever elite school you pick, Mommy and Daddy will pay for it, no questions asked."

As soon as I'm done, I know I've gone too far.

Angela stares at me, eyes wide, caught between hurt and shock.

My anger recedes and regret descends upon me. "Sorry, I . . ." Just seconds ago, I couldn't stop talking. Now I'm lost for words.

I take the easy way out and run.

15

"LYNDA, WAIT."

Angela's voice is firm yet soft, anchoring me in place as I reach for the front door. Torn between the desire to flee and the need to repair the damage I inflicted, I stand there, wallowing in my indecisiveness as the silence expands between us. I want to fix this, but my thoughts keep colliding with one another, scrambling my brain, congesting my throat with words that can't seem to form. Suddenly, it's hard to breathe.

Am I jealous of Angela? Of her so-called aptitude and family?

If not, how could I use them against her?

Ugh. There I go again, lashing out. What's wrong with me? I don't want to put other people down to lift myself up. Maybe that's the kind of person I am, though. Otherwise, I would've kept all those awful thoughts to myself.

"Hey." Angela touches a hand to my back. "How about I make some tea and we talk this out? Besides, it's freezing out, you're miles away from home, and you don't have your phone."

She makes a good point. Several, actually.

"You're right," I finally say, lifting my eyes to hers. Even though I was the one acting out, she's the one trying to mend things. "I wasn't thinking."

"I don't care about being right. What I care about is this misunderstanding we're having." Angela loops her fingers around my wrist and escorts me back to her room. I feel like a lost puppy trailing after her. "Now then, how would you like your tea?"

"However you make yours." I'm not in the position to be telling her what to do.

"I'll pick what I think you'll like, then."

Several minutes later, after I've steeped long enough in my thoughts, she returns with a serving tray laden with a porcelain tea set. I rush to clear the table for her.

"Hope you like Assam," she says, picking up the teapot. Steam emanates from the spout as she pours me a cup. "Help yourself. There's sugar, oat milk, and honey."

"Thanks." I take the cup from her and try not to spill anything as my nerves rattle down my arm and into my fingertips. I drop two heart-shaped sugar cubes into my tea, nearly missing the first time, and stir. "You really went all out."

"My way of compensating for what I said. It was . . . insensitive of me to invalidate your aspirations."

"Still, I overreacted." Now that I've calmed down, I owe her an explanation. "Sorry for blowing up like that. Things between my dad and me have been . . . rocky."

I start from the beginning, when Dad introduced me to Amy—and the whirlwind that followed. I mention the agreement we had, how he'd do his best to help me pay for art school if I also did my best. Then, with restraint, I tell her about Josie's new violin teacher before finally concluding with Dee Dees. Dredging up the past unearths my resentment. My chest heaves at the weight of it, and I do my best to tamp down those unpleasant feelings before they overtake me again.

For my sake and Angela's.

Listening to my family problems is awkward enough without me yelling. I don't want to burden her with too many details. Hopefully she has enough backstory to understand where I'm coming from. I *want* her to see where I'm coming from.

"When you made that comment about RISD, all I could think about was my dad and how it seemed like you were unknowingly siding with him." I twirl a sugar cube between my thumb and forefinger, and when the edges start to melt, I drop it into my second cup of tea. "But that was me projecting."

As much as I hate to admit it, I'm projecting a bit of Claire onto Angela as well. If Claire did get into RISD, I bet her parents wouldn't hesitate to hand her their credit card. Meanwhile, if I were offered a place in their freshman class, I'd have to worry about whether I could afford it.

Yet, *not* going isn't an option. If I'm willing to go into debt for a school, I should have compelling reasons for attending. Are my reasons for wanting this so badly . . . superficial? People have gone to college for less.

Angela cradles her face in her hand and drums her fingers on the table. Her lips part, and my body seizes. I curl my fingers around my cup and brace myself.

"Your parents didn't do you or Josie any favors," she says, the *tap tap* of her fingers petering out with each word. "They should've realized they were pitting you two against each other by hiring that teacher, even if that wasn't their intention. It was unfair to the both of you."

"Equal isn't fair, is what my dad said. He doesn't think I need the help."

That's how he's always been. In the past, it was work first, Lynda last. Now Amy and Josie come first and Lynda last.

Angela takes a dainty sip of tea. "Prestige is nice and all, but at the risk of sounding patronizing, I'm confident you can do well at any art school."

I steel my expression and suppress the happiness swelling inside me. "I feel like you're a guidance counselor padding my ego to make me feel better."

"I'm being sincere. Just remember . . . no matter how talented you are, RISD might not want you." Angela's expression darkens. "You can do everything right and still fail."

It's a hard pill to swallow, but not one I haven't taken before.

"Dreams don't end because you didn't get into your first choice, not unless you want them to," she continues. "Your stepmother's fixation with Curtis is unhealthy, although I can somewhat understand the reason behind her obsession." Angela shifts uncomfortably in her seat. "Based on our tutoring sessions, Josie's grades aren't going to get her anywhere—not anywhere she wants to be, anyway. All she seems to have is her violin."

Art is all I have, too. It's what I want to do for the rest of my life, but I understand what Angela's getting at. Although I have no intention of giving up art, if I had to choose something else, there are other things I could learn to excel at. I wouldn't be completely lost. Meanwhile, Josie's never struck me as someone who likes school. If not music, what else?

"What about you?" I probe Angela with my spoon. "What do you see yourself doing after graduation?" This time, I'm not asking out of spite.

"Not sure," she says, sitting back, hands folded behind her head. "I'm not interested in law or medicine, and finance sounds like a slog. Long story short, I'm still figuring it out."

That's shocking. I could totally see her as some hotshot lawyer or neurosurgeon. This whole time I assumed she was working toward a goal in her ten-year plan.

"Does that mean you don't have a specific school in mind?" I ask.

"Nope." She doesn't seem ashamed to admit it. "I still have a year to decide. I'm not in a rush, although . . . I'm no closer to an answer now than I was sophomore year. I guess . . . that's why I wanted to know why you're so determined to get into RISD." She graces me with a timid smile. "Maybe I was projecting, too."

A small, almost inaudible laugh escapes me. "We really are alike, huh?"

"And yet so different." A rumbling sound erupts from

Angela's pocket. She checks her phone. "Banquet's ready. Dad says to wash our hands."

It's already six o'clock. Where did the time go?

We start for the door.

"Just for today, Lynda, you won't have to sully your hands. I'll peel your seafood for you. I'll even feed you airplane-style."

"I'll peel yours if you peel mine?" Fair is fair.

"That sounds highly suggestive." Angela cuts in front of me on the stairs, a sly grin on her face. "Are you flirting with me?"

I'm too flustered for words, like my breath has been stolen from me. My face is a blank canvas, but internally I'm screaming, scrambling for a witty comeback.

Then she leans in, her breath featherlight against the tip of my nose. "Well, if you are . . . I like it."

16

AFTER SCHOOL THE next day, I tag along with Bora as she runs errands.

"If that wasn't a come-on, I don't know what is." Bora cackles, slipping a book back into place in the young adult section of the Fallbank Public Library.

Yesterday ended on a high note. Grace returned from work in time to join everyone for the seafood boil Alvin single-handedly prepared. Everything was served on banana leaves that spanned the entire dining table. We ate our weight in clams, crawfish, mussels, and shrimp while chatting about everything and nothing. There's something about Angela's parents that make them so easy to be around.

Bora hands me a pile of books to hold while she continues browsing the shelves. "Angela sure is forward. First she treats you to Korean barbecue, then an all-you-can-eat buffet."

"Angela's just being friendly," I say.

"She encouraged you to flirt with her. What kind of friend does that?"

I follow Bora upstairs to the new display in adult fiction. "Don't you flirt with me sometimes?"

Bora guffaws. "Have I ever gazed longingly into your eyes and talked sexy to you?"

"Not that I recall."

"Then I've never flirted with you."

"Okay . . . so Angela was teasing. You and I tease each other."

Angela isn't very approachable, but she's thoughtful and quirky once you get to know her. It would be easy to mistake her sense of humor for flirting, and I don't want to assume she's into me just because she's bi. She probably has very high standards anyway.

Bora sticks out her tongue and blows a raspberry, attracting the attention of other patrons. "Fine. Let's assume she was *teasing*. She was at least receptive to you flirting with *her*. She said she liked it, for crying out loud."

"I wasn't flirting with her." Bora shoots me an incredulous look. "I didn't *intentionally* flirt with her." Angela has this magical way of getting me to engage, to be silly and honest. What's going on between us is nothing more than harmless banter.

Bora flips through a paperback with two women on the cover waltzing on top of a giant wedding cake. She adds it to the pile in my hands and thumbs through more books. "Let's forget about Angela for a sec. How do *you* feel about her?"

"I enjoy hanging out with her. . . ." I trail off until Bora urges me to go on. "Our dynamic isn't the same as when I'm with you. I also haven't felt the urge to . . . kiss her."

I liked hooking arms with Melody and relished those delightful flutters whenever she touched my shoulder. While we did kiss, I recall wanting us to *be* more but not necessarily wanting to *do* more.

"You are vanilla—not that there's anything wrong with that. We can't all be into bodice-rippers," Bora says way too loudly. "Sexuality is a spectrum, and sometimes the slow-burn romances are more intense than the smut—"

"Bora, this is a library."

"I know, and what we're having is a book discussion." She speed-reads a random page of a hardcover titled *Acing Love* and then recites a line: "'Seeing her there in the rain, water droplets glistening in her hair . . . I didn't know if I wanted to kiss her. But I also didn't *not* want to.'"

I rub my temple. "What does that even mean?"

"Romantic attraction can be bewildering and amazing. Are you always this bad at reading comprehension?" Bora says with mock outrage as she insistently taps her finger against the book. "You need to read this."

"When am I supposed to find time for that?" I haven't read a book for fun in ages, and if I had to pick a genre, it wouldn't be romance—with its unrealistic expectations and even more unrealistic happy endings.

"You'll make time. That sentence was too on the nose to be a coincidence. Maybe the characters in this story parallel your life."

"Give me a break." I haul her books to the self-checkout station.

"As someone who cares about you and will root for whoever your love interest is, I'm simply suggesting some . . . educational resources for you." Bora scans the barcode to *Acing Love* and slides it toward me. "Do it for me, please?"

I stare at *Acing Love* with its minimalistic cover of a report card marked with hearts instead of letter grades. Sighing, I grab the book and slip it into my bag.

• • •

Nick, Josie, and Amy are in the living room when I return. I acknowledge them with a small wave before retreating to my room as Nick rambles on about the winter recital. I toss my copy of *Acing Love* onto my bed and turn on Henry.

After giving my eyes a little time to adjust, I'm happy with how Xiaohua turned out. Her petite stature makes a humble impression, while her military posture alludes to her efficiency as a royal servant. It's her slightly arched brow and sweet yet secretive smile that reveal a hidden nature. The more I admire her, the more confident I am that Angela will approve. Unlike Li Fang, Xiaohua will impress the first—

And then I see it.

How Xiaohua and Angela look alike. They aren't the same height or weight, but Xiaohua's face is basically a cartoonish rendition of Angela's. There's no mistaking it.

I slump into my chair, my feet hitting the wall as my arms dangle uselessly beside me. My mind is a feedback loop of what, why, and how.

What is wrong with me?

Why am I drawing Angela?

And how did I not notice this sooner?

I try to remember where my mind was when I envisioned Xiaohua but fail to retrieve the memory. Maybe reasons don't matter. Angela occupies so much real estate in my head, and rent-free, at that. As I'm thinking about her now—how she annoys me, surprises me, delights me, and charms me—I realize that . . . while I don't want to kiss her, I also don't want to *not* kiss her.

I snatch *Acing Love* off my bed and start reading.

•••

Perhaps to no one's surprise but mine, after staying up all night to finish *Acing Love* and relating a little too much with the main character, I realize I'm crushing on Angela.

Crushing on her badly.

Angela's my client and my boss. I shouldn't mix business with pleasure by acting on my feelings, and for all I know, she might not reciprocate.

"Oh my god, Lynda." Bora is not shy about expressing her exasperation after I call her and spill my heart out. "Angela likes you. I repeat, Angela likes you!"

"But I have so much to do as it is with school and the otome game." I haven't told Bora about Xiaohua. "I might lose focus if we start dating."

"Not like you're focused now. Better to act than continue to let this distract you."

Curse you, Bora, for being right. What would I do without you?

"If you need more time to collect your feelings, take it," Bora says, "but you're making this harder than it needs to be. Asking her out isn't asking for her hand in marriage, and remember, the early bird snags the worm."

"*Gets* the worm."

"You know what I mean. Don't keep delaying. Be too indecisive and someone else will make the decision for you. Also, if you're coming to me for emotional support, I'd appreciate it if you'd follow my advice."

Ouch. Can't fault her for saying her piece. Still . . .

She carries on. "Anyway, I'm glad you enjoyed the book. How many stars would you rate it?"

"Four out of five," I say. "I would've given it full marks if it hadn't taken a hundred pages of pining for the MC to act on her feelings. Talk about frustrating."

Bora snorts. "Jeez, Lynda, imagine how I feel."

17

EVEN IF ANGELA does like me back, I don't know if I want to change what we have now. I don't want to compromise our partnership because of a bad romance.

Also, I really do need to focus on school. I don't want to slack off, let my grades slip, and then have my dad use that against me. But if I don't act on my feelings until senior year, I'll probably lose whatever chance I have with Angela.

"Lynda?" Josie's voice ropes me back into the present, where I sit seiza-style on my bed, my phone burning in my grip. I've barely moved since getting off the phone with Bora.

Josie cautiously circles the bed. "Everything okay? You've been staring into space."

"I'm just having an internal monologue," I say.

"Oh . . . okay."

I throw my blanket aside and slip into a pair of fuzzy slippers. "So, uh, did you need something?" I eye the violin in her hand and the bow in the other.

"I've been rehearsing for my recital, and Mom wants me

to perform at Thanksgiving." She starts to fidget. "I'm kind of . . . nervous. Do you mind if I practice in front of you?"

"Not at all," I say. Although I've heard Josie play many times, I've never watched her. She's performed in front of people far more knowledgeable in classical music than I am.

What does she have to be nervous about?

I follow Josie to her practice room and make myself comfortable on the love seat. There's a shelf on the wall behind me bearing accolades from local and state competitions. Her previous successes don't seem to instill much confidence in her. She switches her sheet music, turns on the Bluetooth speaker on her desk, and hands me her phone.

"First up is Wieniawski's Polonaise Brillante No. 1 in D major," she says. "I'll be playing with a backing track. Can you hit Play when I give the signal?"

"Sure." I'm musically illiterate and have no idea what D major means.

Josie shakes out her shoulders and, after a deep breath, positions her violin under her chin, steadies her bow, and gives me a small nod. I press Play.

The song announces itself right away with a piano opening that calls you to attention. The real magic happens once Josie joins in, her bow dancing in short and long fluid strokes while her left hand slides up and down the neck of her violin, her fingers skipping and lingering with the tune. She makes being ambidextrous seem effortless.

"That was brilliant," I tell her after the song concludes. Her performance was lovely to the eyes and ears, though I was too fascinated by her finger work to fully appreciate the music.

Josie relaxes her arms and smiles. "It's one of my favorite songs. It's fun and versatile, and I've practiced it a million times. It would be embarrassing if I couldn't play it perfectly . . . you know?"

"I could never do what you just did." I can't even draw Buncleaver with my left hand.

"Thanks. . . . Can I play a few more songs?"

"Go for it."

Up next is Vivaldi, followed by Beethoven, and then Brahms's Violin Sonata No. 3, Op. 108. Slow, dense, and somber. There's an almost dreamlike quality to the way Josie plays it, so much so that I find myself sinking into an abyss.

Just as I begin to doze off, Josie suddenly stops playing.

"Ugh!" She brandishes her bow, slicing the air with it. "I can never get this right!"

"It sounded right to me." Like a dark, heavy lullaby.

"Nick keeps reminding me to take it slow—to lean into the notes—but I always find myself rushing."

"How long is the song supposed to be?"

"Twenty minutes."

"What?" I deadpan. "In that case, who wouldn't want to get it over with?"

Humor tugs at Josie's lips. "Nick keeps insisting that I inject my heart and soul into the song, that I personalize it with my own interpretation—as if I'm a robot or something."

"Can't rushing some notes count as your own interpretation?"

"But it doesn't sound *right*." Josie massages her temple. "Sorry, I can't explain it."

"I think I get it." I hug my knees to my chest. "It's the same with visual arts. A painting might seem perfect to someone, but as the artist, you know something's lacking. You can't describe what's missing. You just know."

"Exactly." Josie eases her grip on her bow and sets down her violin.

"Are you feeling more . . . confident about Thanksgiving?"

Josie exercises her jaw. "Once I decide how I want to play Brahms's sonata and commit to it, I should be golden. I don't want to butcher it . . . and have the whole family question my ability to get into Curtis."

"Don't dignify those kinds of comments with a response." I can already hear Aunt Val's nagging voice. "They're not the ones practicing three to five hours a day."

Josie starts fidgeting again. "It's hard when it's your family. I don't want to disappoint them. At the end of the day, I know they mean well."

I disagree with that sentiment. Family shouldn't get a pass for being insensitive just because they're coming from a place of concern.

But I'm not Josie, and Josie isn't me.

"Keep practicing," I tell her. "I'm sure you'll blow everyone away."

"I'll try," Josie says as I push myself up from the love seat. "And good luck with Angela."

I stop dead in my tracks and whip my head in her direction.

Her smile drops. "I—I didn't mean to eavesdrop! I was in the hallway and heard you through the bedroom door."

I tug at the collar of my shirt. Suddenly it's hot in here. "Don't sweat it. I shouldn't have been so loud. I'm gonna go . . . now."

And then I hightail it out of the room.

...

While I don't have any intention of asking Angela out the next time I see her, I won't avoid her either. I have too much anxious energy to do nothing, so sometime before bed, I email Angela my files for Xiaohua and hope she doesn't notice the similarities between them.

Two NPCs remain and I still need to do the CG for Sun Hong and Meng Li and finalize their in-game files. I won't be tackling any of that until next year. After Thanksgiving, Bora and I will be cramming for the SAT. Whatever free time I have, I'll be spending it with Buncleaver. My Instagram backlog is running low, and I want to draw him doing winter things, like eating a yule log cake while wearing an ugly holiday sweater.

Here's hoping I meet Angela's standards and don't have to redo Xiaohua.

Unfortunately, I don't hear from her all weekend.

On Monday, I'm back at the school library, editing an essay, when the table suddenly shifts. I look up and choke on my spit.

Angela's sprawled across the tabletop, lying on her side with her head propped in her hand. "Draw me like one of your French girls," she coos, conjuring a paper fan from her pocket. She snaps it open. "Only your pen can do my beauty justice."

She flutters the fan in my direction, the cool air flicking against my skin.

I blush despite myself.

"Then again . . ." She scoots into a new position, her knees pointed toward me as she shuts my laptop and leans in to whisper, "I suppose you already have."

I clamp a hand over my ear as a tremor ripples through me. "Ever heard of personal space?" I ask, sitting as far back into my chair as possible.

"You can't base a character on me and not expect a good ol' teasing," she says. "It's payback for giving me more cosplay ideas."

"Payback, huh? Is that what this is?" I try not to sound disappointed.

Angela tilts her head, innocent yet coy. "What else would it be?"

"You should get down before the librarian sees you," I say, powering my laptop back on.

Angela hides the bottom half of her face behind her fan and observes me. I try not to cave under the scrutiny of her gaze. I hit some random keys on my laptop and wait it out.

After an uncomfortably long moment, she relents and slides into the chair across from me. "Good work, by the way. You nailed Xiaohua's character. Her color palette is good to go, and you're free to render."

"Thanks . . ." I should be overjoyed by her approval, yet . . .

"Something on your mind?"

"I've been wondering. . . ." I think back to my failed attempt at getting Angela to share the script with me. "There would be less ambiguity if I got to know these characters through their dialogue and actions."

"I'm always available to talk if you need more direction."

"I know, but it's not the same as reading the script."

Angela clicks her teeth. "The script isn't final yet."

"You said it was in its second stage of editing *back in September.*"

"There've been delays. It'll be ready by the deadline, just not as soon as I anticipated," she says breezily. "Enough about that. I'm not done gushing over Xiaohua. After all, she and I look so much alike. How can I not talk about myself?"

There it is. That smugness I used to find so grating but now can't seem to get enough of. I watch as she tucks a strand of hair behind her ear before fixating on her lips. Today they're a glistening shade of cranberry plum.

"Should I chalk up the similarities as a coincidence and not some subliminal message?" she asks, a playful gleam in her eyes. She tilts her head downward, her eyelashes in full view. So close I could count them.

I swallow the lump in my throat and try not to match the color of her lip tint. "Which would you prefer?"

"Oh? A trick question, is it?" Angela flicks her eyes to the ceiling, thinking.

I told myself I wouldn't ask her out, but she's making it impossible. Like Bora said, this doesn't have to be complicated. I like Angela, and I want her to like me back. We can go on a date and take it from there. Question is, how exactly do I ask her out? If life were an otome game and I had three choices, which would award me the most love points?

> A) Hey, I like you. Want to go out sometime?
> B) Go out with me.
> C) Want to get bubble tea after school? My treat!

I'm leaning toward A or C. I try to sound the words out in my head. My delivery won't be perfect, but as long as I don't make a fool of myself, I'll consider it a victory.

"I prefer whatever you prefer," Angela says, her voice strangely passive while the look on her face is all hope and a pinch of unease.

"I . . ." The words linger on the tip of my tongue. I wring my hands under the table as the world presses in on me—on this very moment. I forget everything I rehearsed seconds ago and just say what naturally comes to mind. "How about we change the subject and grab bubble tea?" After a few beats, I realize I was too vague and hastily tack on, "Like a date."

Smooth, Lynda. Smooth.

Now that I'm blushing to the roots of my hair, I brave a glance at Angela.

She's smiling.

"I would love to get bubble tea with you," she says. "Like a date."

18

FOR ONCE, I wish my wardrobe consisted of more than cropped sweaters, cardigans, and jeggings. It's not what I'd wear on a first date, casual or not.

After canceling my plans with Bora, who nearly fainted the second I told her about the date, I take Angela to a bubble tea shop outside of town. (She drove, so technically she took me.) The shop is a little out of the way, but their menu is massive. There's something for everyone, no matter how picky you are. Plus, they use fresh fruit and various dairy substitutes. Wouldn't hurt to cater to Angela's . . . sophisticated palate.

Inside the decor is mostly sleek black countertops and matching bar stools. The back wall is a rainbow mural of sticky notes. K-pop plays overhead as we wait for our drinks: a rose lychee green tea with boba for Angela and a classic milk tea for me.

"Thanks for treating," she says after we settle into the faux leather couch by the mural.

I shrug. "How can I not pay after asking you out?"

"Next one's on me."

My heart flutters at the promise of a second date. All of this is new to me, and I don't quite feel like myself. Angela, however, doesn't seem the least bit frazzled.

"So . . . is there something you want to talk about?" she asks.

"I mean . . ." I shift nervously in my seat. "It goes without saying. I sort of . . . like you."

Angela's eyes twinkle with laughter. "I like you, too. I was . . . really happy when you popped the question. I was hoping you would."

"Really? But you're such a go-getter. I thought you'd—"

"I like it when others take the initiative and . . ." Angela toys with her straw and wiggles it around in her cup. "I wasn't sure how you felt. I didn't want to get rejected if . . . you know."

So even Angela is afraid of rejection.

Her confession is so disarming, I'm momentarily stunned into silence.

"It wasn't all confidence on my end either," I confess, blushing all over again. Is it just me or do people operate at a higher internal body temperature when smitten? "Bora insisted there was no way you, uh, didn't reciprocate my feelings. Had you proved her wrong, I would've been mortified."

"You two talked about me?"

"Obviously . . ." Can't lie my way out of that one.

"Well, when I confided in my friends, they had mixed opinions about you and I getting together." Angela takes a long sip of tea before continuing. "You see, while I'm attracted to guys and girls, I'm also asexual. Demi, specifically."

My brain short-circuits, and my mind goes blank.

Angela purses her lips, worry creasing her forehead as the silence between us grows. "I assume that's . . . not something you're okay with?" Her voice is soft, her expression faraway, like she's retreating into herself. It's not a face I'm used to seeing on her.

"That's not it!" I blurt out. "I-I'm ace, too!" Angela blinks at me, her unease replaced with surprise. "What are the odds, right?"

It doesn't feel real. Yet the truth is out, and I'm not complaining.

"Some might call this destiny," Angela says.

"Others would call it a coincidence."

"Let's compromise and call it serendipity." Angela and I share a laugh. "If you don't mind me asking, when did you realize you're ace?"

"I can't pinpoint when, but it came naturally," I say. "When I had my first crush on a boy, I realized I like boys. When I had my first crush on a girl, I realized I like girls. When people at school talked about *doing it*, I realized I had little to no interest in it. Dating's never been much of a topic in my family, but I grew up around open-minded people. While I do feel . . . different, I never felt ashamed to be ace or bi."

"Nor should you be."

"How about you? Your parents seem progressive."

Angela tilts her head left and right as if debating with herself. "Believe it or not, my mom was devastated when I came out as bi. She said I'd change my mind once I met the right guy."

Yikes. That's shocking to hear. I've only met Grace twice, but from my interactions with her, I never would've guessed she was capable of such narrow-mindedness.

"After she said that, we got into a screaming match. She fed me some sob story about how she always envisioned me bringing home a nice young man she could one day call her son-in-law. She made *my* sexuality about *her*." Angela heaves a disappointed sigh. "She eventually came around after my dad talked some sense into her. She apologized, but our relationship hasn't been the same since."

"I can only imagine . . ." If my dad had reacted like Grace when I told him I was bi, our relationship would've been even more damaged than it already is. I'm not the most forgiving person, after all.

"You know what takes the cake?" Angela says. "She had the opposite reaction when I told her I was ace. Many parents have a tough time accepting that their children mature into sexual beings. In my mom's mind, asexual equals sexless, so me being ace was a cause for celebration, because no sex means no teen pregnancy."

"Um . . ." I'm not sure what to say other than "That's messed up."

"My mom isn't perfect, but I still love her. And she *is* trying. While she does have her setbacks now and then, I can't fault someone for trying to do better. Some of my friends think I'm enabling her—"

"You're fine the way you are, Angela." It's not easy to set

aside your pride and be the bigger person. Trust me. I know. "In fact, I'd even call you amazing."

"You're pretty amazing yourself," Angela says before plucking a marker out of her bag. She removes a blank sticky note from the mural behind us and starts scribbling. Only when she presses the note back into place do I see what she wrote: *ANGELA & LYNDA*.

"That is so cheesy," I can't help but say.

I hate it and love it all the same.

Angela reaches for my hand, the warmth of her smile exceeding the touch of her skin on mine. It's distracting, maddening, and absolutely delightful. "Let's be amazing and cheesy together."

19

"AW, LYNDA! I'M so happy for you!"

I hold my phone several inches from my ear as Aunt Mindy celebrates on the other end. I thought I'd give her a call Thanksgiving morning to catch up. She and Uncle Ben aren't joining me for turkey dinner, but they'll be returning to Fallbank for the winter holidays.

"Bubble tea for a first date. Classic," she gushes, "and then she repaid you by treating you to soufflé pancakes. Oh, to be young again."

Angela surprised me the other day by taking me to a manga café tucked away on the third floor of a nondescript building with faded signage. For ten dollars, you can read whatever you want from their extensive manga collection (Angela immediately gunned for their josei section). You can also order food and drinks during your stay. Their soufflé pancakes were to die for—light, fluffy, and not too sweet.

"When you first told me about Angela, I thought everything between you two was strictly business. Now you're all lovey-dovey." Aunt Mindy giggles like a schoolgirl. "Will I be meeting Angela over the holidays?"

"We'll see," I say.

"Does Brian know about her and the game you're making?"

My silence is everything.

"Lynda! You haven't told him?"

"I'm not ready to."

Just because Dad and I are back on speaking terms doesn't mean I have anything to say to him. Telling him about the otome game will inevitably lead to talks about art school, and those never end well. Besides, Dad's rarely home. His job has been in perpetual busy season. Amy's more of a parent to me now. She cooks, cleans, and runs other errands while working full-time. Sometimes she divvies out chores to me and Josie but not enough where it interferes with our studies and hobbies. I appreciate her being fair in that regard.

Aunt Mindy sighs wearily. "I don't want to rush you. It's your business—just know Brian wouldn't hesitate to welcome Angela into the family."

I groan. "You're making this more serious than it is."

"Then you should have no problem telling Brian."

"Didn't you just say you wouldn't rush me?"

"I did, sorry." There's a brief pause before she says, "Please keep me in the loop. I'm not usually a romantic, but if it concerns my niece, I can't help but be sixteen again. Can I tell Ben?" And before I get the chance to respond, "Can I? Can I?"

"You can tell him." I distance the phone from my ear

again as she resumes squealing. "Anyway, I got to go. Talk to you later?"

"Good luck with your third date. Put that creative mind of yours to work."

I will. After I survive dinner at Aunt Val's.

. . .

Val's house is perched at the end of a cul-de-sac, among identical ranch-style houses with wide driveways and front lawns turned brittle with frost. After sitting through two hours of traffic, I'm aching for a good stretch. The drive may have tested my patience, but I can always count on my family to push me past my limits.

I first met Val last year at Christmas. She was hosting, and after introducing herself, she told me I had to adopt her family's traditions if I wanted to be a Koh. I didn't care about any of that, but I couldn't exactly admit that to someone I just met, much less under their own roof. So I behaved myself—even after discovering that these so-called traditions were simply a code word for housework. While Luke got to goof off, I had to set the table, fix the old folks a plate, and demolish the tower of dishes in the kitchen sink.

This year, I refuse to partake in such blatant sexism.

I can be rebellious without making a scene.

I can stand by my principles without compromising the peace.

Easy.

Val's husband, What's-His-Name, welcomes us inside,

and immediately I am seized by the aroma of deep-fried peanuts and incense. Dad and Amy go off on their own while I follow Josie into the living room, where a bunch of kids sit around a giant flat-screen. Luke peels his eyes away from the TV to look at us, and seconds later, he's hugging Josie.

I haven't seen Luke since he killed Henry. Before I can find a quiet corner to hide in, Luke latches on to my cardigan and says, "Sorry about Harry. Are you still mad?"

"Uh . . ." I look down at him, unsure of what to do as my hands hover over his shoulders. Josie gives me an encouraging nod, and I stroke his back in what I believe is a cousinly gesture. "Don't worry about it. I have a new *Henry* now."

"I can't pay you back, but you can pick tonight's movie," he says, releasing my crumpled cardigan. "I'll watch what you pick."

That's very . . . sweet of him.

No one here except Josie is around my age. If I want to keep myself entertained, I'll have to either rely on my phone or be sociable for once. When Luke hands me his holy grail, the TV remote, I take it. On the couch, as I'm scrolling through a list of animated films, I lean toward Josie and whisper, "What kind of movies does Luke like?"

"He's a big Studio Ghibli fan," she whispers back.

"Got it."

• • •

Before food is served, Val summons everyone into the dining room for an obligatory prayer. Once that's over with, she instructs each of us to share one thing we're grateful for, like we're a bunch of six-year-olds, and since there's seventeen of us, the whole exercise is long and tedious.

After Val's husband thanks her for cooking all day, we finally dig in. Like last year, the adults claim the dining room and relegate us kids to the kitchen, where we all bump elbows with each other at a folding table. I plow through a pile of roasted veg and mashed potatoes. Only when I'm scooping up the last drops of gravy do I notice Josie's plate—three-quarters of it still untouched. I gesture vaguely toward her plate.

"Not hungry?" I ask.

She rakes her fork through her sweet potato. "Just nervous."

About what? I almost ask, until I remember her violin in the foyer.

"You got this," I assure her.

Tonight, Josie will be covering Debussy, Beethoven, and Wieniawski. In the interest of time, she removed Mozart and Brahms from her repertoire. She played flawlessly in front of me and Amy before we left the house. Surely she can replicate her performance.

My beliefs are put to the test once dessert is served. Everyone's making themselves comfortable in the living room while Josie tunes her violin. She catches my eye from across the room, and I flash her a smile. She returns one in kind.

Up first is "Clair de Lune." A nice warm-up piece, according to Josie—calm, serene, and makes you feel weightless, like you're suspended in moonlit waters. I overheard Amy telling her Debussy was "too easy" and not reflective of her true abilities. I don't know the entirety of their conversation, but Josie evidently put her foot down. The girl's been practicing three-plus hours a day. Let her play what she wants on Thanksgiving.

Next is Violin Sonata No. 7, a twenty-minute piece Josie shortened for the sake of our attention span, followed by Polonaise Brillante No. 1. Her performance is effortless, nothing short of bold. There's a lively flare to how she maneuvers her bow and glides her fingers along the strings. You can feel her passion radiating through her music.

"That new teacher is paying off," I hear Val's husband whisper behind me. "She's a shoo-in for Curtis, no doubt about it."

I don't know who he's talking to until Val tuts, "I wouldn't say that, but she's certainly improved." Her tone is as judgmental as ever. "Can you believe there are children who play as well as her? Sometimes I wonder if it's worth it—working this hard while others don't even have to try."

So what? Because other people have it easier, Josie shouldn't bother trying? News flash: There will always be people better than you. Comparison is the thief of joy. I wouldn't be where I am today if I gave up the first, second, or hundredth time I felt inadequate.

Suddenly, I'm transported back to Angela's room, to that moment where we talked about Amy's obsession with Curtis. *"Josie's grades aren't going to get her anywhere—not anywhere she wants to be, anyway. All she seems to have is her violin."*

Perhaps my anger is misplaced. Considering my track record, I have no right to feel offended on Josie's behalf. Even so, I can't let Val get away with that comment.

"They're called child prodigies," I hiss, pivoting my head just enough for Val to know I'm talking to her—Angela's signature move. "They're one in a million. Sorry you're not one of them. Welcome to the party."

I turn back around in time to witness the end of Josie's performance as Val huffs angrily behind me. I give Josie a standing ovation and others follow. Josie beams at us, her lips breaking into a wide smile as her eyes search the crowd to land on me.

Something passes between us, and for a fleeting moment, we feel like sisters.

20

I REGRET SIGNING up for the SAT in December. It's a struggle to not get caught up in all the holiday cheer when your neighborhood is electrified with string lights.

On the last day before the test, Bora and I spend our lunch period trying to make sense of the practice problems we got wrong. At this point, there's not much we can do that will have any significant impact on our scores. Still, I'm not a quitter.

"Put me out of my misery! I want to get this over with already." Bora yawns into her elbow before taking two large gulps from her thermos. Her coffee breath is especially pungent today. "Watch, after all this torture, I'm going to score below a thousand."

"Don't talk like that," I say, snapping my fingers to get her to focus. "You're going to hit a home run."

Bora rubs her eyes and sighs, her voice thick with exhaustion. "A home run would be a perfect score, and that's never happening."

I give her shoulder a reassuring squeeze. "You've been

scoring between twelve and thirteen hundred on your practice tests. Those are winning numbers."

Bora doesn't need a sixteen hundred and neither do I. Art schools don't care that much about whether you can crack a tricky multiple-choice question, but if I want to make myself more appealing to the admissions committee, a high SAT score will do that.

"How come Josie isn't taking the SAT with us?" Bora asks.

"I think she plans to take it in May."

"During AP exams?"

"She's not taking any AP classes," I remind her.

"Oh, right." Bora smacks herself upside the head before getting up to throw out her trash. As soon as she's gone, Claire Lipkin sweeps by and extends an Art Club flyer my way.

"I'm sure you already heard about the charity auction," she says, carefully enunciating each word. "Here's a reminder in case you forgot."

"Thanks. You can leave it on the table," I say, picking at a hangnail. She pins the flyer to the table, rotates it one hundred and eighty degrees, and slides it toward me. I briefly catch a line of bolded text, something about hors d'oeuvres and refreshments.

"My dad's bringing his friends," she says airily, basking in her own self-importance. "They're antiques collectors. They know priceless art when they see it. If you or your dad know anyone, feel free to spread the word. This is for a good cause, after all."

"Will do." After I slay the SAT, Claire's next on the chopping block.

• • •

I do slay on Saturday. Well, I won't know for certain until I receive my score.

Still, I'm confident Bora and I did well. There were a few questions I hastily answered in a mad dash against the clock, but I'm not going to dwell on that for long because Angela and I are going on another date, which is a pretty decent distraction.

Bora helped me pick out an outfit: high-waisted jeans paired with an orchid-pink sweater that she bought for me. It has a Chinese proverb printed across the chest that translates to "If you bow at all, bow low." She thought it suited me.

I told Angela to dress casually and that I'd pick her up from the public library after her tutoring session. Dad's working despite today being a Sunday, so Amy's letting me borrow her car. I vacuumed the floor mats and cleared old receipts from the cracks between the seats.

Once Angela gives me the green light, I head out. Soon I'm reaching over the center console to hug her, her breath tickling my ear as I catch a whiff of brisk winter air emanating from her clothes.

"How did tutoring go?" I ask as we pull out of the parking lot.

"Could've gone better," she says, loosening her scarf. "I met with a nine-year-old boy and his overbearing mom." The library is far behind us by the time she finishes recounting how awkward and tense their encounter was. "So, what are we doing today?"

"First, we're grabbing lunch at Tastea." My chest swells with pride when Angela clasps her hands together and beams at me. Tastea is a café that sells traditional Taiwanese bites and is known for their homemade soy milk. I hope they don't sell out by the time we arrive.

Angela leans toward me, eager for more details.

"The rest is a surprise," I say.

"This is why I hate being on the receiving end." She pouts, her enthusiasm waning a little before she points at my chest and barks out a laugh. "What's with your shirt?"

"Bora got it for me."

"A fitting proverb. She knows you well."

"I didn't know you could read Chinese."

"There's a reason I'm taking French instead of Mandarin."

"Humblebrag much?" Her confidence inspires an idea in me. "Should we try speaking only in Mandarin during lunch? First to use English has to treat the winner to bubble tea?"

Having learned Mandarin for almost three years, I'd like to say I'm fluent enough for everyday conversation.

"Lunch *and* a game?" Angela arches a brow as a mischievous glint illuminates her eyes. "Don't threaten me with a good time, Lynda."

Our game starts off easy. We order drinks and food, gush over how delicious the soy milk is, share our upcoming holiday plans, and discuss the new route that was released in *Romancing the New Moon* (which I heard about from Bora). Nearing the end of lunch, Angela steers our conversation toward Model UN and our country's international trade policies. Something I am not knowledgeable about at all.

"Oh crap." My last words before defeat.

"That was fun," Angela says when we're leaving. "It's even more fun when you win."

"I should've known your Mandarin's better than mine."

A blast of frigid air greets us as soon as we open the lobby door. I recoil from the wind and hastily zip up my jacket. "You need to layer up," Angela says, wrapping her scarf around my neck. "Where are your gloves?"

"I forgot them at home."

She clicks her teeth. "I guess that means we have to hold hands."

Even though we're only a short trek from the car, I take her up on her offer.

Our next destination is a secret. I almost do the whole blindfold thing but don't want to overhype the surprise in case it flops.

"Are you taking me to a museum?" Angela asks. I shake my head. "The movies?" Again, I shake my head. After several failed guesses, she snaps her fingers as if to say *eureka*. "I know! We're going to an escape room."

Puzzles and riddles would've been the perfect choice. Except it's still a no.

Angela purses her lips. "I'm wrong? I feel like I've listed everything."

Doubt begins to creep in, and my confidence cracks. Did she list everything she wanted to do? She did sound particularly keen on the escape room. . . .

Suddenly, the ghost of my morning coffee comes to haunt me, and it takes everything in me not to gag. I put a lot of thought into today . . . Was it enough? Did I make the right choices? Either way, it's too late to change course. All I can do is stick to my plans and hope for the best.

I'm a bundle of nerves for the remainder of our drive, and as we enter a shopping plaza, the urge to vomit intensifies. Before my lunch can come back to say hello, Angela points to the store at the end of the plaza, MUSE & SIP, a BYOB art studio.

"Are we painting?" She searches my face for confirmation, and as soon as she has it, she claps her hands and releases a cute little squeal. "Oh my god, yes, we're painting!"

"We can do something else if—"

"This is perfect! I can't believe I didn't guess it."

And just like that, the nerves retreat like vampires fleeing the sun, and I mirror her excitement. Unfortunately, we're not old enough to bring our own alcohol, so we'll have to make do with ramune and flavored seltzer. As soon as I fetch them from the trunk, Angela rushes me into the store even though we have ten minutes before our class starts.

The interior is reminiscent of many art studios I've seen: vinyl flooring the color of wet concrete, wooden countertops that could use some sanding, and long tables arranged parallel to each other, a patchwork of spilled paint running up and down their legs. The walls are plastered with paintings from previous classes, the canvases coming in all shapes and sizes. There's no uniformity, but it's not chaos either—and I feel right at home.

Angela and I squeeze through a cluster of people milling about and claim the table at the very back, where two pre-sketched canvases await us on tiny easels. We each get three different paintbrushes and our own disposable plate preloaded with acrylic paints.

"Have you been here before?" Angela asks as she takes in her surroundings.

"Bora and I came here several months ago," I say. "She was in an artsy mood."

"The last thing I painted was a portrait of a Shiba Inu back in sixth grade. My dad had one growing up. I wanted to gift the painting to him on Father's Day."

"And what did he think of it?"

"He said, *That's a nice fox you got there.*"

I pinch my nose to stop myself from snorting.

Angela snaps to attention as our instructor, distinguished by the paint stains on her apron, saunters in and assumes her position at the front of the room.

Today we're painting a field of wildflowers under a purpling, star-spangled sky. A full moon looms overhead, casting intricate shadows across the landscape. The composition might seem intimidating at first, but once our instructor demonstrates her technique, replicating the scene should be as relaxing as a stroll in the park. There's no need to be sober for this. . . .

But when I peek over at Angela's canvas to check on her progress, I instinctively take a whiff of her ramune bottle to make sure there isn't any alcohol in it.

"Why don't you rub salt in the wound while you're at it?"

She pouts, leaning back on her stool to assess her painting. "This is a disaster."

"I wouldn't call it a disaster. . . ." I search for a more adequate adjective and come up short. Her flowers, silhouetted against the moonlight, do appear a bit . . . charred. Their wilted form and thin petals remind me of stick figures writhing in pain. "There's a morbid charm to it."

"That wasn't the mood I was aiming for. Why doesn't mine"—she gestures at her canvas and then at mine—"look like yours? Am I that bad at following instructions?"

"I'd have no business applying to RISD if I couldn't paint this." If Angela could paint as well as I can despite her last attempt dating back to middle school, let's just say I'd be questioning my life choices.

"Sorry, I didn't mean to imply anyone can be a master class painter as long as they follow a how-to guide."

"You're not exactly wrong," I admit. Many people give up on art because they don't know where to start or how to keep going. "Unless all you want to do is forge famous paintings, it's essential to have your own artistic flair."

"My artistic flair belongs in a horror film." Angela sighs. "I'm much better at taking up the pen than a paintbrush. Words over pictures."

"You don't need to be skilled at something to have fun with it."

"Who says I'm having fun?" she says pointedly. Something a lot like dread grips me by the neck. "Lynda, I'm kidding! No need to look petrified!"

"So . . ." I clear the rasp in my throat. "You are having fun?"

"Of course! Now I need rack my brain over how to outdo you."

"We can just stay in. . . . You know, watch a movie, make some hot chocolate, talk . . . Easy stuff." While I do want to impress Angela, this isn't a competition.

"That wouldn't bore you?"

"No?"

"And why's that?" There's a devious tic to her brow as she smirks at me.

I see the trap she's laid out for me, and I walk right into it.

"Because . . ." I stroke her cheek with the end of my brush, leaving a swirl of magenta in its wake. "Even the everyday stuff is a lot more colorful with you around."

21

CHRISTMAS EVE IS finally here, and Dad just returned from the airport with Aunt Mindy and Uncle Ben. As soon as they walk through the door, I launch myself into Aunt Mindy's arms. She catches her footing and hugs me back.

"Hello to you, too!" she says before kissing me on the head. She smells like spiced wine and holiday cheer, a scent I grew up with and adore.

Ever since she moved away, Christmas has been hit-or-miss. Last year Dad and Amy asked me what I wanted, since, in their words, I'm difficult to shop for. Despite being upfront about wanting cold hard cash, I received a gift card to a craft store. So while I did get a little something for everyone this year, I'm not expecting much in return.

That said, I've been anticipating Aunt Mindy and Uncle Ben's visit. Their presence is like a breath of fresh air on this white wintry morning. Snowfall started around midnight and petered out near dawn. Dad was up at six, shoveling and scraping ice off the cars.

Uncle Ben reaches a gloved hand toward me and ruffles

my hair. His clothes reek of that distinct airplane cabin smell. "Are you trying to blind me, Lynda? I feel like I need sunglasses."

I do a little twirl in my fleece pajamas, the shirt and pants an obnoxious pineapple yellow patterned with mini Buncleavers. "Bora got them custom-made for me!"

She knows me so well. Hopefully she'll feel the same way about me when she opens her present—a gift card to the App Store to fuel her latest otome game craze and a limited-edition pin set of all the love interests from *Romancing the New Moon*.

Amy shuffles out of the kitchen. "Mindy! Ben! So wonderful to see you. Please excuse the mess." She twiddles her sauce-coated fingers and gestures toward the stains on her apron. "It's been a hectic morning."

Aunt Mindy kisses her once on each cheek before shimmying out of her coat. "I hope my brother hasn't shackled you with all the cooking."

Dad grunts disapprovingly while pouring himself a cup of tea, the dark circles under his eyes exacerbating the severity of his expression.

"Brian's done his share. No ball and chain here." Amy laughs, waving her wrists and ankles. "Anyway, make yourself at home and help yourself to whatever you'd like."

"Lynda told me you've all been baking," Aunt Mindy says. "I'd like to have a taste."

"You can't," I say. "Not until we have a decorating contest."

A baking craze swept through our house yesterday,

transforming our kitchen into a sugar and spice wonderland while leaving our pantry flourless. Now that we have enough cookies to feed an entire village—sugar, gingerbread, chocolate chip, butter pecan, and oatmeal raisin—it would be a waste to just eat them.

"Judging will be blind," I explain. "Since Amy won't be participating, she'll choose the winner. Whichever design she likes best wins."

"Seems rather arbitrary," Aunt Mindy says, rolling up her sleeves.

"Afraid you'll lose?" I quip, hand on my hip, eyes on the prize.

There's no real prize on the line. Only my pride.

Aunt Mindy does her best impression of an evil stepmother and laughs into the back of her hand. "May the odds be ever in your favor, Lynda. Let the cookie games begin."

● ● ●

This is an outrage. A scandal.

How could Uncle Ben win with his sloppy handiwork? He drew two orange circles with no attempt at symmetry whatsoever, and below them, he added a lopsided yellow crescent moon bisected by a brown line. I get that it's a smiley face made out of fruit, but this is something you'd expect from a first grader.

"I thought it was funny," Amy said after she declared Uncle Ben the winner.

In other words, it's so bad, it's good.

Meanwhile, I painstakingly outlined Buncleaver in royal icing and colored him in. Even Josie demonstrated more finesse and creativity by sculpting Beethoven's wig on a cookie—out of frosting! As for Aunt Mindy . . . She talked a big game, but her gingerbread people are drowning in edible glitter. The white chocolate pearls she used for their eyes and the red shoelace candy she used for their lips remind me of something out of a horror movie.

Aunt Mindy bites off the head of a gingerbread man and glares at Uncle Ben. "You win some, you lose some."

Since there are still a few naked cookies, I dress them up with some *Love Takes Root* character art to later gift to Angela. With Henry propped up on the table to provide me with a visual reference, I use edible ink to sketch Meng Li's headshot. Once I have an outline, I trace it over with a piping bag.

"Who do we have here?" Aunt Mindy asks, peering over my shoulder.

"Her name's Meng Li," I say. "She's one of the love interests in that otome game I'm making with Angela."

Before I can divulge more details, Dad inserts himself into our conversation. "Do my ears deceive me or did someone mention they're making a game?"

"It's nothing." I shrug.

"Doesn't sound like nothing to me," he says, bright-eyed and curious.

"I'm kind of in the middle of something. Aunt Mindy can, uh, loop you in." I flash her an OK sign before flooding Meng Li's hair in careful segments and smoothing out the surface with my piping needle. Still, my brain refuses to completely disassociate from my surroundings, and I catch my dad as he says, "That explains her new iPad."

He sounds genuinely impressed, if not baffled. "Good for Lynda, but what teenager has ten grand at their disposal?" And then, as if remembering we're in the same room, he says, "Lynda, why didn't you tell me? This sounds like an awesome—"

"I didn't think it was worth sharing," I say, refining the edges of Meng Li's shoulder before setting her aside on a sheet of parchment paper to dry.

It's getting awkward in here.

Dad frowns. "But you told Min?"

"She supports me going to art school, so . . . why wouldn't I tell her?" I didn't intend to drop a truth bomb, but the words just . . . slipped.

I steal a glimpse at my dad. A dozen or more emotions are twisting his face one way then another. Before the ticking bomb detonates behind me, Josie suddenly chimes in.

"Angela's making an otome game? I didn't know she liked them." Her voice is like an arctic breeze cooling the moment. She drops into the chair beside me and points to Henry. "May I?"

"Go ahead." I hand Henry over to her.

She swipes through my character sheets and concept sketches. A goofy smile overtakes her face when she lands on Sun Hong.

Aunt Mindy claps Dad on the shoulder and ushers him into the living room.

"Thanks," I whisper to Josie. "You saved me."

She shakes her head as if to say *No problem*. "Mind if I watch you draw Sun Hong?"

"We can draw him together," I say, grabbing a spare piping bag. "I'll walk you through each step. We must do his beauty justice."

"But what if he's too pretty to eat?"

I scoff. "Eating beautiful people? Sounds badass to me."

Too bad this badass needs her sister to save her from her own battles.

22

ALTHOUGH THE MOOD does lighten up in the afternoon with card games and a movie, everything comes undone after dinner.

Aunt Mindy and Uncle Ben give me and Josie two hundred dollars each, leaving both of us awestruck. Any amount helps after all my spending, though I wasn't expecting anything in that range.

Dad and Amy got me a Zen coloring book and a backpack to replace the one I've been using for years. A rainbow backpack with donut cats on it isn't something I'd pick for myself, but I can't complain. It's on par with what I gifted them: a cycling jacket and pair of socks for my dad, and a neck pillow and ergonomic mouse for Amy since her wrist has been aching. They're over the top in their reactions, in the same way parents gush over a stick figure their toddler drew and then hang it on the fridge.

That part of the evening is pure cringe.

Unfortunately, things go from cringey to bad.

So bad.

Dad and Amy aren't the type of parents who think dictionaries make terrific gifts, so imagine my complete and utter horror when Josie tears into an envelope and pulls out a brochure for a tutoring center.

The realization hits her in slow motion. As her eyes roam over the brochure, her excitement dulls, and a tremor passes through her lips. The house is nothing but crickets.

A chain reaction of secondhand embarrassment.

I feel for her then. I sort of save the evening with the digital character portraits I painted of Marlo Montgomery and Theodore Tudor from *Romancing the New Moon*. At first I feel cheap for gifting Josie PNG files, but she loves them—almost enough to forget how, starting in March, she'll be attending Saturday tutoring sessions.

"It's my fault," Josie says once we're in bed. "Mom's been hounding me ever since my grades started slipping." This is news to me. "I wanted her to back off, so I told her about this new tutoring center I wanted to enroll in, except . . . I didn't think she'd actually sign me up."

"Why's that?" I ask.

"Because they're expensive."

"Oh."

"I oversold the online reviews, and, well, you know the rest. . . ."

Josie did shoot herself in the foot with that one. Still, our parents should've known better. Of all the things they could've given her . . . Tutoring sessions? Really? Also, it does not escape me that they will now be paying for two private instructors. But I'm not mad. I don't envy Josie and certainly don't wish to be in her shoes.

"I thought Curtis didn't care about grades," I say. "Aren't you better off focusing on your violin lessons?"

"Curtis doesn't care, but other schools do."

There's been so much fixation on Curtis, it never occurred to me that she'd have fallback schools. After her mesmerizing performance at Thanksgiving, I can't imagine her not getting in.

"Sorry, I don't mean to sound ungrateful," Josie says. "I should be happy for all the help I'm getting—and I am—but I barely have any free time as it is. I see Nick more than I see my friends. Don't get me wrong. I don't have anything against—"

"Josie." Her name leaves my lips like a command, and she immediately quiets. It was rude of me to interrupt, but I couldn't keep listening. "The problem isn't that you're ungrateful. It's that you can't be honest."

The silence that follows is harrowing. Josie's lying flat on her back, so I have no way to gauge her reaction. Perhaps I assumed too much and said too much. I wasn't exactly gentle in my delivery. . . .

"You're right," she finally says. "I just don't want to upset my mom."

"I know it's easier said than done, but you have to speak up for yourself or else no one will."

"Aren't you speaking up for me now?"

"Not really?" It's not as if I'm publicly defending her, and even if I did, I question the effectiveness of my intervention. I can't seem to advocate for myself without making a scene.

"If you say so." Josie turns to look at me. "Maybe admiring Marlo's portrait every morning before school will motivate me to do better in math."

"Are you really lacking motivation, though? You're a hard worker."

She gives me a close-lipped smile. "Thanks. That means a lot."

"I'm just calling it as I see it."

Josie giggles. "The way you compliment people is funny."

...

Around two a.m., I wake up, parched. I pad into the kitchen for a glass of water and notice that the backyard light is on. Voices sound from outside, muffled and distorted. Curiosity gets the best of me. I crack open the window above the kitchen sink and listen.

"It's not a competition," I hear Aunt Mindy say. "Ben and I thought the girls deserved a reward. Amy told me they've been going the extra mile this year."

Damn right I have. I scored a 1350 on my SAT.

"A reward doesn't have to be two hundred dollars," Dad hisses. "Half of that would've sufficed and wouldn't have made Amy and me look—"

"Two hundred should compensate for that tone-deaf present you two gave Josie. Even Lynda made more of an effort, and that's saying something."

Part of me wants to be offended, but Aunt Mindy's right. Compared to last year, when I got Josie a mug and some dollar store candy, I did invest more effort this time.

"Amy said she *raved* about the tutoring center! Believe it or not, I genuinely thought Josie would appreciate our gift. In hindsight, it was a mistake, but that's beside the point."

"Right, we're here to talk about *my* spending habits." Aunt Mindy steps in front of the window, and I retreat farther into the dark, preparing to duck if necessary. "You didn't seem too concerned about my overly generous nature when I lent you money for your honeymoon—not that I expect you to pay it back at this point."

Yikes. I have never heard Dad and Aunt Mindy bicker like this. Ever.

"Amy and I are in a tight spot right now, and I know we put ourselves there. No one forced us to have a lavish wedding or honeymoon, but it's been so long since either of us had someone . . . special in our lives."

Aunt Mindy tugs her shawl tight around her shoulders and sighs. "I get it. I'm not trying to upstage you by throwing my money around. All I want is for Lynda to feel appreciated."

"I do appreciate her! She's very capable for someone her age."

"I'm not the one who needs to hear that. While Lynda does relish her independence, perhaps she would include you in her life if you would validate her now and then."

"How can I when every time I talk to her, she brushes me off?" I can tell without looking that my dad's throwing his hands up in the air. "After the wedding, I thought the four of us could be a family, but Lynda—" His voice cracks, and he stops to collect himself. "She always seems to have an attitude when I'm around."

"Welcome to having a teenage daughter," Aunt Mindy says emphatically.

Excuse me? Aunt Mindy, I love you, but I don't have an attitude just because of my age.

My bad moods are justified.

"Fiona was a fireball, and she gave birth to one," she says. "As Lynda's dad, you're going to get burned, and let's be honest, she inherited some of her fire from you, too."

Fiona is my mom's name. I haven't heard it in a while. Even though Aunt Mindy and I can talk about anything and everything, my mom rarely comes up in conversation—not that I ask about her often. I always thought I took after Aunt Mindy. Does Dad see a bit of Mom in me too? Is what he sees good . . . or bad? Given our fights, being described as a fireball doesn't seem like a positive thing.

"Keep trying, Brian. That's all you can do," Aunt Mindy continues. "Lynda will come around when she's ready. Now let's head inside before I turn into a human Popsicle."

And that's my cue to leave.

• • •

Late in the morning, I find Dad hunched over the stove, stirring a pot of xifan. Everyone else is still in bed despite it being a quarter to eleven.

"Look who's finally up," he says when I walk in. "Hungry?"

"I'm still full from yesterday," I say before drawing the curtains over the sink. It's extraordinarily bright from all the sunlight reflecting off the snow.

Dad bangs his wooden spoon against the pot and turns off the flame. "Help yourself once you work up an appetite. I added taro and pork, so it's a bit on the sweet side."

"Sounds good." I grab a bag of ground coffee from an overhead cabinet while Dad washes the dishes, the sound of rushing water compensating for the ensuing silence.

I'm conflicted.

While I do feel guilty for giving him a hard time, I also don't think I should feel bad. Neither of us has owned up to anything. How can he acknowledge his mistakes with Aunt Mindy but then act like his decisions are justified with me? If he's using his parental status as leverage, maybe he should be the bigger person and admit when he's wrong.

Maybe then I'd admit when I'm wrong.

Dad turns off the faucet and dries his hands with a dish towel, his movements slow and deliberate, like he's stalling. "I never got to ask . . . how's that project coming along? Min said you're making an oto . . . ottoman . . ."

"Otome game," I supply. The coffee machine rumbles to life and spews caffeinated goodness into my mug. "It's a work in progress. I'm on deadline, so it keeps me busy."

"What's the game about? The way Min explained it to me, it sounds like a choose-your-own-adventure story."

"Basically, yeah." I do not want to talk dating games with my dad.

"Well, this sounds like an amazing opportunity. I don't

know much about video games, but this Angela seems like a bright kid with some big ideas."

"She's something all right," I say.

Dad chuckles. "What's with that tone? Have you and Angela been butting heads?"

"Not lately." I think back to what Aunt Mindy said. *It's your business—just know Brian wouldn't hesitate to welcome Angela into the family.* I'll have to spill the tea eventually, and now seems like an opportune time. "Angela and I are dating, actually."

Dad blinks at me with his mouth agape. As soon as he recovers from the shock, a huge grin splits his face. "Th-that's great!"

I think back to Calvin and Josie. "You don't think she's a . . . distraction?"

"Not at all. You've accomplished a lot this semester, and from what I know about Angela, she sounds good for you," Dad says, beaming. "I'd love to meet her." His enthusiasm feels rather performative after his talk with Aunt Mindy, but . . . I'll cut him some slack.

"Maybe I'll bring her around sometime." I spoon some sugar into my coffee and absently stir. "Just so you know, I recently asked her out, so we're not that serious or anything."

"Serious or not, give me a heads-up when you have her over. I want to meet her."

"Sure . . ." I grab my coffee and make my exit. As soon as I step out of the kitchen, Dad starts whistling.

That wasn't so bad, I guess.

23

"SHOULD WE TURN back?" I ask Angela as she activates her windshield wipers against the sudden onslaught of snow that greets us midway through our trip to Fallbank High.

"I've driven through worse," Angela says, slowing to a stop at a red light.

After much convincing and some bribery, Angela and I are on our way to the Art Club's charity auction. I'm in no mood to see Claire, but Angela promised to share the script for Meng Li's route in exchange for my cooperation. So here I am.

"I'm surprised Ms. Friedman didn't postpone the auction," I say, checking my phone. "The forecast says we might get five to six inches."

"Enough with the excuses." Angela rubs my shoulder, sending a flurry of emotions down my arm and straight to my heart. "Relax. It'll be a good time. Look"—she directs my gaze to the back seat, where a giant thermos sits nestled in one of those camping quilts—"I even brought hot cocoa."

"Made from the finest chocolate, I'm sure."

Angela winks at me. "Nothing but the finest for you."

Fallbank's football field, coated in a thin layer of snow, soon emerges into view. We glide into an empty spot in the staff parking lot. As soon as the passenger door shuts behind me, Angela loops her arm through mine and leads the way.

People are clamoring in the art wing while student-volunteers thread through the hallway, balancing platters of mini quiches, cucumber sandwiches, and fruit tarts. It's a departure from the greasy slop served in the cafeteria. The auction was advertised as a "formal casual affair," and I spot few attendees in cocktail dresses and blazers.

"Lynda!" Ms. Friedman swoops in out of nowhere and welcomes us with open arms. "What a pleasant surprise. I wasn't expecting to see you."

I scratch my head. "I thought I'd show my support."

"That's very sweet. I had an inkling you weren't completely done with Art Club. Now then . . ." Ms. Friedman claps her hands in the way teachers do when they mean business. "The auction will commence shortly in the museum. Coat check is in the music room. Food and drinks are in the ceramics studio. Enjoy!" And with that, she sashays off.

Most of the attendees here seem to be on the older side. Realistically, they're the ones who can afford to contribute, although, come to think of it, does Angela intend to participate in the auction? She has the funds. I'd rather she didn't make the Art Club look good by giving them money, but what she does with her wallet is her business.

After checking our coats, Angela and I head for the ceramics studio. As soon as we enter, Owen dips into our path, one arm folded behind him as he presents us with a tray of filo cups dressed in melted cheese and caramelized pear.

"Ladies, can I interest you in some sweet and savory tartlets?" he says, feigning an aristocratic accent.

Angela helps herself to one. "You're volunteering?"

"Just helping out my buddy Miguel," he says. "He has a photograph up for auction. I'm broke, but maybe one of you ladies will appreciate his creative genius and buy it."

Miguel is a member of the Art Club. He's also the guy who called me uptight and bossy during my short-lived presidency. His love for minimalist art is reflected in his minimalistic effort to do anything meaningful for the club.

"I thought this sort of thing was beneath him," I grouse.

Owen, either oblivious or ignoring my hostility, shrugs and says, "He's just here to see if he can outearn Claire."

Wouldn't that be a doozy?

"By the way . . ." Owen looks back and forth between me and Angela. "Are you two together?" He points to our hooked arms.

Angela answers right away. "We're dating."

"I knew it!" Owen punches the air like he just scored a home run. "I knew there was something going on ever since I introduced you to Buncleaver. You were—"

Angela shoves her hand into Owen's face before dragging me over to the buffet table. "I don't know about you, Lynda, but I'm feeling peckish."

"What did he mean by that?" I ask, helping myself to

the cheese platter as Angela piles her plate with cucumber sandwiches. I click my tongs at her when she doesn't respond. "Well?"

She purses her lips and stares intently at the wall. "Owen and I bumped into each other at a party back in sophomore year. He shared one of your Buncleaver posts with me. That's how I discovered your art."

"Why are you acting so weird about it?"

"Because by then, we'd been in a few classes together, and I didn't even know you were an artist. After seeing your art, I started to . . . notice you more."

"Ah . . ." Now I see where she's coming from. "I guess I should thank Owen for being our unintentional matchmaker."

"I'm sure I would've discovered your art without him."

"Of course . . . and I'm sure you would've commissioned me for your game even if I hadn't needed a new iPad, and we would've fallen for each other all the same."

I'm expecting a smooth comeback or witty retort, but when all I get is silence, I turn to look at her. Angela's cheeks are a vibrant shade of rose and her eyes are smiling.

• • •

Ms. Friedman ushers everyone into the Kirby Museum, a boxy art gallery fitted with ambient light fixtures. Angela and I shuffle into the back row while others populate the front. Projected onto a large screen at the very front of the room is a slideshow presentation:

FALLBANK'S WINTER ART AUCTION:
A NEW YEAR FOR A NEW AESTHETIC

Claire's seated to the left of the screen, tinkering with the laptop that controls the slideshow. I don't know which I dislike more: the title of her presentation or the bubbly font she used for it.

A few chairs remain vacant once everyone settles in. The turnout is modest for a school event but above average for the Art Club, and if what Claire said was true, her dad and his highbrow art collector friends should be here.

Ms. Friedman steps up to the lectern and explains the auction. Participating members of the audience each have a unique identifier in the form of a numeric card, which they will raise anytime they bid on an item. They must voice their offering price out loud and must not bid any amount they are not prepared to pay. The item then goes to the highest bidder. Simple.

Ms. Friedman signals Claire to begin the presentation.

Up first is a watercolor landscape of a marshy grassland cloaked in fog by Blythe Savin. The atmosphere is bleak, the effect unearthly, and Angela appraises it with a contemplative nod. Ms. Friedman recites a few details regarding the composition and the artist's intent before bidding commences. The landscape goes for twenty dollars, thirty, then thirty-five—and is sold for forty in the blink of an eye.

Next is Constance Shi's three-piece set of matte ceramic teacups, painted charcoal black with traditional Chinese characters etched into the surface and outlined in red. The calligraphy is clean and fluid, and the finish smooth. Her skill is almost that of a professional's. I'm tempted to bid on the set until Angela cackles.

"How brazen of her," she says under her breath. "The writing on the cup says *I am the best. Everyone should follow me.*"

The set is sold for one hundred dollars. A few more rounds go by with the lowest winning bid at thirty dollars and the highest at two hundred.

"Miguel should be up soon," Owen says, spooking Angela and me as he suddenly appears behind us. "It's here! Look! Look!" He repeatedly points at the projector screen as if our eyes aren't already there, and what I see is a photograph juxtaposed on another photograph.

"Uh-huh . . ." I tilt my head this way, then that way and take a moment to absorb what's in front of me. Something a lot like awe begins to consume me the longer I stare at it.

But not the good kind.

Miguel drew a possum—not a very good one, I must say—on a sheet of yellow notebook paper, the kind you get from the dollar store. He then used a Polaroid to take a close-up shot of the possum. Once the photo developed, he pinned it to his fridge with a magnet and took *another* photo, this time with his smartphone. The final product is what we see now.

"Very meta," says Angela, her tone edging on sarcastic.

"It's funny," I admit, "and crude."

The possum is identifiable, but barely. Overall, not much artistry was involved compared to the other pieces I've seen today. I'm not saying splattered paint on a canvas doesn't belong in a museum or that a photo of some mundane object can't be valued at millions. Landscapes and teacups aren't groundbreaking or original, but Miguel's entry for the auction feels somewhat like a mockery. I doubt anyone here would want—

"One hundred!" someone shouts.

"Huh?" Owen, Angela, and I balk. We watch as a collective murmur ripples through the crowd. An intense volley of bids ensues, the offering price increasing in five-dollar increments before settling at $250. All in the span of a minute.

I'm gobsmacked. "What the hell just happened?"

"Chef's kiss is what happened." Owen searches the room for Miguel and blows him a kiss, which he returns with the middle finger. "Can you believe his photo's a year old? He forgot he had it saved on his phone."

I have nothing against modern or minimalistic art, but is something that took less than ten minutes worth more than Constance's handcrafted teacups? Ms. Friedman even said that Miguel printed the final photo on glossy paper using a home printer. I've had strangers on Instagram hound me over my commission rates when the projects they propose require hours, if not days, to complete.

Angela shakes her head. "What a joke. Is the Art Club facilitating money laundering?"

"Don't be such sore losers," Owen says. "All the money goes to charity, remember?"

Leave it to Owen to be the sensible one.

Finally, it's Claire's turn. She's impassive as the projector displays an impasto painting of a sun beginning to set over an abstract field of poppies. The spiraling sky and psychedelic sun are overpowering; the colors all seem to blur together, setting the entire composition ablaze. The piece is provocative, dizzying, and experimental—for Claire, anyway. She used thick acrylics to achieve a textured effect. You can literally count every brushstroke she made.

"What are your thoughts?" Angela asks, prodding me. "A bit garish, don't you think?"

"I . . . like it," I confess. "Reminds me of a fever dream."

"A surprisingly mature response," Owen teases. He backs away as if I'm about to punch him, which of course would be the farthest thing from a mature response.

A gentleman up front starts the bidding at two hundred, a humble amount after all the smoke Claire blew up her you-know-what. I lean forward, hovering a few inches off my chair as I crane my neck to get a better look at him. Apart from his lavender blazer and the silver streaking his hair, I can't discern much with all the heads obscuring my view.

Claire observes the crowd, appearing more pensive than smug. If her rich daddy and his distinguished art buddies are here, they should be flaunting their wealth soon enough and kicking Miguel off his pedestal. If bidding soars to the thousands, I'm not sure whether to be livid, jealous, or perplexed.

Ms. Friedman surveys the audience, and after a considerable pause, somewhere in the middle row, someone says, "Two hundred and fifteen."

Hardly a noteworthy counter to stir a bidding war. The gentleman in the lavender blazer increases the stakes to three hundred. The whispers begin once more as people start weighing their opinions. The lady seated right in front of me slowly raises her arm, but then her companion lowers it back to her lap.

The voices thin out and the room quiets.

Claire's face is drawn tight. Ms. Friedman reaches for her gavel, and in that split second where her hand has yet to depart from the lectern, a crack begins to form in Claire's armor. That one minuscule flaw is enough to reveal her disappointment—and her shame.

Before the gavel can strike, I leap to my feet, raise my bidding card high over my head, and shout, "Four hundred!"

All eyes turn to me. I think I even hear a gasp.

Angela tugs the hem of my sweater. "Lynda, what are you—" I give her a pleading look, and immediately she raises her own card. "Five hundred!"

Confusion overtakes the crowd, followed by curiosity.

"Uh . . ." Owen, cardless, waves his hand. "Five hundred and ten cents?"

The room springs back to life, and the gentleman in the blazer escalates his bid to six hundred, only for Angela to outdo him with seven hundred. The lady in front of me finally raises her card and, with an air of finality, shouts, "Nine hundred."

Ms. Friedman slams her gavel. "Sold!"

• • •

A steady snowfall continues to blanket the town as the sun dips behind the trees. Angela and I stop in the middle of the parking lot to admire the landscape. The sky is a breathtaking mixture of pinks and blues, the clouds soft and voluminous like cotton candy, while snowflakes descend upon us like a sugar storm.

If this isn't romantic, I don't know what is.

Just as I'm about to dust the snow off Angela's nose, Claire suddenly cuts in front of me, but not without slipping on a patch of ice. I yank her up by her jacket before her feet slide out from under her. Once she regains her balance, she rips her jacket out of my grasp and takes a moment to catch her breath.

I signal Angela to go ahead and start the car.

"Do you need something?" I ask Claire.

She starts to say something and then stops. The longer she takes to reply, the more I expect her to show some gratitude—until she blurts, "What the hell was that?!" She carries on before I can get a word in. "Don't think you did me any favors, Lynda. Count your lucky stars you weren't stuck with the bill."

I resist the urge to roll my eyes. "Whatever. Are we done here?"

"Not until you answer my question."

"Oh, that was a legit question? It sounded like you were telling me off."

Claire glowers at me. Despite the murderous intent radiating off her, her conviction is somewhat endearing, so I dial back the sass.

"Answer my question first," I say. "What happened to your dad and his friends?"

"They couldn't make it," she grumbles.

Clearly there's more to the story. I dig my feet into the snow and wait. The wind picks up, whipping my hair in all sorts of directions as the cold seeps through my clothes and my toes begin to numb. Still, I refuse to budge.

"Ugh, fine!" Claire throws up her hands and sighs dramatically. "My dad backed out last minute to attend some gala in New York, and since he dropped out, his friends did too."

Her dad must've known how much this auction meant to her. I'm sure she couldn't stop gloating about it to him. Dropping out says a lot about his priorities—and a lot about him.

Parents shouldn't make empty promises.

"What about your mom?" I ask. "Did she come tonight?"

"Only my brother showed up."

"The guy in the lavender blazer?"

"If you mean the *lavender-blue* blazer, then yes, that was him, and he's broke." Claire crosses her arms and kicks the snow. "I almost had a heart attack when he kept bidding money he didn't have."

Well, what do you know? I have something in common with Claire.

"That's three questions, Lynda. Now answer mine."

I don't think telling Claire I felt bad for her will be appreciated. We might be enemies, but I know her well enough to understand she doesn't want my pity. She's not one to sugarcoat, so if there's anything she could possibly want from me, it would be my honesty.

"I don't like you, and I might like Miguel even less," I say, "but you know what I *hate*? Seeing someone's hard work go unacknowledged."

Claire gnaws on the inside of her cheek. "That's all?"

"That's all."

She appraises me with an unreadable expression before turning back toward the school. I watch as her silhouette fades into the distance.

"That was interesting," Angela says, sidling up to me. "She has a point. You could've saddled us with a hefty bill."

I dip my head in an apologetic bow. "I'm sorry! I got caught up in the moment."

Angela hooks a finger under my chin and lifts my gaze to hers. "While you were getting caught up in the moment, I was getting caught up in you," she says, taking my hands in hers and raising them to her lips, her breath hot against my fingers. "Who knew Lynda Fan could be reckless and noble for someone she doesn't even like?"

The friction between us is unsettling yet . . . enticing. A delightful shiver courses through me. It's such an unfamiliar sensation. I don't know what to do with it.

"I wasn't trying to be," I sputter as she inches her face closer to mine. "Wh-what is it? Is there something on my face?"

"Lynda." She sighs. "I'm trying to kiss you right now."

"Oh."

"Please hold still . . . if that's okay with you?"

"S-sure. Hopefully my breath doesn't—"

She silences me with a kiss, stealing the words from my lips and the breath from my lungs. All at once, the world slows, and time becomes an inconsequential thing. I am blissfully unaware of my surroundings yet all too cognizant of my hands as they linger over her back, grasping at nothing, and of how her lips taste like candied apples. Even after we part, the dreamlike bubble I'm floating in refuses to pop.

I didn't know a kiss could be so . . . innocent yet intimate. But now I do.

Angela smiles sheepishly at me, then braces herself as a gust of wind sends ice crystals into the air. Night has fallen, and glitter is everywhere. I wrap my arms around her and hug her tightly, savoring the moment for as long as I can. All that matters right now is the two of us, here, rendered white by the snow.

Right where we should be.

24

LONG AFTER OUR kiss, when the snow has ceased and we're settled into a camping quilt laid over a bench at the local pond, Angela pours me a cup of hot cocoa from her thermos.

"That's some high-tech thermos you got there," I say as the cup warms my palms and a ribbon of steam flicks the tip of my nose. "Does your family go camping often?"

"My dad does every now and then." Angela drills her thermos into the snow and drapes a heated blanket across our laps to seal ourselves from the cold. "He purchased all this camping gear two winters ago to attend the Harbin Ice Festival."

"Guess we should be thanking him. Else we wouldn't be here."

"Don't give him all the credit. I still would've come prepared if I was planning to make you sit out here." Angela side-eyes me. "You're not . . . cold, are you?"

"Far from it." Even with my ears and fingers exposed, I feel like I'm lounging by a fire, the invisible flames intensifying as Angela snuggles against me. I sip my hot cocoa and let the sweet, molten liquid ooze down my throat.

Despite all the rom-coms I've watched with Bora, I could never understand how a single person could become your entire world. Overromanticizing someone and pinning all your hopes and dreams on them doesn't bode well for a healthy relationship, yet . . . when I look at Angela, she does feel like a dream come true.

"Why are you looking at me like that?" she says.

"Like what?" I ask.

"Like you're captivated by me." Angela takes a sip from her cup and licks the chocolatey residue off her lips.

I instinctively look the other way. "So . . . when are you sending me the script?"

Angela playfully smacks my lap. "I'll email it once I get home. Happy?"

"Very. How long is it anyway? Is it like a novel?"

"It's written as a screenplay." A plume of condensation hangs in the air as she sighs. "Just so you're aware . . . I'm the one writing the script for *Love Takes Root*. I originally said my brother's friend was responsible for it, but that was . . . another lie."

Her confession is like a raindrop hitting the pond, the impact rippling toward me as my mind struggles to catch up, until finally, understanding hits.

"You're a writer?" I ask.

She traces a finger along the rim of her cup.

"I am," she says after a pause. "It's not something I'm . . . open about."

Angela's been up-front about liking otome games. In fact, she's been up-front about a lot of things. It seems out of character for her to be so secretive about being a writer.

"I don't write anything weird or depraved, if that's what you're wondering," she adds. "I enjoy a smutty story now and then, but nothing . . . hard-core."

"Thanks for the clarification. You sure are full of surprises."

And white lies . . .

Angela squares her shoulders and wears my statement like a crown. "I started writing fan fiction in middle school before graduating to more original works. Short stories, mostly. *Love Takes Root* is my first attempt at a mobile game."

"Are otome games usually written as screenplays?"

"I'm not . . . informed enough to answer that." Angela seems embarrassed by her own admission. "Some people write and code as they go, into whatever visual novel engine they're publishing on. I prefer writing everything in Word first."

"So . . . is the game actually a graduation gift from your brother?"

"Yes and no. It's really a gift to myself, since I came up with the idea. When *Romancing the New Moon* was still in development, I thought, why not make my own game? I've written and trunked so many stories that no one will ever read, but to see my characters come to life in an otome game? That would be . . . something."

Something or everything?

"What else have you written?"

"You sure are full of questions. . . ." Angela tugs her scarf farther up her face. "I wrote a ninety-thousand-word fake dating rom-com in eighth grade, and no, you can't read it. It's a dumpster fire."

"Come on. It can't be that bad."

"Believe me, you'll want to claw your eyes out. I had fun writing it but cringe whenever I revisit it." She shudders at the recollection. "I'm baffled by how I could produce something so . . . unrealistic and cliché."

Great. Now I'm thinking back to my own art as a kid. Like in third grade, when my class covered a unit on fairy tales and folklore, and I drew a princess riding on the back of a dragon as part of a group project. The only reason I remember this is because, years later, I stumbled upon the drawing while cleaning out my closet and noticed the, uh, ample bosom I'd bestowed on the princess and how her royal scepter was a bit too . . . phallic.

Angela presses on. "Anyway, I started a second book during sophomore year. I reached forty thousand words before giving up."

"Why?" I ask, my tone bordering on accusation.

Angela? Give up? This does not compute.

"I . . . ran out of steam. When you're juggling school, extracurriculars, family, and hobbies, something has to give. Even I have my limits. There aren't enough hours in the day to do everything you want to do."

Time waits for no one, not even the capable.

"Have you considered writing professionally? I mean,

you're already on your way, developing an otome game and all."

"Writing is more of a hobby for me. An outlet."

"So if a publishing house approached you and offered to buy your book, you wouldn't jump on that opportunity?"

"That's not how the publishing industry works, Lynda."

"You've researched it, then?"

She side-eyes me. Checkmate.

"You understand how competitive the art industry is. Writing is no different. I don't share the same drive as you," she says. "Not enough to fight for it."

"Angela Wu, future valedictorian of Fallbank High, isn't driven enough?" I jest, but the humor doesn't seem to land, as Angela remains impassive. "Now I'm really eager to read Meng Li's route."

"I think . . . that's enough questions for tonight. Remember, this is all fun and games. I didn't write *Love Takes Root* with the intention of winning a literary honor. Enjoy it for what it's meant to be."

"Still, I'm sure your writing will blow me away."

I deliver a quick kiss to her forehead, and her eyes light up with renewed confidence. I even see a smile peeking out from under her scarf. Although writing might not be her passion in the same way art is mine, Angela is the kind of person who always strives to do her best.

What's not to love about that?

• • •

I spend New Year's Eve reading Meng Li's route.

The MC is a silk weaver who resides in the far west region of Lianhua Po. After catching the attention of a visiting noble, MC is forced to marry a man thirteen years their senior. On their eighteenth birthday, MC will have no choice but to abandon their hometown and move across the country to play bride to a stranger. News of this unfortunate affair spreads throughout the land and reaches Meng Li, MC's childhood friend.

Meng Li hasn't seen MC in two years due to her lifestyle as a traveling performer. The pair have always dreamed of settling down and opening a teahouse together. Keen to save her friend and the future they long for, Meng Li hires the infamous thief Sun Hong to steal MC on the night they're to be delivered to their betrothed. The heist proves successful but not without incurring a hefty bounty and the wrath of the nobleman they've slighted. The penalty for their crime is death. Meng Li and Sun Hong have no intention of dying, while MC has no intention of marrying someone they don't love. But the three can only be on the run for so long.

Then a solution presents itself.

The empress is on her deathbed. If they can find a way to reverse her illness, the emperor will pardon them. And so, this unlikely trio embark on a journey to retrieve the Golden Lotus, a mythical flower said to cure any disease if you consume a single petal. Their search is not without trial and tribulation, but where there is pain and suffering there is also love and devotion.

Meng Li is a determined individual who possesses a bottomless reserve of optimism. She is a force to be reckoned with, and it's impossible not to fall in love with her. Her route was an entertaining ride that had me racing toward the finishing line.

In the happy ending, the trio saves the empress, and the emperor not only pardons them but also rewards them with a lifetime supply of gold. MC and Meng Li open their teahouse with Sun Hong as their supplier, and everyone lives happily ever after.

In the bad ending, Meng Li retrieves the Golden Lotus, nestled into the outer walls of a cliff, and hands it to MC. At that very second, a nameless bandit, who's been stalking the trio to obtain the flower for himself, directs his bow and arrow at MC. Meng Li blocks the lethal blow with her body, slips off the cliff, and plummets to her death. In the end, Sun Hong and MC deliver the flower to the emperor—without Meng Li.

After dinner and a round of card games with Aunt Mindy and Uncle Ben, I text Angela. *Did you have to do Meng Li dirty like that in the bad ending?*

Meng Li dies courageously but gets taken out by a random character.

It's a bad ending for a reason, Angela responds. *Did I trigger your tear glands?*

Maybe . . . Does Sun Hong also die in his bad ending?

Three dots appear on-screen as Angela types. They seem to linger there forever, until finally—*He doesn't, but after an explosive battle against Xiaohua, he has burn scars over half his face and goes blind in his left eye.*

That's when I call her.

"You can't do this to me!" I scream as soon as she picks up.

"Well, I am. Sorry not sorry?" She laughs. "I guess you liked what you read?"

"I loved it!"

"You're not just saying that to boost my ego?"

"Angela, please, your ego doesn't need boosting. I really did love what I read. The bad ending emotionally destroyed me; it was wild, sad, and bittersweet—and it got me thinking that maybe we should illustrate the bandit who kills Meng Li. Right now, he's a faceless, nameless nobody."

The emperor and nobleman are the last two NPCs I've been assigned. Drawing them should be a breeze now that I'm well acquainted with them. Although there's still much to do, I'm confident I can fit in one more character.

"I don't know if that's a good idea," Angela says unexpectedly. "Other characters have more lines than him. Singling him out doesn't make much sense. If anything, you should draw the empress."

"Okay, I see what you mean, but giving the bandit a stronger presence in the game would make Meng Li's death feel less—I don't know—bleak."

"Are you suggesting that I rewrite the ending?"

"No, I'm suggesting we make the bandit an illustrated NPC. I'll even draw him for free. As creative director, you have the final say, so the decision is yours."

Angela's quiet for a moment.

Maybe I managed to convince her. After all, including more illustrations can only improve the game.

Then she says, "I think you should stick to our original agreement and focus on the remaining characters and CGs."

"Oh." I can't help but sound disappointed. Who declines free labor? "Sure, if that's what you want . . . I'll probably work on the emperor next."

"Great! Can't wait to see him, and . . . Lynda, if I do change my mind, we can renegotiate the contract. I want to compensate you properly if you draw more characters."

I brighten at the possibility. "Keep me posted! You've written something special, and I want to do it justice."

"And I want to do your art justice. Amazing and cheesy together, remember?"

"Of course."

Although, for a minute there, it almost seemed like Angela forgot.

25

RETURNING TO SCHOOL after winter break is like taking part in a funeral procession. Everyone moves at a glacial pace, as if the weight of their backpack equals that of a casket. I too mourn the loss of sleeping in and doing whatever I want. To ease the pain, I surprise Bora with egg tarts and tea in the school parking lot.

"You're a lifesaver," she says, hugging me.

"We could all use an extra boost this morning." Including myself. Just an hour ago, I had to say goodbye to Aunt Mindy and Uncle Ben before Dad took them to the airport. I hand Bora a cup of milk tea. "Made with Darjeeling and honey, exactly how you like it."

Bora touches a hand to her heart. "You know me so well."

We each help ourselves to an egg tart as cars continue pulling into the lot. A few of them stop to beep at us even though we're not in their way. Then, as Bora and I traverse the crosswalk, a silver car speeds toward us—before swerving into the lot at the very last second.

If that was a joke, it wasn't funny.

I trail after the car with my eyes and barely make out Arun in the driver's seat.

Bora hooks her arm though mine and yanks me toward the school.

"Come on," she says. "Let's get this day over with."

The start of a new semester is a somber affair, yet I can't shake off the impression that people are staring at me. My paranoia is confirmed during first period, after some freshman approaches me in the locker room to ask, "Is it true you're dating Angela Wu?"

"Yeah," I answer while changing into my yoga pants. "What's it to you?"

"My friend saw you two at the Art Club auction." The girl looks around before leaning in with one hand over her mouth as her voice drops to conspiratorial whisper. "Just so you know, I heard Angela has a history of leading people on."

"Okay, bye." I exit into the gymnasium and catch up with Bora.

Who's dating who is a daily topic that circulates the halls of Fallbank High. Common as it is, it didn't cross my mind that Angela and I would be a source for gossip.

Unfortunately, the gossip continues to follow me.

Today we're playing badminton, and Arun keeps spiking the birdie at my face. Not once has he acknowledged Bora standing next to me on the court. He isn't giving his partner a chance to play either. He's intent on making this a one-on-one, and I'm not the type to back away from a challenge— not when he's coming at me with so much inexplicable aggression. He already got my knee, so I dished it back by aiming for his neck.

Now we're both out for blood.

I need to make him pay after that little stunt he pulled this morning in the parking lot.

Bora idly swings her racket and shouts, "Arun! What gives? Am I supposed to stand here all day looking pretty?"

With Arun distracted, I deliver the birdie straight to his face. Before it can nail him between the eyes, his partner parries my shot, driving the birdie into the net.

"Hey!" I run across the court as Arun retrieves the birdie. "That point was ours. It's our serve." He turns his back on me and starts to walk away. "Fine. Whatever. We don't have to play by the rules. I'll win regardless."

"Lynda!" Bora grabs my arm. "Let's not go overboard."

"What are you talking about? This is just the tip of the iceberg." And since I don't know when to stop, "It's no wonder Angela never gave him the time of day."

Arun starts to backtrack.

"Oh my god . . ." Bora face-palms. "Lynda, he looks like he wants to kill you."

So he does. Still, I don't back down as he meets me at the net. He sizes me up, and something changes in him, his hostility waning with what seems to be resignation.

"I don't get it," he grumbles, dropping the birdie into my outstretched hand. "Why did Angela choose you?"

And there we have it, the source of his frustration.

"I don't know about you, Arun, but I wouldn't date

someone who used to make fun of me in middle school," I quip as Bora tugs incessantly on my sweatshirt. "Karma's a bitch."

"I already apologized to her for that."

"And you storming out of Owen's party isn't a sign you might have anger issues?"

Arun makes a sound halfway between a laugh and a scoff. "Right, 'cause you're just so *nice*, Lynda. Get over yourself. Angela will drop you the same way she dropped the rest of us."

· · ·

After several people ask me about Angela, some more well-meaning than others, I finally reach my boiling point. On my way to lunch, I spot Angela in the hallway and shove my way through the crowd to reach her. Her gaze is open and curious as I lock hands with her in the middle of a busy intersection and lead her into an empty classroom.

She smirks as I close the door and move us away from the window looking out into the hall. "You're awfully bold," she says. "Can't say I hate it."

I have no brain capacity at the moment to understand what she's implying and just say what I came here to say. "Are you okay?"

Angela squints at me. "Yes. Why wouldn't I be?"

"People are talking. About us."

There's a subtle shift in her expression before Angela pantomimes a yawn. "Are they, now? I must not have been paying attention." She rocks back and forth on her feet, more amused by the world maps on the wall than what anyone has to say about her.

The bell rings, though neither of us is in a rush to leave.

"I thought you had something romantic in mind when you brought me here," she says with a hint of mischief.

"Sorry to bore you, but I'm here to talk."

Angela visibly wilts and dismisses me with a wave of her hand. "At least talk about something that isn't so . . . mundane. Two girls dating is hardly news."

"Not to you, but Arun—"

She snaps her head in my direction. "What did he do?"

Her voice is an octave too low to belong to the Angela I know.

"Nothing, really . . ." After our confrontation, he sulked off and had his partner play for the remainder of class. I pushed one too many buttons, and instead of exploding, he turned off like a defused bomb. "He's being passive-aggressive and mopey."

"Don't listen to sour grapes." Angela relaxes and tosses her hair back over her shoulder. "They can make a tempest in a teapot and sip it all they want. Their opinions don't matter."

"They matter to me," I counter. "I don't like it when people speak badly of you."

"Oh, so they're saying *negative* things about me?"

"Angela. I'm being serious."

Finally, she drops the pretense and speaks honestly. "I know people are whispering and dredging up my freshman

year . . . antics. I'm sorry you're getting caught up in that."
She cuts me off before I can tell her she has nothing to apologize for. "What's important to me is that people aren't giving you a hard time. It's enough that you think well of me."

"Arun's the only one with a bone to pick. He'll probably get over it soon. . . ." I didn't appreciate how he tried to make me out to be the bad one. Nor did I appreciate the implication that I somehow don't deserve Angela.

As for Angela breaking up with me . . .

I shake the thought out of my head. "Anyway, I know you can look out for yourself just fine, but I'm here if you need me."

"Good." Angela crosses her arms and nods affirmatively. "Everything else is noise."

I guess that's that, and now Angela's late to class. Still, she shows no sense of urgency as she presses a finger to my lips and disarms me with a few words.

"You look very kissable right now."

And in a span of a second, I go from kissable to kissed.

• • •

While Angela did alleviate some of my unease, something else lingers in its place, because I am dreading Art & Design. Upon entering, I take a cursory look around the art studio.

Ms. Friedman rises from her desk, positively beaming. "Lynda! You created quite a stir the other day."

She's referring to the auction. I evaded her after the

event, but there's no escaping her now. I unload my belongings into the wooden cubby by the door and give her a nonchalant "I guess I did" before sliding into my usual seat.

Gale Sullivan, a sophomore I shared a table with last semester, turns to me. "My grandma was at the auction, said someone ignited a bidding war. That was you?"

"Uh, yeah . . ." I tug my ponytail loose and let my hair down to hide my face.

"Damn, wish I was there to witness it."

"Believe me, you didn't miss much," I tell Gale as more faces file into the room.

At least in this corner of the school, people are more interested in the charity auction than my relationship status. Still, the auction is old news. Why haven't people found something else to clamor about? It's not like Claire's painting sold for thousands of dollars.

Claire arrives after the bell and hands Ms. Friedman a late slip while she's explaining a light and shadow exercise. Today we'll be splitting into groups of three. One person will be the photographer, another will be the subject, and the other will control the lighting. The assignment is to capture our subject's face under various degrees of light.

Gale raps his knuckles on the table. "Want to work together?"

"Sure," I say. The two seniors who usually sit with us left to find other partners. As I skim the room for any stragglers who might want to join Gale and me, the chair across from me rattles on its legs.

Claire has claimed the seat.

"Looks like we have our group," she declares.

"Fine. You can be our subject," I say, opening the camera on my phone while Gale turns on his flashlight and angles it at Claire's face.

Once everyone is settled in, Ms. Friedman turns off the overhead lights, throwing Claire's profile into stark relief, highlighting the incline of her cheek while carving deep shadows around the grooves of her lips and the valley of her nose.

The room is nothing but disembodied, half-formed heads. What terrifies me, however, is having photos of Claire saved on my phone. I will be deleting them as soon as this torture—I mean, exercise—is over.

"So, Lynda . . ." Claire starts to speak, eyes closed as Gale positions the flashlight a few inches from her right temple. "I forgot to thank you the other day."

I take a couple photos before instructing her to lower her chin.

"Are you listening to me?" she snaps.

Gale shines the flashlight at himself and shakes his head as if to say *Don't mind me!*

"What happened to thinking I was doing all that for clout?" I finally say.

"I changed my mind, okay? I'm trying to be real with you here."

"Right now?"

"You did the Art Club a favor, and me a personal one. Is a thank-you too much for you?"

Leave it to Claire to make a thank-you sound like an insult.

"You pack a lot of attitude into your gratitude," I say. "I suppose the polite response would be *You're welcome.* So. You're welcome."

This seems to appease her, and we continue our assignment without speaking to each other. At the end of class, Claire comes up from behind me as I'm collecting my things. She reaches into her own cubby to grab her messenger bag.

"By the way, I'm not applying to RISD anymore," she says without looking at me. "It's too cold up there. I belong at CalArts. They need me as much as I need the sun." She pauses, and I prepare myself in case she has something new to brag about.

But then the bell rings, and she concludes with, "Just thought you should know."

26

DAD'S HOME EARLY when I return from school on Thursday. I find him hunched over the dining table, sifting through a mess of paperwork. Judging by the mugs cluttering the table, he's on his fourth cup of coffee. Once the front door shuts behind me, he rubs the fatigue from his eyes and greets me.

My confusion gives me away, and he jumps right into an explanation.

"I took the afternoon off so we could visit the mausoleum," he says.

It takes a shamefully long minute before I realize today's the anniversary of Mom's death. I completely forgot.

Dad presses on while I grapple with my awful memory. "Maybe we can grab some food while we're out. How does that sound?"

"As long as we're back by six," I say, depositing my backpack at the foot of the couch. "I have to get started on a group project, and we're all meeting virtually."

Dad flashes me a crooked grin before retrieving the car

keys from his briefcase. "Let me know when you're ready to head out."

I don't keep him waiting too long.

After a bathroom break, we hit the backroads to avoid after-school traffic and wend our way up a mountain before passing through the iron gates of Fallbank's Garden Mausoleum. An expansive field looms ahead, punctuated by a granite structure set far back behind a frozen pond. We follow the footpath laid out for visitors and enter the main building. The thick carpeting of the ceremony hall eventually gives way to marble floors and a maze of columbarium walls. Our footsteps echo throughout the cavernous space as we find Mom's little square engraved with her name: FIONA FAN.

Her ashes weren't always kept here.

Dad had removed the door to a spare closet in our apartment and erected a memorial to house her cremation urn. He used to burn incense every morning until a neighbor complained about the smell. While I did pay my respects now and then by plating some fruit on the altar and keeping the area tidy, I couldn't help but feel detached from the whole practice. Her memorial was a constant reminder of someone I should've *felt* more for—but didn't.

Eventually Dad thought it was best to move her elsewhere, long before he started dating again. I'm not familiar with . . . grief. I suspect the art of moving on is far more difficult to achieve when you enshrine the memory of your late spouse in a closet that you pass by every day. Whatever memorabilia remains of my mom is tucked away in the attic, out of sight though not always out of mind.

Dad places a bouquet of tulips on the floor, directly below Mom's name, and closes his eyes in silent prayer. I pretend to focus on my own thoughts despite the blank canvas in my head. My phone vibrates in my pocket, and in this too-quiet room, the sound is amplified to a startling degree. I swiftly mute my phone and watch as an elderly couple walks by, arm in arm, bearing colorful perennial blooms.

"Hey, Dad." I wince as my voice echoes throughout the room.

He throws a curious glance in my direction.

"Can you tell me about Mom's side of the family?"

A strangled sound escapes him. I can't blame him for being surprised. I rarely ask about Mom. Most of what I know about her is through photographs and stories. Dad and Aunt Mindy do occasionally share a fond memory or two, but they haven't been forthcoming about the not-so-fond ones.

"What exactly do you want to know?" he asks.

"Her side of the family never talks to us, and we never talk to them. I assume . . . our relationship is strained for a reason?"

I only met my mom's parents once, and I was too young to remember it. They used to live in New York, somewhere near the Canadian border. After Mom passed away, they retired to their hometown in Taiwan. She was their only child, and after she departed, I suppose they didn't have a reason to stick around.

"Fiona's parents didn't support our marriage," Dad tentatively says. "Still, they're your grandparents, and I'd rather not speak poorly of them to you."

"No need to shield me from the truth. There's not much love to lose between us." I laugh, hoping to cut through this oppressive atmosphere, but as my voice echoes throughout this bright yet sterile room, I succeed in only making myself uncomfortable.

Dad produces a handkerchief from his pocket. Panic strikes and I frantically search his face for tears, but then he removes his glasses and starts polishing the lenses.

"I suppose you're old enough to know," he says, angling his glasses to catch the sunlight pouring in through the windows. "Fiona's parents didn't approve of her life choices. They had a specific future planned for her, and she deviated from it. They wanted her to attend college in New York; instead, she went to Virginia. They wanted her to become a doctor, and she became a teacher. They wanted her to marry someone of their choosing, but she chose me."

"Quite the rebel." I'm impressed.

"Maybe one day Min can tell you about how they tried to separate us."

"Why didn't they want her to marry you?"

"Because I wasn't rich," he says evenly. "I didn't come from money or have a lot of it, so they thought I couldn't make her happy."

"Mom wouldn't have married you if she wasn't happy."

And based on their wedding photos, she was *very* happy.

If I'm being honest, though, while money doesn't guarantee happiness, it does solve a lot of problems.

Dad stares lovingly at Mom's name engraved on the wall. "She knew what she wanted. No amount of parental disapproval could dissuade her."

I guess I do take after her.

"Once you were born, her parents found more things to nitpick—what to name you, what to feed you, how to discipline you. The list goes on." The recollection of it exhausts him. "Fiona and I knew it would get worse, so we went low contact. No more phone calls or visits unless we initiated them."

"How did low contact go to no contact?"

Dad flicks his eyes to the ceiling. "After Fiona was diagnosed with cancer, she spent a lot of time in and out of the hospital. Her parents offered to pay for her treatment under the condition that she . . . move back to New York and receive treatment there. Of course, they wanted you to come along, too."

"But . . . they wanted you to stay in Virginia?"

Dad forces a smile and nods stiffly.

Well, isn't that despicable?

"Fiona refused, and she cut them out of her life for good. Her parents tried to salvage the relationship by rescinding the condition, but by then Fiona had had enough." Dad drags a hand down his face, looking pained and haggard. "We figured out our finances without their help."

That's . . . a lot to digest. I did ask for the truth, and I got it. Mom fought tooth and nail to be with Dad, and in the end, it wasn't even her parents that separated them. It's sobering how some things just . . . aren't in our control. I can see why Dad and Aunt Mindy never mentioned this part of our family history.

"Cutting them off was the right choice," I say after a moment.

"It was for us, but . . ." Dad touches a hand to my shoulder. "If you want to reconnect with your grandparents, I won't discourage it. Now that I'm several years removed from everything, perhaps they were more misguided than malicious in their intentions."

"No thanks." I shake my head, as if my words aren't enough to get my point across.

"Well, let me know if you change your mind."

I doubt that'll ever happen.

Life is trying enough as it is without your family holding you back.

27

AS JOSIE'S RECITAL nears, I see Nick more often than I'd like to. Her lessons last longer these days. Some nights she doesn't even come to bed, preferring to sleep in her practice room instead. She seems on edge, so I try to give her space by spending my afternoons out of the house.

Friday night, I pick up a pizza on my way home from Angela's since Dad's working late and Amy's celebrating a coworker's retirement. Nick's car is still in the driveway when I arrive. It's seven p.m. I thought he'd be gone by now. I mentally prepare myself before entering the house, and right away, I hear Josie's violin—which means the door to her practice room is open. I clear the dining table and fetch some plates from the kitchen.

"There's pizza!" I shout. "Get it while it's hot!"

The violin screeches to a halt, and I expect to hear footsteps.

Instead, I get Nick's voice.

"How many times do I have to tell you? Relax your hand

but don't move it. Keep it in the same spot and stretch your fingers to reach the strings. Now take it from the top."

I sneak down the hallway and catch a glimpse of Josie's back through the two-inch gap between the door and the frame.

"We've been at it for hours," she says, exasperated. "Can't we call it a day? I don't . . . I don't feel too good."

"Neither do I," says Nick. "Your recital is next Saturday. A Curtis faculty member will be there, and if you can impress her, she'll meet with you one-on-one. She might even vouch for you to the admissions committee. If you fail—"

"I'm doing the best I can!" Josie sounds like she's on the verge of tears.

"Your performance today doesn't reflect that."

Whatever fight Josie had left in her gives out. Her shoulders slacken and her bow slips through her fingers, hitting the floor with a thud. Nick sighs and starts to speak, but before he can add salt to the wound, I swing the door wide open on its hinges. They startle at the sound, neither of them relieved by my intrusion.

"Everything okay in here?" I ask lightly.

Josie looks away and swipes a hand across her eyes before gathering up the sheet music scattered on the floor. Nick packs his violin, sweat beading on his forehead as I track his movements across the room. They avoid my question, both equally stiff as I lurk in the doorway, expecting an answer that is eventually lost to the silence.

Nick tries to slink past me without so much as a goodbye.

I step back and extend my arm, blocking his path. "Are you sure you don't want to stick around?" I ask, my tone sweet as sugar. "There's pizza."

"I ate before I got here," he mutters. "Have a good night."

And with that, he's gone.

My eyes dart back to Josie still scrambling to pick up the mess. I get down to help her and reach for the music sheet pinned under her knee. Tears blot the page, warping the surface.

"I got this," I tell her. "You should go eat—"

She's out the door before I can finish.

. . .

Josie's curled up in bed when I finish my shower. She hasn't said a word to me all night. When Amy asked how lessons went, she completely glossed over what happened with Nick. I thought I was helping her by interrupting. . . . Perhaps all I did was humiliate her. There are some things we simply don't want other people to see.

I fan my hair out with a towel, my nighttime routine a welcome distraction from the persisting silence that bothers me way more than I want it to. Josie's problems are her own. If she doesn't want to talk, that's her right. Still, it feels wrong to leave her alone.

Josie rolls onto her side and tucks her pillow under her chin. "I heard you visited your mom last week," she mumbles, her expression taut. "How'd it go? I meant to ask sooner, but . . ."

"It was like every other year." I shrug. "We paid our respects, and that's about it."

"Can I . . . ask you something? It's kind of invasive."

"Ask away."

"Do you ever wonder what life would've been like . . . if your mom were still here?"

"Sometimes." I drape my towel over my chair and grab a tub of moisturizer from the top of the dresser. "If my mom were still alive, Dad wouldn't have married your mom, and I'd probably still be living in my old apartment."

Although I'm not happy with my current living situation, I don't necessarily believe my life would've been a fairy tale had cancer not taken my mom. If she really was as stubborn as Dad described her, she and I would've butted heads. Even so . . . Dad probably would've been home more often, and I would've had more people to rely on than Aunt Mindy and Uncle Ben. Things might not have been perfect if Mom were still here, but they could've been . . . better. Happier, even.

But who's to say? The grass isn't always greener on the other side, and what's the point in dwelling on what could've been? I can't rewrite the past. What's important is what happens now and what *can* happen. I should focus on the things I can control.

"Do you miss her?" Josie asks, eyes pooling with sympathy I don't need.

"Not really," I say. I know I sound callous. At this point, it wouldn't surprise me at all if Josie were to call me a sociopath. Try as I might, I can't help the way I feel. My mom's death wasn't a heavy loss for me, not in the way it was for Dad.

How can you lose someone you didn't know you had? And what if I did miss my mom? She's gone. Secondhand memories and photographs can't give me the whole story. I won't ever know her. Not truly. I have no memory of her, only an idea. She'll never be more than that. She can't be. Better not to feel anything at all than hope for something that can only exist in my imagination.

"I see. . . ." Josie doesn't seem too disturbed by my answer.

"What about you? Do you miss your, uh, birth dad?"

I know Amy divorced her first husband and that he walked out of Josie's life before she was potty-trained. That's the most I've heard, and it isn't pretty.

"Not really," she says, mimicking my tone from earlier.

"I see. . . ."

We share a laugh. The humor is fleeting as Josie hugs her pillow and says, "Lately I've been thinking . . . about how things would've turned out if people had made different choices."

"Uh, my mom didn't *choose* cancer."

"Oh god!" She blanches. "That's not what I meant!"

"I know, I know." I rush to reassure her before she can feel even worse about herself. "I was kidding. Sorry, it was a poorly timed joke."

Josie relaxes her grip on her pillow, but her mind seems to be elsewhere. She's probably stressing out about her recital. Having lived together for a while now, I've noticed she's someone who likes to simmer in her thoughts but never lets them boil over.

"Anyway . . ." I scratch my head and start to flounder. "Tomorrow I'm going to a board game café with Angela and Bora. Wanna come?"

Josie's eyes widen with excitement. Then she deflates. "I do, but with the recital coming up, Mom probably won't let me go."

"She will if I tell her we're going to Bora's house to study."

Josie sits up and releases a delighted gasp. "No! You can't lie to her!"

"I can and I will. If we get caught—which we won't—I'll tell her it was my idea."

"I don't want you to get into trouble."

"What trouble?" I scoff. "My dad has never grounded me. He's not going to start now just because we lied to play board games."

I don't disclose the part where Aunt Mindy used to be the discipliner whenever I misbehaved.

"If you say so . . ."

"Don't worry. I got this."

• • •

"That sounds like a wonderful idea!" Amy practically swoons at my suggestion.

After buttering Dad and Amy up with homemade blueberry waffles this morning, I casually mentioned going to Bora's place for a study session before asking Josie if she wanted to tag along. Josie tried not to sound too eager when she said yes, just as we rehearsed.

"Be back by four," Amy says to Josie. "Even though Nick isn't coming today, you should still practice for an hour or two."

"Do you need money for gas or lunch?" Dad asks, reaching into his pocket.

"Bora has it covered," I tell him.

"Don't goof off too much," Amy chimes in. "Homework first, fun later."

And just like that, Josie and I are on our way. We convene at Bora's and take a thirty-minute ride in Angela's car to a neighboring town with a bustling main street. Nestled between a post office and spice shop, Game Master's Café is a tight squeeze for a group of four. Board games crowd the storefront window, and the seating arrangement doesn't leave much elbow room. At least the hot chocolate here is aromatic and the company is good.

We order drinks from the coffee bar and claim a super cozy table in the back corner.

"How's math treating you this year?" Angela asks Josie.

Josie tilts her head side to side. "Could be better. Are you still tutoring at the library?"

"Every now and then. How's your mom doing?"

"Same as always." Josie silently communicates something with her eyes. "Anyway, thanks for having me."

"The more the merrier."

"Angela's a regular," I interject. Coming here was her idea. "She knows all the best multiplayer games."

"Let's play a game we all have an equal shot at winning."
Bora shoots me a knowing look. "No Pictionary."

"Why not?" I ask. "That's a collaborative game."

"Girl, please. Anyone who has you as a partner will win."

"Fine. Josie can pick the first game." I give her a friendly
tap on the shoulder, and she squirms as all eyes turn to her.

"Oh, don't mind me." She fiddles with her drink, clearly
uncomfortable in the spotlight. "I can play anything as long
as someone explains the rules to me. The only game I really
know how to play is Monopoly. . . ."

Bora makes a face. "No Monopoly. I'm not going to jail
again."

I shake my head. "So what can we play? Candy Land?"

Bora playfully backhands me in the chest. "Like you're
one to talk. I know you're a sucker for Old Maid."

Creases form on Angela's face as she brainstorms some
suggestions. (She's taking this very seriously.) A light bulb
seems to go off as she visibly brightens.

"I know just the game!" She maneuvers herself through
the cramped space and returns with a box. We all scoot
higher into our seats. "You'll love this. It's about budgeting
and running your own opera house."

• • •

"That was fun," Josie says during our drive back home.

"It was." It's a shame we had to cut the day short because
of Josie's curfew. "I didn't know you were such a good liar."

While Angela proved herself to be a walking dictionary

by dominating every word game we played, Josie reigned supreme in every game where we were required to bluff our way to victory. It was hilarious, if not a bit unsettling, how Josie managed to convince everyone there was a movie about a mermaid falling in love with a robot pirate.

"Thanks?" Josie says with a nervous laugh.

As we pull into the driveway, my mind flashes back to the scene I walked in on yesterday, between Nick and Josie. I should probably mind my own business, but I feel like if I don't say something now, I never will.

"It doesn't hurt to take a break now and then," I say just as Josie reaches for the passenger door handle. "Self-care is important."

That came out way more patronizing than I intended.

I let my words hang in the air before braving a glance at Josie, hoping I didn't spoil the mood and ruin her day.

Josie closes her eyes and sighs. "Tell that to Nick."

"Do you want to talk about what happened?" I ask. "You know me. I would never miss an opportunity to bad-mouth him."

"It's not a big deal. Really, it isn't. I was in a lousy mood yesterday. That's all."

"I'm all ears whenever you want to vent. No need to hold back."

She manages a small smile. "I'm fine, Lynda."

The next morning, Josie wakes up with a fever.

28

"THERE'S ABSOLUTELY NO way you can reschedule?" Amy asks, pacing back and forth in the kitchen, clutching a glass of wine in one hand and her phone in the other.

Up until today, I thought Josie was supposed to have a solo recital. Turns out, a group of Nick's students will be performing, although I'm not sure Josie will be one of them. . . .

She developed a fever overnight. I heard her tossing and turning in her sleep but chalked it up to bad dreams. It was only after I woke up at around nine that I noticed she was short of breath and her clothes were damp. Despite her body aches, Amy insisted that she eat something. After gagging on her first bite of chicken ginger soup, Josie's back in bed with the windows open and a trash bin within arm's reach.

"I understand. We hope to see you Saturday." Amy tosses her phone onto the counter as I steep myself a cup of jasmine tea. "I can't believe this is happening," she groans. "Of all times to get sick . . ."

Murphy's law: Anything that can go wrong will go wrong. Josie seemed fine while we were hanging out yesterday.

Was it only last night she started feeling unwell or . . . was she hiding it the entire time? Why didn't she say anything? She could've asked for help.

Maybe she has a higher pain tolerance than I do. Whenever I'm down with the cold or flu, I am the biggest crybaby and need to be waited on hand and foot. Aunt Mindy can attest to that.

"Be careful, Lynda," Amy says as she replenishes her wineglass, the liquid sloshing around as she tips the bottle too far. "I don't want you catching what Josie has. Eat some soup and take your vitamins. I know you're working on that . . . that . . ."

"Otome game," I supply.

"Yes, that otome game . . ." She nods as her memory clicks into place. "I know you're juggling a lot these days. Don't overexert yourself."

Then, without waiting for my response, she retreats into her office.

Now that I'm alone, I take a moment to bask in the peace and quiet.

This house has been under damage control all morning. Dad rushed to the pharmacy to stock up on over-the-counter meds while Amy called every doctor's office in the area to see who could book Josie the soonest. Then she spent twenty minutes on the phone with Nick, failing to convince him to reschedule the recital. If Dad hadn't left for work to clock in that sweet, sweet overtime, he could've reined in the madness and brought Amy down a notch. You'd think the world was ending with the way she's acting.

Although this recital is a golden opportunity for Josie to showcase her skills, it's not her only chance. I'm sure there will be other opportunities. That said, I hope she recovers soon. She's put so much into this. I want her efforts to pay off.

• • •

Armed with my tea, I take up my position at the dining table (which will temporarily serve as my drawing station while Josie's sick). Flu season waits for no one, and Emperor Feng isn't going to draw himself. He has the most elaborate attire of all the characters. I've lost count of all the outfits I've sketched for him, and after debating the style of his sleeves for almost a week, I'm ready to make a decision.

He is royalty, and now I must make him look the part.

The sun is setting by the time I start refining the line art. As I'm stretching out my back, I receive a text from Bora: *I'm stranded. Can you pick me up?*

I nearly drop my phone in shock and immediately write back. *Where are you?*

Seconds later, I'm borrowing Amy's car to pick Bora up in the middle of the highway, thirty minutes from her grandma's house. I spot her waiting at the underpass wearing a bright orange jacket and ease onto the shoulder. She races into the passenger seat, rubbing and blowing into her hands. I blast the heat and take us to the nearest drive-through.

After ordering her a large hot chocolate, I merge back into traffic and wait for Bora to thaw before asking, "What happened?"

"My mom," Bora grumbles. "I don't want to talk about it right now."

"Did you call me because you don't want Halmoni finding out?"

"Sort of . . . Halmoni's in the middle of cooking. It's bingo night at the senior center." Bora turns down the heat as color finally returns to her face. "Wanna come?"

The senior center isn't a place I frequent often, especially not for fun, but I'm worried about leaving Bora by herself. "Sure. Whatever you need."

She looks out the window. "Thanks."

Halmoni's in the kitchen rolling up her signature pork cutlet kimbap when we arrive.

"Long time no see, Halmoni!" I swoop in to give her a hug. "That's a lovely shade of lipstick you're wearing. Is there someone you're out to impress?"

Halmoni peels off her cooking gloves and pinches my cheek. "Only you, dearest."

I place a hand over my heart, and she hand-feeds me a fatty piece of deep-fried pork.

Halmoni's real name is Min-Jung, but no one calls her that. She wears her grandma title like an honorary badge. Food is her remedy for most problems—jajangmyeon for a broken heart, hotteok for stress relief, and samgyetang for a weak immune system. Her cooking has gotten Bora through some harsh times.

It's confounding how Bora's dad turned out the way he did. How could someone like Halmoni raise a son who grew up to be an uninvolved father? Maybe it's a nature versus nurture thing. You can do everything right and your child can still be everything you didn't want them to be. Like Mom. Her parents had a specific life script for her, and instead of following it to earn their approval, she forged her own path. That is, until cancer cut it short.

"Bora told me all about your dad's new wife," Halmoni says while I assemble the sliced kimbap in an aluminum tray. "How are you getting along with your new family?"

"I'm . . . acclimating" is all I say.

"You know I don't like it when you girls beat around the bush." Halmoni cracks her knuckles. "Do I need to fight someone?"

"Let's not get into any fistfights. It's bad for your arthritis," Bora says. "Bingo night starts in twenty minutes. Make haste, Halmoni, or you'll miss the first game."

"You're the one who was supposed to be back two hours ago to help me." Halmoni tuts as she takes off her apron and hangs it on the pantry door. "What did my daughter-in-law want with you anyway?"

I trade a look with Bora. "That's my fault, Halmoni. Bora meant to come back sooner, but I wanted to stop for hot chocolate."

"And you didn't bring me any?" Halmoni jokingly shakes her head before waddling out of the kitchen. "Let me re-apply my lipstick, then I'll be good to go."

Outside the senior center, I escort Halmoni up an accessibility ramp while Bora carries the food. Entering the main lobby is like crossing into a time capsule, to an era where lava lamps were groovy and color blocking was considered innovative.

"You'll be my lucky charm tonight," Halmoni says, squeezing my forearm. "Twenty-seven will be my winning number. I'm calling it now."

"Why twenty-seven?" I ask, matching her gait as we bound toward the cafeteria.

"Because that's RISD's acceptance rate"—she winks at me—"and you're going to be in that twenty-seven percent."

A smile blooms across my face while Bora rolls her eyes. "Aw, Halmoni! Who taught you that?"

"My favorite granddaughter, of course."

"Bora taught you well." The acceptance rate for this academic term was actually around seventeen percent, but Halmoni doesn't need to know that. "In that case, you're going to be my lucky charm when I submit my college applications," I say—just to be nice.

Luck is an elusive, whimsical thing, and I'm not the kind of person to rely on it. Never put your future in someone else's hands—not unless you want them to throw it away.

• • •

You can't have bingo night without a potluck. Bora and I are seated behind the buffet, munching away on carbohydrates, while a lady in a cheetah-print pantsuit churns the lever to an oversize bingo ball cage stationed at the front of the cafeteria.

"So . . . how are things at home?" I finally ask.

Bora stops midbite and replies somewhat distractedly, "Things are . . . meh."

"And your parents? Are they *meh,* too?" I remember Bora telling me she stayed with her parents during the tail end of winter break. All the holiday cheer put them in a good mood.

"More like *ugh.*" Bora sighs. "I've been living with Halmoni since the semester started. I don't plan on leaving soon, not with the way my parents have been behaving."

"What did your mom do that ended with you stranded on the highway?"

Bora chews on her bottom lip. "She invited me out, said she wanted to talk birthday plans for Halmoni. I was stupid and let my guard down because Mom treated me to lunch and a mani." She twiddles her fingers at me, and I notice how the nail polish is already chipping away. "On the drive back to Halmoni's, she asked to borrow two grand because Dad got into a fender bender and needs repairs."

My jaw drops.

Bora plops a slice of kimbap into her mouth. "It didn't take long for the tears to start after I refused to give her money. When that didn't work, she tried guilt-tripping me, and when that didn't work, she kicked me out of her car."

"I hate your parents. They treat you like—like you're their punching bag." I know Bora doesn't like it when I get bent out of shape over her parents, but I can't keep my anger at bay, not after I found her freezing in the middle of nowhere. "Why don't you want Halmoni to know what happened?"

Bora picks at her nails. "She's an old lady. I don't want to stress her out and ruin bingo night. Halmoni already threatened to write my dad out of her will the last time my parents acted up."

"Your parents obviously haven't cleaned up their act. Why is it so hard for them to be nice to you when they spoil your brother rotten?"

"I wonder the same thing. What exactly do they not like about me?"

"It's not about what you lack," I say plainly but firmly. "They're miserable people, and nothing will justify how they treat you. Stick to your exit plan and don't look back."

"You're right," Bora concedes. "I know I'm better off without them. . . ."

"If they ever pull a stunt like this again, call me." I grab Bora by the shoulders and make her look me in the eyes. "I don't care if it's two a.m. or if I'm out of town. Call me, okay?"

Bora laughs and shakes me off. "Okay, okay."

"I'm being serious."

"And I appreciate it. Now, enough about me. What are you doing for your dad's birthday tomorrow?"

I give her a blank look.

"Lynda. Don't tell me you forgot."

"How do you know when his birthday is?" I practically shriek.

"Because his birthday is a week before my brother's."

"I'll, uh, have to think of something . . ." A stifling sensation begins to creep up my neck the longer I flounder. I snatch a paper plate from the buffet and fan myself with it. First I forget the anniversary of Mom's death, and now this.

"Maybe Amy has something planned. Last year she made reservations at his favorite restaurant."

"Lynda, I don't like my brother, and even I know when he was born."

"It's not like I forgot on purpose!"

Aunt Mindy planned all my birthday parties when I was a kid. I remember her birthday like it was tattooed on my brain. If Dad had put in the effort all those years, I would've too, and it's not like I don't do *anything* for him. I'm just . . . not as proactive as I could be.

"You didn't set a reminder on your phone?" Bora asks.

"Apparently not," I mutter as I indiscreetly enter it now.

"Do you know how old he's turning?"

"Forty . . . ," I start to answer, then pause. "Forty-five."

Bora shakes her head at me. "Maybe you should invite Angela to his birthday celebration. Your dad did say he wanted to meet her."

"That's kind of intense for a first meeting."

Bora makes a sound halfway between a snicker and a scoff. "I doubt Angela will mind. What's your dad going to do? Interrogate her?"

"I'll . . . think about it," I say dismissively. Bora narrows her eyes, and I repeat myself with more conviction, "I'll think about it. Better?"

"Better is what you need to do."

"Jeez, Bora, do you think I'm a bad person?"

"Not exactly. It's just . . . when I watch you with Halmoni, I feel like you're missing out on the kind of relationship you could have with your dad."

I laugh, partly because it's funny but mostly to hide my discomfort. "My dad and your grandma are nothing alike."

"You know . . . things don't need to stay the way they are." Bora taps her fork against her plate and gives me the side-eye. "Your dad did a poor job assimilating Amy and Josie into your life, but now that they're going to be around for a while, maybe you should make the most of it."

I can envision Josie and I becoming closer the longer we live together, but—

"Does it matter if I'm leaving for RISD?"

Bora bites her lip and shrugs. "Only you can decide if they're worth it."

29

ON MONDAY, JOSIE'S racked with sniffles and a sore throat. I overheard Dad checking in on her at least twice last night before I conked out on the couch. Needless to say, she did not go to school with me.

The house was a low-key mess when I left and still is when I return. Recycling needs to be emptied, laundry needs to be folded, and the floors could use a sweep. Angela will be coming over for Dad's birthday dinner, and right now, this place is unfit for guests.

I start tidying up while Dad and Amy grab coffee at the café where they had their first date. They both took a half day off from work to spend some love-dovey time together.

Before heading out for their coffee date, Amy left me Dad's birthday card to sign. She already took up an entire side while Josie left me ample space below her message: HAPPY BIRTHDAY! CHEERS TO TURNING 45—which is more than I intended to write.

What else do you put on a birthday card?

After searching my brain for synonyms and generic

greetings, I end up drawing an elephant blasting confetti out of its trunk. That should earn me points for creativity; plus elephants are my dad's favorite animal.

I've never been good with words.

But as the saying goes, a picture is worth a thousand.

The door creaks open while I'm folding laundry. Josie emerges from around the corner, her complexion an improvement from yesterday, though her movements remain sluggish.

"Need me to bring you anything?" I offer, poking my head into the kitchen to maintain a respectable distance between us. She coughs into her elbow and pours herself a cup of hot water before mixing in a teaspoon of honey.

"No," she croaks, wrinkling her nose, the skin around her nostrils red and flaky.

"How are you feeling?"

"Gross. But better," she mutters. "Can you save me a slice of cake?"

"Amy ordered an entire sheet cake. I'm sure there'll be leftovers." I don't know if Josie was looking forward to Dad's birthday, but it feels wrong to celebrate without her, especially with Angela coming over.

Josie tests the temperature of her honey tea before taking a hefty gulp. I can hear the liquid traveling down her throat, unclogging her windpipe. We don't say another word to each other as she drains her mug and then waddles into the bathroom for a shower. I take that time to strip her bed and replace the sheets with freshly laundered ones still warm from the dryer.

"Thanks," Josie says when she returns, wearing a new set of pajamas. She twists her hair into a towel and climbs into bed.

"You shouldn't sleep with your hair wet," I tell her.

She whines into her pillow. "I'm tired."

"You have all day to sleep." I grab the hair dryer and plug it into the outlet between our beds. "Get up. It'll only take a minute."

When she doesn't comply, I shake her by the shoulder until she brushes me off. Then I poke her in the stomach, and she instinctively curls in on herself with a squeak.

"I'm going to tickle you if you don't listen," I say. "On the count of three. One, two . . ."

Josie quickly sits up. "Okay, okay! But just so you know, sleeping with your hair wet isn't bad for you. It won't make you sick or give you a brain tumor. That's all a myth."

"You'll sleep better with your hair dry."

Whatever else Josie has to say is drowned out by the roar of the hair dryer.

"I didn't know you could be so maternal," she says once I'm done.

"The sooner you recover, the sooner I get my bed back."

Josie shimmies under her blankets, toasty and content. "Don't catch what I have," she says. "You were doing a good job social distancing in the kitchen."

"So you noticed."

"I notice a lot of things."

"Yeah? Like what?" I observe Josie for a moment, but she doesn't elaborate. "Well, if I do get sick, it'll be your turn to take care of me."

· · ·

Now that the house is presentable, I spend what's left of my afternoon finishing the line art for Emperor Feng.

"Thanks for cleaning up," Amy says as I safely stow Henry away. She returned sometime after four and started prepping dinner. It's now a quarter past five.

I respond with a shrug.

"Can you pick up the cake?" she asks.

"Sure." I open my hand and signal Amy to toss me her keys.

"Do you need my credit card? The cake's already been paid for, but if you want to pick something out for Angela—"

"The cake will suffice." Just because I forgot my dad's birthday doesn't mean I want to hijack it by making it about Angela. She wouldn't want that either.

Amy offers me an encouraging smile. "I know high school girls don't like to talk about their love life with their parents, but Brian is very excited about tonight. Meeting Angela is a birthday surprise of its own."

Oh, jeez, I hope they don't say this kind of sentimental stuff in front of Angela. The secondhand embarrassment might kill me. Then again . . . Angela was over the moon when I invited her for dinner, and, in her words, she absolutely can't wait to meet my dad. Whatever she knows about him, she heard from me, and I haven't been too forthcoming.

There's not much to say, really.

Angela arrives at six o'clock sharp bearing a bouquet of lilies and a box of taro mooncakes.

242

"No one's gotten me flowers before!" Dad exclaims, taking a customary whiff. Then he holds up the box of pastries like it's a trophy. "And taro mooncakes? My favorite!"

I thought Dad's reaction to the cologne I gifted him (last-minute) was over-the-top, but this is superfluous. Since when does he love taro so much?

"You can't go wrong with flowers and sweets," Angela says as she hands me her coat. "Nice to meet you, Mr. Fan, and a very happy birthday to you, too."

"I'm glad you could join us," he says warmly. "Lynda's been so secretive about you."

"Oh?" Angela casts a backward glance in my direction. "I'm a secret, am I?"

"That's not what he meant," I hastily explain, all too aware of the negative connotation. "You're more like a . . . mystery, since I haven't told him much about you."

"A mystery, huh?" Angela ponders this for a moment. "I like that."

As soon as she turns back around, I shoot Dad a wide-eyed look, and he clams up. He hurries off to find a vase while Angela and I claim our seats at the dining table.

"Thanks again for coming on such short notice," I tell her.

Angela raises a spoon to her face and admires her reflection. "The pleasure is all mine. I wouldn't pass up a dinner party."

"Don't make it sound so formal," I say, despite the fact I asked Amy for permission to set the table using her crystal glassware and expensive china.

243

In true Angela fashion, her hair is immaculate, parted down the middle and oiled to a soft shine. Her outfit—a ribbed turtleneck paired with a formfitting overall dress—looks quite fetching on her. I tear my gaze away before I make her uncomfortable.

"Your dad seems like a funny guy," Angela muses, tenting her fingers.

"Cheesy is more like it. As you probably noticed, he was looking forward to meeting you."

"Why wouldn't he be? I'm your girlfriend."

"Yeah, I get that—" I cut myself off and repeat her words in my head. "Wait. Does that mean . . . I'm *your* girlfriend?"

Angela snorts with laughter. Before I can prod her further, Amy interrupts by serving an entire braised duck. Dad follows with a plate of stir-fried vegetables in one hand and a bowl of mei fun in the other.

"Someone here has a huge grin on their face," Dad says teasingly.

I look around to see who he's referring to and realize all eyes are on me.

"Lynda's delirious from hunger," Angela says. "I don't blame her. This all smells divine."

"There's more where that came from. Eat up!" Amy laughs while Dad grabs the remaining dishes. I nudge Angela with my foot and make a face—not because I'm annoyed but because I'm flirting.

With *my* girlfriend.

30

STRANGE HOW A single word can make the world sing with color.

An antsy yet delightful feeling courses through me, delivering a fluttery sensation to my chest—as if I'm housing a terrarium inside me and all the flowers have bloomed. I take distracted bites here and there, conflicted as to whether I'm lovestruck or experiencing a medical condition. I'm like a giddy schoolgirl who finally got noticed by her crush. It seems so childish to assign so much weight to relationship statuses. My self-worth isn't validated because Angela acknowledged me as someone worthy enough to be her girlfriend. Yet part of me glows with pride at the thought that I *am* her girlfriend, and I can now call her *my* girlfriend.

What did Arun say again?

"*Get over yourself. Angela will drop you the same way she dropped the rest of us.*"

I love proving people wrong.

Not that I have any doubts about me and Angela. Our relationship can only get stronger from here.

Angela's proven herself to be quite the social butterfly, chatting up my parents. I'm astonished by how effortless it is for her. Meanwhile, I can't carry a conversation to save my life.

"Are you into sports?" Amy asks.

"Not anymore. I was in cheer freshman year," Angela says with a hint of reservation. Imagine if she told the whole story. "I used to take gymnastics lessons as a kid. It was fun, but my days of handstands and somersaults are over."

That's news to me. I thought she joined cheer solely to get back at Arun and his friends. I didn't know she *liked* sports. She always struck me as the type of person you'd find in a bookstore or museum, not in the gym. Now that I think about it, though, not anyone can wake up one random day and become a cheerleader. You need to possess some level of physical fitness.

"Any interest in computer science?" Dad asks. "I heard from Lynda that you're making a mobile game. Doesn't that involve coding?"

"My brother, Andy, is responsible for the coding," Angela explains. "My role is more management oriented."

"Leadership skills are always in demand," Amy chimes in. "Have you decided what colleges you'll be applying to?"

You can always rely on adults to bring up college. This conversation is becoming more and more like a counseling session.

"I'm still exploring my options." Angela serves herself a second helping of mei fun. "I'm not married to any school or major."

"What about something math related?" Dad says, sitting a little higher in his seat while I sink a little lower in mine.

"I've considered it, but like I said, I'm exploring my options." Angela pushes the noodles around on her plate before abandoning her fork altogether. "At least Lynda isn't as indecisive as I am," she adds, not without humor.

Dad takes a sip of water while Amy dabs the corners of her mouth with a napkin.

Cue dessert time. I clap my hands and thank Amy for the delicious meal, and all at once, the room bustles with activity as everyone pitches in to clear the table.

Amy brings out a vanilla sponge cake layered with whipped cream and taro pudding. We skip the singing and go straight into cutting. Dad devours two slices with gusto and helps himself to a mooncake. I guess . . . he *is* a big fan of taro.

Funny, the things you learn after so many years.

• • •

I escort Angela to her car, which is parked across the street. The sky is a void, the neighboring houses are asleep, and the air is sharp and brisk with fleeting notes of chimney smoke. Angela and I linger on the sidewalk, both of us reluctant to say goodbye even as the night sinks its icy claws into us.

"I had a lovely time," she says, smoothing down the lapels of my coat.

"There must be a more suitable adjective than that," I quip.

"Excuse my vocabulary." Angela slaps herself upside the

head. "I had an exquisite evening. This commoner's hospitality exceeded my expectations."

"Wow." I laugh. "I don't know if I should be flattered or insulted."

Angela catches my hand in hers, and my chest tightens with sweet anticipation. Her gaze is earnest and unsettling in the way it affects me so. "Well, I for one am flattered. I know you don't have the best relationship with your family . . . so thank you."

She delivers a featherlight kiss to my fingertips, a whisper of affection that tingles with unspoken words. I instinctively tuck my hair behind my ear, my cheeks warming as I divert my attention toward the house next door.

Who cares for honeyed words when honesty is enough to make me melt? Unfortunately, I'm too frazzled to return the gesture. Angela has that effect on me. I embrace it wholeheartedly, yet I can't deny how vulnerable it leaves me feeling.

"Now that you've met my dad," I all but announce to the entire neighborhood in a flimsy attempt to mute my thoughts, "feel free to come over more often."

"Sounds like a plan."

"I learned something today," I tell her. "You're more athletic than I gave you credit for. I didn't know you were into gymnastics."

"I tried all sorts of things as a kid—swimming, soccer, piano, and even violin—mostly because of my parents, and surprise, surprise, I lost interest. I like poetry readings and book festivals, not swim meets and soccer games."

"Giving me date ideas?"

Angela winks at me. "Was I not subtle enough?"

"Well, don't give me too many. I need to focus on finishing those character sheets."

"About that . . ." Angela's expression falters. "Andy's girlfriend was supposed to do the background art. Sad to say, they had a falling out. Now she doesn't want anything to do with him or *Love Takes Root*."

"Sorry to hear that." I suppose there's no good news without bad news, though it could be worse. If I were reeling from an ugly breakup, I wouldn't want to work on an otome game either, much less with my ex.

"I'm now without a background artist, and my brother is without a girlfriend."

"At least you have me?" I jest.

This elicits a small smile from her.

"That is a comforting thought," she says. "Unfortunately, what I don't have is time."

"Does this mean you have to postpone the deadline?" If memory serves me correctly, once I complete all the character art by April, I'm supposed to start rendering the backgrounds and have them finished by the end of July.

"Probably. I'll keep you posted." Then, after a measured breath, she says, "Have you ever heard of Heart-Eye Games?"

"The name sounds vaguely familiar. Bora might've mentioned them to me once."

"They're a small gaming studio that specializes in mobile otome games. Andy met the founder, Hugo, at a recent virtual conference and pitched *Love Takes Root* to him.

Hugo's now offering to supply us with a background artist and voice actors—at no cost."

"Really?" My interest is piqued, to say the least. Giving the characters voiced lines would bring the game to another level. "Has Hugo read the script?"

Angela shakes her head, and my curiosity deepens into suspicion. Why would some random entrepreneur invest in a game they know almost nothing about?

"What's the catch?" I ask.

"Not only do I have to make the game commercially available, but I have to give him a forty to fifty percent cut of all sales."

Forty is offensive. Fifty is exploitative.

Angela must sense my apprehension because she then follows up with, "Andy vetted this guy, and I did my own research. Hugo is a well-known name and has the connections to hook us up with professional voice actors and artists. I don't have to pay him a single penny until after the game is released and *if* it sells."

The idea of *Love Takes Root* becoming a commercial success excites me more than ever. Before, it was just a possibility, an afterthought. But now? Now it feels real.

"Maybe you could negotiate the terms," I suggest. "I know you're not making this game as a get-rich-quick scheme, but what Hugo's asking is ridiculous." Angela tilts her head side to side, and I can't tell if she agrees or disagrees with me. "How does Andy feel about this?"

"He'll agree with whatever I decide."

"If you do partner with Hugo, maybe it will lead to other

opportunities." I give her a meaningful look. "For your writing."

Angela crosses her arms and sighs. "I write for fun, Lynda, remember?"

"You can have fun and get paid for it. And who knows? This could be the beginning of something big."

Angela gnaws on her bottom lip. "What if I decline? How would *you* feel about that?"

Good question. How would I feel? Even if the game were to become a commercial hit, the earnings wouldn't go to me. Angela's only paying me for the art. Still, a rising tide lifts all boats. If Hugo is as well known as Angela says he is, making friends with him wouldn't hurt. While I am against working for exposure, a partnership with Heart-Eye Games could boost my college applications, my portfolio, and my commissions. I could even increase my rates.

But I'm getting ahead of myself.

Love Takes Root belongs to Angela.

It's her dream, her vision, and her story.

My desires shouldn't come at her expense.

"I'm with Andy," I finally say. "Your decision is my decision. Just promise me you'll make the choice that makes you happy."

• • •

The week flies by in a flurry of snow and pop quizzes.

Despite several invitations, Angela can't seem to find room in her schedule to come over. She did squeeze in a couple minutes to get bubble tea with me after school, but other than that, we haven't had much time together—especially with her skipping study hall. At the risk of sounding clingy, I assumed we'd see each other more often now that we're official.

"Got any dates lined up for the weekend?" Bora asks during gym class on Friday.

"No," I grouse while planking. I'm not angry, just working out my core. "Angela has Model UN on Saturday, and Josie has her violin recital."

Josie returned to school on Wednesday and resumed violin lessons yesterday. She still has lingering cold-like symptoms, but Amy didn't want her missing any more days.

Bora crab-walks over to the empty spot across from me as I splay my legs out and reach for my toes. "You're going to her recital?" she says.

"She's been practicing her butt off since forever, so why not?"

"*Why not?*" Bora snorts. "This is like an accomplishment for you—supporting your sister even though it doesn't benefit you."

"I may be an egoist, but I'm perfectly capable of empathy and emotional support."

"I know you're there for me when I need you. Your family, however . . ."

"No sixteen-year-old should have to emotionally support their parent."

"You're missing the point." Bora shakes her head and sighs. "Anyway, wish Josie good luck for me. It must be tough jumping straight into rehearsal after being sick, knowing your fate rests on this one performance."

"I don't think this recital is a make-it-or-break-it kind of deal," I say. "If she nails it, then it helps her stand out. If not, she can audition at Curtis like everyone else."

Honestly, Nick and Amy are blowing this way out of proportion, and they're completely ignoring the fact that Josie isn't back in tip-top shape. She seems to be lost in a mental fog, bogged down by her sinuses and all the schoolwork she has to catch up on. Impressing some industry hotshots is probably the last thing on her mind.

But I suppose that's the price she must pay for Curtis.

Nothing worth having comes easy. If you want something, you have to fight for it, or else you're nothing but a dreamer.

• • •

Angela surprises me by waiting outside my classroom after the last bell.

"Hey," she says, roping me in for a hug. "Mind if I walk with you?"

"Of course not," I reply. "Do you even have to ask?"

What should be a short trek to the main lobby takes forever as we make a detour through the science wing and wander upstairs. Angela gives me a breakdown of her day, and I find the minute details so endearing in how they capture her personality. Only she can make a pop quiz in AP Biology a harrowing experience. We talk about everything and nothing, and the school is all but deserted by the time we find ourselves in the main lobby.

We stop in front of a bulletin board littered with college flyers, their enlarged, bolded text urging us to speak with our guidance counselors . . . TODAY!

"Have you given more thought to what you want to study at RISD?" she asks.

"I still want to take a shot at animation, see if it's for me," I say. "How about you? Are you any closer to knowing what you want after my dad grilled you?"

Angela bites the tip of her thumb, seemingly conflicted. "I've been thinking . . . maybe I don't want writing to just be a hobby."

"You mean you want to be a professional writer?"

"Maybe? I don't know." She rakes a hand through her hair and looks away. "I don't want to be a bestselling author or anything . . . I like reading books more than I like writing them."

"What about otome games?"

"I do have other ideas in the works," she says like it's a confession. "Somewhere down the road, I'd also like to add more routes to *Love Takes Root*."

I haven't read Sun Hong's route yet and already I'm eager to learn more about these new potential love interests. I wouldn't hesitate to work on more projects with her. We make a great team even though we aren't always in sync. Where there's creativity, there's possibility, and something about Angela inspires me to dream big. There's so much we have yet to do and so much we could do. If she's considering the long term, then—

"Does this mean you're partnering with Hugo?" I ask.

"That . . . remains to be seen. Like I said, I've been thinking."

Thinking is what she does best. She's not the kind of person to blindly agree to something, especially when the terms aren't in her favor. I'll have to trust Angela to know what she wants. That said, I don't understand why writing is a source of uncertainty for her. I don't know what I want to study at RISD, but nothing can dissuade me from pursuing art. What's holding her back from committing herself to her writing? She's self-assured in nearly every other facet of her life.

"Perhaps it's time I called Hugo for a little negotiation," Angela says with an air of resolution that catches me off guard. "I'm in Model UN. I should be able to convince him to see things my way—with diplomacy."

Her lips form a small but smug smile, and in her confidence, I find safety. It wraps around me in the same way I wrap my arms around her, warmly and securely.

"That's the Angela I know and love!"

31

JOSIE'S RECITAL IS finally happening. She was a little too quiet throughout dinner, but the frantic tapping of her foot during our drive to the playhouse is enough to compensate.

"You got this," I whisper as she stares out the window at the blurry landscape speeding past us as we careen down the highway.

We hit a bump in the road, but her eyes remain unblinking. Amy drums the steering wheel, the pitter-patter of her fingers combined with her humming grating to my ears. I don't know if she's humming to calm Josie or herself. Either way, it's not working.

Dad made the last-minute call to stay home after nursing a migraine all day. Although Josie doesn't seem bothered by his absence, Amy exchanged a few words with him behind closed doors. Can't say I blame Amy for being disappointed. If Josie can pick herself up after the flu, surely my dad can pop some painkillers and endure a migraine for her sake.

That's what it means to be a parent, right?

"Now, Josie, don't forget the breathing exercise Nick

taught you," Amy says as a brick building begins to take shape up ahead, shining like a candle in the dark before emerging into clarity the farther we advance.

The Autumn Song Playhouse is a modest one-story structure cast in warm yellow lights, its windows decked with bells and holly. It reminds me of one of those cozy winter landscapes commonly found on seasonal greeting cards. I snap a photo to use for later. It'll serve as a nice reference for my next Buncleaver piece.

"Don't let nerves get the best of you," Amy continues, trying to catch Josie's attention in the rearview mirror. "Remember, mind over matter. You've been rehearsing for months. Each song should come to you like muscle memory."

Josie worries her lips, more interested in the decorative buckles on her shoes than in whatever Amy has to say.

We file into the playhouse and check in at the box office. An attendant at the coat check escorts us to the reception area. There, I take a look around. Most of the people in attendance lean a bit older. The ones performing tonight, Josie's competition, are around my age, and they're easy to spot, with their evening dresses and tailored suits. There's a refined if not snooty air about them that reminds me of Angela—without the self-aware charm.

"I'm going to throw up." Josie crosses her arms over her stomach, her complexion ghostly pale as she doubles over and wheezes.

Before I can search for the nearest bathroom, Amy grabs Josie by the shoulders and corrects her posture. "Don't stand like that," she says to Josie. "Just because you're not onstage doesn't mean you're not being judged."

Josie complies but not without muttering something under her breath. Nick waves at us from across the room and tips his champagne glass in the direction of a young lady wearing a mustard-yellow jumpsuit and tasseled earrings. She must be the one to impress tonight.

As soon as Amy leaves to introduce herself, I wrap an arm around Josie and coax her into the hallway. We fumble past several doors until I find an unlocked room cluttered with headless mannequins and garment racks. The space is tight, but at least Josie can practice her breathing exercise in peace while I get her a drink.

"Still feel like throwing up?" I ask after she chugs a glass of cranberry juice.

"Not anymore," she says with relief.

"Are the nerves always this bad?"

"They've gotten worse over the years." She leans her head against the wall behind her and shuts her eyes. Slowly but surely, a healthy color begins to return to her cheeks. "Give me another five minutes and I'll be set."

"Good luck."

"Thanks, I'll need it."

"Forget Curtis. Marlo Montgomery is the only person in the audience, and you're going to blow him away. Remember, love conquers all."

For the first time tonight, a sliver of a smile breaks through the pinched expression that has carved itself into Josie's face, and she releases a breathy laugh.

"Of course," she says, more to herself than to me. "Love conquers all."

• • •

Except it doesn't.

Because Josie's performance is a disaster—at least, according to Nick.

She had a promising start but apparently rushed her third song. She didn't play a particular note as intended and "visibly panicked." I didn't notice anything off about her performance. To the musically trained ear, however, the mistake was jarring. On par with an out-of-tune violin, as Nick so kindly phrased it. He didn't stick around to congratulate Josie after the program concluded.

Amy didn't have much to offer her in terms of praise either.

Nothing I said could make up for it. I tried, but Josie wouldn't listen.

I don't care if she made a mistake. She did a good job—no, an excellent job, despite the circumstances—yet all she got was criticism and silent judgment. If she wasn't already defeated by her own performance, then the lukewarm response she received certainly did the trick.

Amy is five steps ahead of us when we return home. Josie hasn't even unbuckled her seat belt and already Amy's wrestling with the house key. Like she's ashamed to be seen with her own daughter. A bolt of fury strikes me then, and I can't help but glare at her.

Josie is clearly distraught. Why is Amy kicking her while she's down?

I want to give her a piece of my mind, but picking a fight would probably make Josie feel worse, so I bite my tongue and flick on the indoor lights.

Dad's nowhere to be found—guess he's sleeping off his migraine.

Amy unwinds her scarf and musses her hair, shaking out whatever has her preoccupied. "Well," she finally says, "at least Aunt Val wasn't there tonight."

Never mind. I can't stand by and let this go on any longer.

Before I can get a word in, something sails past me, nearly nicking me in the head as it slices the air and smashes into the closet door, splintering the wood with a deafening crack. I recoil at the impact, flinching as a single black shoe clatters to the floor and lands a few inches shy of where Amy stands with her mouth hanging open.

There's a beat of silence before my eyes cut to Josie.

"Who needs Aunt Val's judgment when you and Nick think I'm a failure?" she says through clenched teeth, her breath coming in short, heaving bursts.

I recognize the resentment blazing in her eyes and instinctively take a step back.

Amy is still reeling with disbelief. It takes a moment for the shock to wear off, and instead of apologizing, she deflects. "Josie! When did I ever call you a failure?"

"Oh please!" Josie kicks off her other shoe and shoves past us, turning this way, then that, as if her anger has nowhere to go. Her tears are relentless, and her voice isn't hers. "I make one mistake and that's all anyone cares about! As if the person who played before me didn't mess up! As if the guy after me didn't play easy songs! As if—"

Amy clamps a hand on Josie's shoulder, anchoring her in place. "Josie, you're not a failure," she says with an imploring look, her face as white as a blank canvas. "I'm sorry I made you feel that way."

"Whatever." Josie yanks herself free and dries her eyes with her sleeve. "Forget Curtis. Forget music school. I'm done."

Amy starts to protest, then thinks better of it and takes a deep breath. "I understand your frustration, but let's not let emotions cloud our judgment." Then, very softly, she adds, "I think we've both said enough for tonight. Let's talk about this when we're in a better mood."

"I meant what I said." Josie's voice breaks and she swallows the last of her tears to say "I don't want to do this anymore. No matter how hard I work, it's never enough."

· · ·

Part of me thinks Amy got exactly what she deserved. You can't disparage your daughter with passive-aggressive comments and then act surprised when she retaliates.

Another part of me agrees that Josie shouldn't throw away all those years of learning the violin because of one recital. I'm sure every musician has a history of bad performances.

Their mistakes probably outnumber their accolades. While I sympathize with Josie, the solution to her struggles isn't to give up. She's come too far to quit.

As my favorite inspirational quote goes, "Nothing in the world is worth having or worth doing unless it means effort, pain, difficulty."

Dad and Amy are having a hushed conversation behind closed doors. Every now and then someone raises their voice. Emotions are running high, and the house feels more tense than ever.

It's been a long night, to say the least.

Josie's holed up in our room. As much as I don't want to disturb her while she's having a good cry, I also need to sleep. I announce myself with a knock and give her ample time to collect herself before entering. Leaving the door ajar, I use the hallway light to guide me through the dark. I'll just grab my blanket and settle on the couch. No questions asked.

But as I pass Josie's bed, she releases a sad sniffle, and something tightens in my chest. I'm not the best at damage control, especially when it comes to familial fights.

Still, I can at least try.

"Here." I perch on the edge of her bed and offer her a tissue box.

She swipes a couple of tissues and blows her nose.

"Are these angry tears or sad tears?" I ask, trying not to stare too long at the swollen pockets under her eyes.

"Both." Josie scratches her nose, her nostrils rimmed

with flakey skin. "Sorry you had to witness that. I just . . . lost it."

"You had a rough evening. I'm glad you stood up for yourself." I think back to the night I walked in on Nick and Josie and the tension that existed then. "It seems you've been bottling this up for a while."

"I have," she mutters. "I'm so done."

"Are you really?" Then, silently, *It wasn't a spur-of-the-moment decision?*

"I didn't say all that just because I'm mad."

"So . . . if you're no longer pursuing music, what will you be doing?"

"I don't know. I just . . . I just want to be sad right now." Josie's expression crumbles with a fresh wave of tears that she manages to keep at bay. "I have another year to think it over . . . I'm only sixteen. It's not the end of the world if I don't know what I want to do for the rest of my life . . . right?"

"No, it's not. . . . I imagine most people don't know what they want to do five or ten years from now." I absently tug at a loose thread dangling from her bedsheet. "How long have you been thinking of quitting? Nick didn't ruin the violin for you, did he?"

"I was having doubts before Nick," she confesses.

And then it all comes spilling out—how Josie considered quitting as early as freshman year. Back then, it was just a seed of doubt. It only blossomed into a fully grown thought once our parents got engaged. To avoid raining on their parade, she chose to wait until after the honeymoon to broach the subject, but the longer she did nothing, the more Amy seemed to fixate on Curtis. By the time she fired Ms. Chen, Josie had lost the courage to say what she'd been meaning to say for over a year.

All that money washed down the drain because she didn't speak up sooner.

"I knew how you felt about my private lessons. I didn't want to come across as ungrateful by backing out," Josie sobs. "So I chose to grin and bear it, but . . . I can't anymore. I'm sorry."

Her apology means little to me.

She *should* be sorry.

I leave before I say something I'll regret.

32

I THOUGHT AMY would insist that Josie continue her lessons on a less rigorous schedule—or that she would compromise on another music school. Instead, she puts an indefinite pause on all lessons and will be meeting with Josie's guidance counselor.

All the talk about Curtis?

Gone overnight.

How anticlimactic. Can you imagine if Dad took out loans to send me to RISD, and then after a year, I transferred to community college to study accounting? I would never hear the end of it. So why does it feel like Josie's getting rewarded?

I'm two blocks from home, stooped on the sidewalk, bundled in my heaviest down coat as I recount the events of last night to Aunt Mindy. The walls in my house are too thin for venting, and I'm too riled up to keep my voice down.

"Can you believe it? All that money wasted, and for what?" I exclaim, my phone burning in my grip. "I understand why Josie didn't speak up sooner, but she could've at least asked Amy to pause the lessons while she sorted out her feelings."

"Sometimes it takes courage to be honest," Aunt Mindy says.

I fail to see how Josie's actions were anywhere near courageous.

"It sounds to me like Josie was worried about disappointing Amy and scared of angering you," Aunt Mindy continues. "She thought she could continue the violin out of obligation, but in the end, she reached her limit."

"Well, she had an obligation to be forthcoming."

"I'm sure Josie regrets waiting this long to come clean."

"Give me a break. She had one foot out the door before Nick was hired—and what about Ms. Chen? Josie didn't feel bad enough about her getting fired to say something? She should've known this—"

Aunt Mindy cuts me off. "Josie didn't do anyone any favors by delaying, but it's good that she *did* speak up." She releases a frustrated breath that I can only interpret to mean she's annoyed with me. Not with Josie, not with Dad, and not with Amy—with *me*.

"Sometimes you have to cut your losses," she says. "Just because Brian and Amy spent a fortune on that violin teacher doesn't mean Josie should pursue something she's no longer committed to."

I know what the sunk cost fallacy is. I know Josie was in a lose-lose situation. But that's not enough to extinguish the wildfire raging inside me—or stop the charred remains from cooling into disdain. Josie squandered the opportunities that were so generously afforded her, and what does she get for giving up?

Permission to do whatever she wants.

How is that fair?

"If her heart isn't in it, then so be it," I snap. "There's no use forcing yourself to do something you don't want to do." And that's the extent of my charitability before the flames lick it up. "But giving up is the easy way out."

"Is it?" Aunt Mindy's voice is tinged with sympathy. I don't understand why she doesn't share my indignation. She's the one who raised me to be the strong-willed person that I am, after all. "How would you feel if you got into RISD and suddenly found yourself falling out of love with art?"

"That would never happen. Art is everything to me." I'd laugh if her hypothetical weren't so ridiculous.

"And music wasn't everything to Josie?"

"If it were, she wouldn't be quitting."

There's a lengthy pause before Aunt Mindy says, "It's not all black-and-white. Our greatest joy can also bring us the most pain. Think about how lost Josie must feel."

"Yeah, yeah, yeah. If I called it quits every time I got—"

"Lynda." The sound of my name commands me into silence. "Josie isn't you."

Of course she isn't me. To suggest otherwise is an insult to me.

I would hate to be Josie. Despite all the help she received, where I got nothing, she still couldn't keep it together. She has so much potential, yet she'd rather bow to the pressure than rise above her limits—and everyone around me has no problem with that. They're so ready to accept her surrender. Only Josie can wave a white flag and come out victorious.

"I'm not Josie, and Josie isn't me, but we're sisters, and Dad and Amy placed all their bets on the wrong daughter," I say, all in a single breath.

"Lynda, I know how you must feel. . . . I don't agree with every decision Brian and Amy make, but this isn't about favoritism." Aunt Mindy's words sound shallow to my ears, like she's trying to overwrite my feelings with a hollow pencil. "There is no competition between you and—"

"How would you know? You're not even here!"

And then I hang up.

• • •

Anger can be destructive and productive. When I'm in a mood, I don't bake or clean. I draw a scheming cartoon beaver doing a bunch of things menacingly: Buncleaver trimming the hedges with a giant pair of gardening shears; Buncleaver sharpening his sushi knife; Buncleaver wielding a chain saw—because why not?

Amy and Dad can continue to support Josie while I continue to rely on myself. That's how it's been and how it always will be. I don't know why I ever thought otherwise. I don't understand why Aunt Mindy isn't on my side. She knows firsthand how Dad was never around during my childhood. It's like he didn't even want a daughter. That is, until he met Amy. Since then, he's been trying to be a good dad to Josie even though he had so many years to try with me.

Not like I need him anyway.

I have my art, I have Bora, and I have Angela.

The weekend concludes with little fanfare, as if the recital never happened, as if Josie's life hasn't revolved around Curtis for the last two years. I avoid her as much as I can, which isn't easy when we share a bedroom. On the bright side, I no longer have to see Nick. As far as I'm concerned, he doesn't even exist.

Thursday afternoon, Bora and I are at my house doing homework when Josie returns. Now that she doesn't have to report straight home for violin lessons, she's been coming back at all hours. When she's not out with friends or chilling at the library, she's glued to her phone, playing otome games and reading fan fiction.

I don't know what she discussed with her guidance counselor, but I assumed she'd use her newfound freedom to discover another passion—not to kick back and relax.

"Hey!" Bora waves to her with a huge grin on her face. "Did you see the news? They're adding a female route to *Romancing the New Moon.*"

Josie looks at me, then at Bora. "I did! I watched the trailer this morning," she says with increasing excitement. "Her name's Gloria Rose Clementine, and I love her design."

"Her cherry blossom eyes are so—ugh!" Bora flings an arm over her head and goes limp in her chair. She straightens as Josie drags her backpack across the floor by its straps. "What do you have in there? A bowling ball?"

It would be an unexpected turn of events if Josie developed an interest in sports, but alas, that is not the case as

Josie drops a stack of books onto the table, the impact redirecting the course of my pencil as I complete my Mandarin worksheet.

"I don't know how much you've heard, but . . . I'm not taking violin lessons anymore," she says timidly. "Now I have time to catch up on my reading."

"And otome games," Bora emphasizes.

I told Bora everything. She understands why I'm bitter, but she won't pick sides. As much as that irks me, I'm not going to start a fight over it, not after my conversation with Aunt Mindy. I know Bora. Nothing will stop her from bonding with another otome gamer.

While I can't control what Bora does, what I can do is keep my interactions with Josie to the bare minimum. I'm not trying to punish her with the cold shoulder. Whenever I see her, though, my resentment begins to bubble, and I need to disengage to stop myself from boiling over.

I don't want to be nice, nor do I want to be mean.

So I choose apathy.

"By the way." Bora swivels toward me. "How's the game going? I haven't heard any updates lately."

Oh, right. I was so quick to tell Bora about my family drama that I forgot to tell her about the background artist dropping out.

"It's going," I answer vaguely. "I'm almost ready to send Angela my character sheet for Emperor Feng." I was supposed to sooner. Unfortunately, things happened.

"I can't wait for the game to be finished!" Josie says with

a happy little clap. "I'll be the first to download it if it hits the App Store."

Before there can be any awkward silence, Bora saves me from myself and chimes in. "Same! Like, take my money already. With Angela and Lynda working together, the game's guaranteed to be a runaway success."

Maybe. So long as I don't implode first.

Angela said she would negotiate with Hugo. I don't know anything beyond that. She hasn't consulted me on what the updated terms should be, nor has she given me a date for when she plans to reach out to Hugo. I understand she's the creative director and that this is a sensitive issue to navigate, but I wish she'd be more transparent.

We're supposed to be a team.

My phone rumbles in my pocket.

Angela must have a sixth sense, because she just texted me: *Hey, can we meet?*

That's cryptic enough to be alarming.

Apart from sneaking a few kisses at school, once again she's been too busy to make time for me. I can't recall when we last had a full conversation in person. She's not the best texter either. For her to suddenly message me after near radio silence . . .

Before my imagination spirals, Angela follows up with *It's nothing serious. Something came up is all. We can hop on a call, but I prefer to talk over bubble tea.*

I relax.

What bad news could she possibly deliver over bubble tea?

• • •

Bora and Josie continue gushing over *Romancing the New Moon* while I head out to meet Angela at the bubble tea shop where we had our first date. A familiar K-pop song greets me as I walk in, and I find Angela at a corner table, my drink already waiting for me.

"Thanks for coming out," she says after we hug. "Sorry I've been so busy."

"No need to apologize. I know you'll make it up to me," I say, half teasing.

"Who needs a hot drink when you have enough sass to chase away the chills?" Angela slides a cup of milk tea toward me. "Everything okay with you? Josie had her recital, right? How'd that go?"

"Let's not talk about it," I say.

Angela winces. "That bad?"

"Long story short, Josie quit the violin, and now she's exploring other . . . things."

"That must be a big change for her." Angela punches her straw through the plastic seal of her rose lychee green tea. "Kudos to her for branching out. I hope she finds a new passion."

Even Angela's patting Josie on the back for giving up.

Her of all people.

Whatever. Right now, all I want is to enjoy her company.

"How's your brother?" I ask. "Does he have a new girlfriend yet?"

"Not unless you count the VTuber he's been infatuated with lately." She sweeps her straw across the bottom of her cup, stirring up the boba. "Bora would make an excellent VTuber. She's got that bouncy personality and a good sense of humor."

"Hey, that's my best friend you're talking about."

"Oh? Did I hit a nerve?" Angela steals a sip of my drink before propping her chin on the back of her hand to stare at me adoringly. I wish I could take a picture of her. "Trust me. You're the only one I want to exchange indirect kisses with."

"Is that why you wanted to meet up? Because Your Highness couldn't bear to be apart from me?" I say while secretly flushing at the thought.

"Her Highness would forgo her life of splendor if it meant being with a peasant like you," she says wistfully before lacing her fingers and dropping the pretense. "In all seriousness . . . I wanted to talk about Hugo."

Anticipation and hope seize me all at once. I could use some good news this week.

"I called Hugo to ask if he was willing to negotiate," she begins with a thoughtful look on her face. "I suggested that he take a fifteen percent cut on sales to start. Only after I make a return on all monies spent to finance the game would I allow him to take thirty percent."

"Sounds fair to me." I haven't done the math to understand the long-term implications. However, I trust Angela to know what she's doing. Thirty percent is better than what Hugo originally proposed.

"It took some convincing, but he agreed and asked to read the script for Sun Hong and Meng Li." Angela scratches the nape of her neck. "Although he recommended tweaking Sun Hong's route, he liked it enough to accept it as is. . . ."

"But?"

"He said he'd only sign off on my terms if I make Meng Li a man."

"What? Why?"

"He thinks the game will have a more promising debut with two male love interests to start. Then, depending on early reception of the game, we can add a female route."

"Does he have any data to support his claim?"

"Even if he did, it's irrelevant. I'm no longer interested in working with him."

I blink once, then twice. This is not what I was expecting to hear, at all. "So . . . because he asked you to make a small change, you no longer want to work with him?"

"*Small?*" Angela scoffs. "It changes the entire dynamic of Meng Li's route. You read it; you should know. Her being a woman is integral to her backstory."

She's right, but . . .

Angela reaches across the table to lay her hand over mine. "I know we've fallen behind, but the game *will* be finished. I'll hire my own background artist, and—"

I don't hear the rest of what she has to say.

The person sitting across from me isn't Angela.

She wouldn't back down from a once-in-a-lifetime opportunity so easily.

She wouldn't give up. Not like Josie.

The Angela I know is somewhere else, and I need to bring her back. Suddenly, I'm gripped by an impending sense of doom and a need to outrun it.

"But this could be our big break," I all but shout. "Who knows when you'll get another chance like this? Is Hugo's suggestion that much of a deal-breaker? You don't even have to change Meng Li's route, just write a different one and save hers for later."

The more I talk, the more I lose control, as if I'm running on my last breath. "I don't know much about publishing, but isn't it normal for subplots and characters to change or get written out? You can't be a writer without learning to take constructive criticism."

Angela appraises me with a cold look.

"I already told you. I don't want to be a professional writer," she says calmly, though the tick of her brow indicates she is anything but. "Sure, I'm on the fence about it, but for now, writing is a hobby. I do it because it makes me happy, not because I want to get rich or famous from it. Finishing the game is my priority. Whether other people get to play it is secondary."

"Well, your parents got the rich part covered," I say flippantly. "Writing might be a hobby for you, but art is everything to me. I need to know you're committed."

"Seriously? You of all people are questioning my commitment?" Angela waits for me to take back what I said, and when I don't, something in her wavers. "Do you honestly believe I invested all this time and energy on a—on a whim?"

"Isn't that what you did freshman year with cheerleading, with Arun, with your friends?"

"Lynda . . . that was different, and you know it."

"Then what's stopping you from taking Hugo's deal? Renegotiate if you don't like his terms. This game could be so much more if you would let it. *We* could be so much more."

Angela pinches the space between her brows and takes a deep breath. "I told you from day one that this game is for *me*."

"And you would be satisfied with just that?" Then, before she can answer, "Admit it. You're terrified of rejection, so you quit before you start."

She bristles at the comment. "I'm not quitting. Did you not hear a single word I said? I don't need to be a commercial success. We're going to finish the game—on *my* terms."

"Settling is no different from quitting."

"Good for you, Lynda, for not knowing when to quit." Angela kicks back her chair and leaps to her feet, fists clenched at her side. "Maybe once you get into RISD and finally decide what exactly it is you want to major in, you'll realize just how steep the competition is. Just how much pressure you can handle. Maybe then you'll understand where I'm coming from."

"I don't have delusions of grandeur," I snap, glaring up at her. "But artists who don't take risks never get close to being the best. Don't let insecurity hold you back."

Angela smacks herself in the forehead before throwing her hands up. "Fine! I'm insecure! There, are you happy now? Happy to use my insecurity against me?"

"That's not what I'm—" I startle at the sight of her tears.

She claps a shaky hand over her mouth, stifling a sob as more tears trickle down her face, revealing a version of herself that neither of us seem to recognize. "Lynda . . . whatever happened to being there for me when I need you?"

"I am here!" I start to get up until she backs away from me.

"How? By projecting your dreams onto me so that *you* can make a name for yourself?" She takes a deep, gasping breath before dabbing the corner of her eyes with her sleeve. "I really thought you'd support my decision."

I stare at the floor, ashamed and unsure of myself.

By the time I look up, Angela is gone.

33

WHEN IT RAINS, it pours. I might as well join the drama club and feed them ideas. Perhaps if I had better control over my emotions, I wouldn't have said all those horrible things to Angela. But how do I apologize for having meant what I said?

"Great way to start the new year," Bora says, stifling a yawn. "Is it your goal to pick a fight with everyone?"

"I'm sorry," I say. "Am I boring you?"

"You're not boring, Lynda, just predictable. I can't leave you alone for an afternoon without you blowing things up."

After my disastrous talk with Angela, I called Bora to ask if she was still at my house. I caught her right when she got back to her grandma's and invited myself over.

"I do think Angela is missing out by not partnering with this Hugo," Bora says, heating up the leftovers Halmoni defrosted before attending karaoke night at the senior center. "It's not like he told Angela she couldn't write a female love interest, so I'll give him the benefit of the doubt and say he's not a homophobe, just a businessman."

"Right? I mean—"

"*But* this project is Angela's baby. Hugo isn't entitled to it, and neither are you." Bora divvies up two bowls of oxtail soup and some banchan for us to eat in front of the TV. "She's paying you to do the art, not to give her career advice."

"I'm her girlfriend," I argue. "My opinion should matter."

Bora points her spoon at me. "As her girlfriend, do you think it was right to call her insecure for deciding what she believes is best for her story?" I purse my lips and pick at a plate of kimchi with my chopsticks. "I know you're eager to go to college and do big things, but you need to slow down. Other people can't keep up as much as you expect them to."

"Angela's different, though. That's what attracted me to her in the first place."

"Well, now that she isn't who you thought she was, have you lost interest?"

"No!" I balk. "I don't want us to break up. I just . . ."

"Just want to convince her to see things your way?"

"Maybe . . ."

Bora makes a face like she just ate something rancid. "Lynda, let's turn this back on you. How would you feel if I offered to invest in your sticker store on the condition that Buncleaver is a rabbit pretending to be a beaver?"

"That's patently false. He's a beaver pretending to be a rabbit."

"Answer the question: Would you or would you not be offended by the suggestion?"

"Okay, yes, I'd be offended."

"And why is that?" she asks.

"Because it ruins the integrity of it."

"Exactly. You get it, so why can't you extend that same courtesy to Angela?"

"Because she's holding herself back," I nearly shout. "Angela and I . . . We're a team! We could achieve so much if she believed in—"

"Holding herself back or holding *you* back? Is that why you resent Josie for quitting the violin? Because all that money spent on her lessons should've gone to you?"

"Well, yeah." I thought I made that clear. "Think about how much further along I could be if I had my own art teacher."

"I feel like your eagerness to excel is its own kind of desperation. I don't understand what you're trying to prove. We both know you're talented. You don't need some fancy tutor, and I know RISD is your dream school, but you don't need it either."

How am I desperate? Desperation is for those who see their hopes and dreams dying right before their very eyes. Mine are just getting started. I made a promise to myself that no matter what life threw at me, art would always be a steady, constant thing.

My thing.

I don't have everything figured out, but I have a map and I have a plan. As long as I keep going, I'll eventually reach my destination. Why slow down?

Bora regards me with a pensive look. "There's a simple explanation for all this," she says. "You, Josie, and Angela all have one thing in common. You're all afraid of failure."

"I am not afraid of failure, Bora."

"Yes, you are, and you're in denial."

I slam my chopsticks down. "This conversation is over. I'll see you at school."

"Seriously? You're running away while I'm giving you some tough love? Is this who you want to—"

I grab my bag and leave the way I came.

Bora's words keep replaying in my head as I drive the backroads, ignoring the speed limit. I know she was coming from a place of concern, but to call me desperate and compare me to Josie? Really?

No one likes to fail, me included, and no one is impervious to failure. That said, it's not like I have this constant fear of it that consumes my life.

I'm confident in what I do.

By getting into my dream school, I'll further prove to myself that I alone can make it and that my art and I are enough. If I can overcome the hurdle of getting into RISD, what's one more challenge? It's up to me to dream big if Angela can't. No challenge is too great as long as I can count on myself to get the job done.

• • •

Even though I'm in no mood to be around anyone right now, Dad wears me down until I join everyone at the table for dinner. I lied and told him I ate at Bora's. Still, he insisted. Now I'm watching everyone else eat while Amy talks on and on about something. Dad taps my arm to get me to listen.

"When I spoke to Josie's guidance counselor the other day, he mentioned how colleges like to see applicants with unique hobbies," Amy says. "Activities like rock climbing, furniture restoration, and even blacksmithing."

Where is this going? Are we seriously having a family meeting about hobbies?

"Amy and I think it would be good for both of you to explore other interests," Dad says to Josie and me. "We don't want you to feel pigeonholed."

Last time we sat down for a lecture, Amy and Dad basically told us dating was off-limits because it's a distraction. Now they want us to broaden our horizons. Are they changing their tune now that Josie quit the violin? Is Dad saying all this because he wants me to find another "hobby"?

As if I'll follow in Josie's footsteps and give up art.

"Josie and I signed up for an indoor rock climbing session. Feel free to join us, Lynda," Amy says. "And let me know if there's anything else you want to try."

"Well, there is one thing," I say, getting her attention. "Now that Josie doesn't need to practice violin anymore, can I finally have my own room?"

"Lynda!" Dad gasps. "How can you talk—"

"It's a valid question. She has no use for it anymore— right?" I swivel in Josie's direction, and she freezes. "You can't have your cake and eat it, too. No one should be rewarded for quitting. I mean . . ."

I look around the table—at Amy, wide-eyed and speechless, at Dad, red-faced and seething, and then at the crystal glass in front of me, the rounded surface distorting my reflection—and finally it sinks in.

"No one likes a quitter," I say. "Giving up your dream is like giving up on yourself, and if you're the only one who ever believed in yourself and your dreams, where does that leave you? With nothing. So excuse me for speaking the uncomfortable truth, but I think we—"

"Enough!" Dad slams his hands on the table and stands up. "Lynda. Go to your room."

"All I'm saying is—"

"*Now.*"

A moment passes as I glare at him.

"Have you even been listening? I don't have a room." And with a swing of my hand, I topple my glass, spilling water everywhere, before storming off.

34

I'M OFFICIALLY GROUNDED. Until I sincerely apologize to everyone, I have to report straight home after school. No TV, no car privileges, and no plans with friends. Dad tried to take Henry away, but Amy talked him out of it.

Confiscating the one thing that brings me joy would have only reinforced my desire *not* to apologize. What is there for me to feel sorry about? Everything I said was true—because I was talking about myself. If I give up on my dreams, I'm giving up on myself, and if I can't rely on myself, I can't rely on anyone.

No one else cares about my dreams as much as I do.

Bora's right. I am afraid of failure.

I can't afford to quit or fail. No one will be there to catch me if I fall.

Even now, as I feel the urge to confide in someone, I realize there's no one. Aunt Mindy and Bora will side with my dad, and I doubt they'll want to hear me out after I left them hanging the last time we talked. As for Angela . . .

I release a heavy breath and try to conjure happy thoughts.

At least I have my art.

I pull up a picture of Buncleaver on my phone and hold him close to my chest.

And then Angela's face emerges, her pained expression louder than everything else crowding my mind. I never thought she could make such a face. She looked so . . . betrayed.

Because of me. I hurt her.

I really . . . messed up, didn't I?

But I'm not going to cry.

I can't, and I won't.

· · ·

I don't see Angela in school for the next week. Her absence is a relief and a red flag. It's not like her to miss so many school days. I hope it's not because of me. I want to mend things, but I'm like splattered paint on the wall and I don't know how to clean myself up. Where would I begin? What would I even say? A sorry would be like applying a Band-Aid to a gaping wound.

I'm an artist, not a doctor.

Still, as the days trudge on, I feel no inspiration to draw.

Even though I'm attending classes as usual, my mind is elsewhere.

Bora and I are ignoring each other. Well, knowing her,

she's ignoring me because I'm ignoring her. I walked out her door, and it's awkward to force my way back in, so I've been avoiding the cafeteria and secretly eating in the library. At least I have a legitimate excuse to avoid her after school, being grounded and all.

When I report to my usual table behind the stacks on Monday, I find Claire occupying my spot. I'm so taken aback by her presence that I almost miss the person seated across from her.

"Angela . . ."

Her name escapes my lips like a long-held breath.

Before I can even think to retreat, Claire and Angela look up from their books, casting me in the spotlight.

"Uh . . ." I search for something to say.

Claire turns to Angela. "Do you need me to move?"

Angela shakes her head and slings her messenger bag over her shoulder. "I was just leaving." Her voice ignites an ache in my chest, and I feel butterflies dropping dead in my stomach as she breezes past me.

I chase her with my eyes and wonder if my feet should follow.

"That was interesting," Claire says, returning to her book. I slip into the vacant chair across from her and put my head down. "Wow, you look pathetic."

Lovely. I'm acting and looking the part.

"Valentine's Day is coming up. You should resolve whatever issues you have with Angela soon—not that I really care about your problems."

"Meh." I can't believe it's February.

"I hope you're not expecting me to comfort you."

"I'd rather you beat some sense into me."

Claire snorts and slides her book toward me.

"Hit yourself, Lynda." The book stops near my face, and I read the spine: *So You Want to Go to Art School.* "Check out chapter seven. The author talks about RISD."

I groan and push the book away.

For once in my life, I don't want to think about art school.

• • •

"Hey," Josie greets me when she returns home from the movie theater.

"Hey," I mumble back from the couch.

I've been camping in the living room since everyone left for the day (to enjoy their fun weekend plans, no doubt). Dad was up first. I heard him reversing out of the driveway at sunrise. Since my house arrest, I've been reading webtoons and zoning out to mobile games. I haven't touched Henry in what seems like forever. Being grounded while still having my phone isn't much of a punishment, but with no one to call or text, it's been . . . lonely.

While Josie hops into the shower, I prepare a packet of instant ramen and dress it up with some side dishes I made earlier in the week. By the time I bring my food to the living room, Josie's on the couch in her pajamas, her hair wrapped in curlers.

I still haven't apologized to her—or anyone, for that matter. At this point, I'm not even holding out because I'm mad.

I *did* say some nasty things. To apologize now, though, feels like a cop-out after getting grounded.

"How was the movie?" I ask her.

She shrugs. "It was your typical rags-to-riches romance."

I could let the conversation end there, but then I say, "You watched it with your friends?"

"I saw it with Calvin." Quickly, she adds, "Don't get me wrong. We're not back together. I just thought we needed closure, and we'd been waiting for this movie to come out back when we were dating. Right now, I really am trying to focus on myself."

"And how's that going?"

"Good, I guess? Wish I had more to share. . . ." There's a prolonged pause before she says, "I noticed you haven't been drawing."

"Sometimes I don't feel like it." I tinker with my chopsticks and aimlessly move the noodles around in my bowl.

"You've been drawing every day since the new year . . . until recently."

Have I? If you count the occasional mindless doodle, then yeah, I guess I have been.

Josie offers me a conciliatory smile. "Like I said, I notice things." Then, more seriously, "Did something happen between you and Angela? I haven't seen you two together in a while."

"We got into a fight and now we're not talking. That's all."

"You know . . ." Josie fiddles with the drawstring of her sweatpants. "When our parents first announced their engagement, all I could think about was how I wasn't going to be an only child anymore. To be honest, I always wanted an older sibling."

"I'm two months older than you," I say. "That's hardly a difference."

"Even though we're the same age, I always felt like you were . . . more mature than everyone else in our grade."

I snort. These last two weeks have cemented the fact that I am anything but mature.

"You speak your mind and go after what you want," she amends. Then her cheeks begin to warm as she hangs on to her next words. "I really . . . look up to you."

"Um, it's nice of you to say that, but I'm not exactly a role model." If only she knew the vindictive things I've thought and said about her in private.

"To be honest, you did hurt my feelings the other day, but . . . it's because of you I finally quit the violin. That night, when we returned from the recital, I could tell you wanted to defend me. That's when I realized I had to speak up for myself."

"Did I also inspire you to kick your shoe into the closet?"

"That was . . . the heat of the moment."

"It was an impressive kick," I say.

"Thanks." Josie laughs.

"So . . ." In the least confrontational way I can think of, I ask, "Do you think you'll ever go back to playing the violin?"

"I haven't abandoned it completely," Josie says as her eyes glaze over. "The violin is the only thing I have a talent for. Making music used to be fun and comforting . . . once upon a time. It was my everything until that everything became

Curtis. All this talk about perfection—it took a toll on me, to the point I was beginning to hate the violin."

I stare at the soggy noodles in my bowl, my appetite gone as guilt eats away at me.

Josie throws her head back and sighs. "Now I'm on the hunt for a new love. It's hard . . . to find something to be passionate about." Then, as if catching herself, "Sorry for the pity party."

"Listen, I've *been* throwing myself a pity party," I tell her. "I'm not qualified to say this, but if you want my advice, start with the things you enjoy. You can't go wrong there and . . . if you ever want to dabble in art, I can teach you a thing or two."

"I have a lot to learn."

"Same." I turn to face her. "I'm sorry, Josie. For giving you a hard time."

Josie starts to say something, then stops herself. After taking a moment to think it over, she accepts my apology with a little nod.

Our greatest joy can also bring us the most pain.

Why am I so dense at the worst of times?

Art is everything to me, but is my ambition worth hurting the people around me? I don't want Angela to hurt because of me, I don't want her to lose her love for writing, and I don't want to put her down to pull myself up. Yet that's exactly what I did. I wanted her to believe in me and what we could achieve together, but when it came time for me to believe in her, I let her down. I made her cry—all because her dream wasn't big enough to suit me.

I thought she had betrayed my trust, when really, I betrayed her.

I smack myself in the face. "I'm such a clown."

"Your makeup looks fine to me," Josie says, confused.

"That's not what I meant . . . and I'm not wearing any makeup."

"Really? Well, your skin looks flawless."

"Thanks. Yours too." I swear, Josie's too kind for her own good.

The front door suddenly swings open. Amy marches inside and trips over the threshold, her purse slipping off her shoulder as she catches herself. Josie and I watch as she lingers in the foyer, looking drained and preoccupied.

"Mom . . ." Josie finally speaks up. "Is everything okay?"

Amy stares at us as if seeing us for the first time.

"Oh, good, you two are home," she says, slowly blinking out of her daze. "I was at the hospital." She raises a hand before Josie and I can interrupt. "Brian fainted at work. He has a broken nose and a concussion, but he should be fine with some rest. The doctors want to keep him for a night or two to monitor his condition."

Dad's worked weekend overtime before and usually returns in the early afternoon. It's now a quarter to eight. If Amy just came from the hospital, that means Dad must've been admitted not too long ago.

"Why was he at work at this hour?" I look at Josie to see if she shares my confusion.

She doesn't.

35

"HE'S BEEN WORKING a second job? Since when?" I ask, alone in my bewilderment as my eyes dart back and forth between Amy and Josie.

"Since October," Amy answers, slipping out of her boots to join me on the couch. "He's been picking up more overtime and freelancing on the side. Unfortunately, he . . ." She measures her words carefully, as if the truth will hurt me. "Let's just say he's bitten off more than he can chew."

"What happened in October that Dad suddenly needed the money?" Did it have to do with the wedding or honeymoon? Josie's lessons? He did borrow money from Aunt Mindy.

Amy massages her temples. "He felt we needed it" is all she offers as an explanation. I stare at her in disbelief, and she caves. "He took another job so he could . . . put more toward your college fund."

Dad's been working a second job . . . for me? I search my memories for all the clues I must've missed—for four months—but I can't recall a single thing.

Was this a secret or did I simply not notice?

Amy nervously wrings her hands and says, "I know college has been a sensitive topic lately and that we . . . haven't been fair to you, Lynda. Money isn't something we want you to worry about. Brian and I felt it was best to keep it between us."

"But Josie knew?" I look to her for confirmation.

"I found out on my own," Josie explains. "Back in December, he left his laptop on the dining table one night with his freelancing website open."

So she knew early on. That must've compounded her fear of quitting the violin. Knowing her, she must feel responsible for Dad's injury, when really, the guilt should be mine.

"I asked her not to tell you," Amy cuts in. "Brian and I . . . We'll have to rethink our arrangement. He can't keep overworking himself, but that's for me and him to sort out." She gives my arm a reassuring squeeze, as if I'm the one in the hospital and need comforting. "You girls keep doing what you're doing and leave Brian and me to worry about the rest."

"I see" is all I say.

Except I don't see.

I haven't seen anything at all. I've been so fixated on the characters living inside my head and the validation they bring me that I've been neglecting the people around me.

It's humbling . . . to realize just how flawed you are.

• • •

The following day, I visit Dad in the hospital. Despite the gray and dreary atmosphere, he's in high spirits when the nurse announces my arrival. I wish him good morning before handing him a large taro milk tea. "Here. Thought you could use a pick-me-up," I say. "I wasn't sure how sweet you take it, so I asked for half sugar."

"Half is perfect," he says, taking an indulgent sip.

"Amy packed you a lunch and some oranges." I unload my things onto a side table. "Josie's planning to swing by later today."

Amy said he'll be fine, but he looks a wreck. His nose is swathed in bandages, and the area beneath his eyes has swelled into hard pillows. Never mind the dark purple bruise on his face that gives the illusion that he's wearing a superhero mask. It's weird to see him all beaten up.

I suppose it's easy to forget parents aren't indestructible.

"What's with the long face?" he says. "Do I look that bad?" When he smiles, his wrinkles deepen across his forehead, and the cracks in his lips become more pronounced.

"You look like you got . . . an involuntary nose job."

Dad snorts and instantly regrets it. His neighbor is fast asleep on the other side of the curtain dividing their beds. I can hear him snoring. "Don't mind Rick. He's passed out from the meds. He won't hear us no matter how loud we are." Dad noisily drinks his taro milk tea and waits for a reaction. "See? Out like a light."

"When will you be discharged?"

"Once my doctor confirms no more dizzy spells, I can check out tomorrow."

I pull up a chair and start peeling an orange for him, to occupy my hands and to mask the sterile smell of cleaning supplies saturating the room.

"I heard about your second job." I let the words hang in the air as I discard the orange rind into the trash. "Amy said it was to help pay for art school. Is there a reason why I was the last to know?"

I already know why, but I want to hear it from him.

Shame and confusion cloud his face. He takes a deep breath before coming clean. "These last few years have been . . . a lot for you. I didn't want to burden you even more by telling you I was working two jobs. I haven't been responsible with my spending, and that's on me."

"Did you work two jobs back when we had the apartment?"

"On and off while you were in elementary school," he confesses. I offer him a slice of orange, and he politely waves it away. "The truth is, after Fiona's death, I was drowning in medical bills. We took out loans, borrowed money from Min, and maxed out our insurance—still, it wasn't enough."

"Why . . . didn't you tell me?" I whisper. "It would've explained so much."

"Because I thought you'd resent your mother," he says after some hesitation. "She refused her parents' help even though we needed it. Your mother had her pride, and she had her hope. She thought she could beat whatever was killing her and that everything would work out in the end. . . ." His voice breaks, and a tear slips down his face. "She left this world when you were so young, Lynda. I didn't want the debt to define her."

Would I have resented her? I suppose it's within the realm of possibility. It's not like elementary school me would've understood anything about the state of health care in this country.

Dad drags a hand down his face and hisses at the pain. "Life was difficult without Fiona. I should've sought help like Min suggested; instead, I buried myself in my work. By the time I paid off the debt, you were already in middle school, and we'd lost so many years together. After Min and Ben moved, I realized I no longer knew how to talk to you and that . . . you didn't need me anymore."

We were like cohabitating strangers.

I wasn't aware he noticed.

"It's my fault you had to learn to be independent."

"Growing up to be a daddy's girl never suited me," I say in an attempt to lighten the mood.

"But I should've been there more," he insists. I can't deny that. "I admit, my relationship with Amy escalated quickly. I was too eager to rebuild our family and stupid enough to believe Amy and Josie could replace Min and Ben."

"That *is* pretty stupid."

"I know you don't have much love for me, Amy, or Josie— and that's on me." Dad's eyes flick to the ceiling, then to me. "I haven't done much to foster goodwill between us. . . ."

I cross my arms over my chest, suddenly feeling exposed.

"You're a capable person, Lynda. You have Fiona's fighting spirit, and you'll succeed at anything you set your mind to, but sometimes . . . I wish you'd slow down." Dad takes a halting breath and tearfully says, "You seem so eager to leave us behind. I'm . . . scared that once you leave, you won't come back. But I don't want to stand in the way of your dreams. Just know that if you ever change your mind or something doesn't work out, Amy and I, we'll be here if you need us."

It never crossed my mind that my dad would miss me. Not after he chose work over me, or after he remarried and found himself another daughter, and certainly not after all our fights.

But I was wrong.

He was always looking out for me. In his own way.

It doesn't excuse his absence, but it certainly puts things into perspective. I just wish we had this conversation years ago.

Better late than never, I suppose.

"I'm sorry, Lynda. I love you. Don't ever doubt that."

My chest tightens, and my vision swims. Everything seems to blend into itself, like an oversaturated watercolor painting. The room is just one big blur until I close my eyes. Bit by bit, the world emerges into clarity, and finally, when I look at my dad, I feel like I'm seeing him for the first time in a long time.

"I'm sorry, too," I say.

And then I hug him.

36

AT HOME, I immediately grab Henry and get to work on the final NPC. If Angela is determined to finish *Love Takes Root*, then I need to uphold my end of the contract. I only hope she hasn't fired me. Even if she has, I'm still going to follow through. It's the least I can do.

I'm on my third concept sketch when Aunt Mindy sends me a video chat request. We haven't talked since the time I yelled and hung up on her.

"Amy told me what happened," she says as soon as I pick up. She's lounging in an armchair with a blanket draped across her lap. Judging by the angle of her camera, she's calling from her laptop. "How's Brian? I heard you paid him a visit."

"He's pretty beaten-up," I tell her. "But he should be back home by tomorrow."

Aunt Mindy shakes her head. "I told him to watch his health. He can't hustle the way he used to, not at his age."

"Did he tell you to keep his other job a secret from me?"

She seems taken aback by my question but not in a guilty

way. She seems more relieved than anything. "He did," she says. "I told him he'd save himself a lot of grief by being up-front. Unfortunately, he's not great at communicating to begin with, and as his older sister, if I tell him to do one thing, he does the opposite."

"Life must be less infuriating when you're an only child."

"You were an only child once. Was life easier for you then?"

"It was easier with you and Uncle Ben."

Aunt Mindy gives me a sad yet knowing smile. "I'll always be here if you need me, and so will Brian. He misses you as much as I do." She glances at the floor before looking back at me. "I know you're in a rush to grow up, Lynda, but . . . adults don't always have it together."

"I kind of noticed."

"You're only sixteen once. Enjoy what you have now."

"Did you get that line from a fortune cookie?" I ask.

"No, I got it from a book Josie recommended to me."

"You two have been talking?"

"Of course we have. I'm her aunt, and she's your sister."

"I know. You don't have to remind me."

"I suspect you might need a reminder now and then."

"Well, I'm going to make an effort, so you don't have to."

● ● ●

Bora eyes me skeptically as I stand in front of her house holding a box of egg tarts fresh from the bakery. She sizes me up before leaning against the doorframe.

"Is there something you'd like to say to me?" she asks while examining her nails.

"I messed up, and I'm sorry."

This must be a world record. I've never had to apologize this much in my life. A few words and a couple of egg tarts might not be enough to earn Bora's forgiveness, but I owe her at least that much.

"Sorry for what?" she asks.

"For walking out when you tried to help me, for not coming to my senses sooner, and for all my bullshit."

"*And* for not eating Halmoni's cooking after I graciously heated it up for you."

"That too."

"Have you smoothed things over with Josie?"

I nod.

"And with your dad?"

I nod, but not without saying "It's . . . a work in progress."

"What about Angela?"

"She's avoiding me, so . . . I'm giving her space. If you, uh, need space too, I can leave. Just eat the egg tarts while they're hot."

Bora grabs the box and peeks inside. "I can't finish a dozen egg tarts on my own. Come in. Halmoni's making tea."

A grin splits my face, and she pinches my cheek.

"Don't get cocky. The next time you shut me down like that, I won't be so nice."

I massage my face. "Thanks for putting up with me."

"What are best friends for?" Bora lifts a finger as if remembering something and smirks. "Oh, but you're not getting off that easy."

"Let me guess. . . ." I follow her into the kitchen, where Halmoni's already pouring three cups of tea. "You want me to play *Romancing the New Moon*?"

"Every route and every ending."

"Deal." I offer her my hand, and we shake on it.

•••

Dad takes the week off to recuperate. His swelling and bruising are down, and to celebrate his release, Amy surprises us on Wednesday with a reservation at Han Seoul-oh. These past few weeks have been trying for everyone. We could all use a treat.

"How does everyone feel about grilled pork belly?" Amy asks, studying the menu.

"Sign me up," I say.

"Can we order some crispy chicken skin?" asks Josie.

"That sounds good," Dad says, looking like he's about to drool. He's mostly been on a diet of soft foods since leaving the hospital. "We should also order a stew, something spicy."

"Dad, the doctor said to avoid spicy foods," I remind him.

"Nothing too crunchy either," Amy chimes in. "That means no gizzards."

After Dad ties up some loose ends, he'll finally shut the doors to his freelancing business, hopefully by the end of this month. Amy's helping him with a few outstanding clients while also worrying about her own job. She's planning to meet with her supervisor to discuss a promotion, and she doesn't want to butcher it. Just the other night, I overheard Amy and Dad role-playing a salary negotiation. I did have my doubts about their relationship, but they're good for each other.

As for Josie, she has an interview with the public library on Friday, and I've been helping her prep. She thought now would be an ideal time to gain some work experience.

All in all, things are beginning to look up. While RISD is still my dream school, maybe I don't need it as much as I think I do. Dad and I will be visiting the campus during spring break, and depending on how that goes, I might ask Aunt Mindy to take me on a tour of SAIC. Who knows? I'll try to take things one step at a time.

Dad and I still have our problems, but this is a promising start.

For him and for me.

Midway into dinner, another family is seated across from us, and I immediately recognize Angela and her parents. Alvin cheerfully waves at me before Angela subdues his arm and whispers into his ear. Dad starts to say something, too, until I frantically shake my head.

Introductions will have to wait.

"You two haven't reconciled yet?" asks Josie.

"It's complicated," I try to explain.

Honestly, I've been too preoccupied with what's going on at home to give Angela the attention and apology she deserves. I don't want to muck it up, but . . . can I really run into her now and not say anything? She could take it the wrong way. Though, judging by her reaction just now, I get the impression she wants me to leave her alone.

Josie pins me with an exasperated look that screams *Really, that's your excuse?*

Ever since we made up, she's been giving me attitude—the good kind. It's refreshing and what you'd expect from a younger sister.

"If this were a rom-com, now would be the time for a grand romantic gesture," she says.

"Well, this isn't a rom-com." Still, there must be something I can do.

"How about if you were in an otome game? What would you do?"

An idea occurs to me then. I grab a napkin and ask if anyone has a pen. Amy fishes one out from her purse, and I start writing. After we grab the check and start to leave, I slither behind the bussing station and tap our waiter on the shoulder. He startles.

"Can you please give this note to the girl in the indigo sweater?" I ask.

"Several girls are wearing purple," he says.

"I mean the pretty one."

"They're all pretty."

"The pretty one over *there.*" I discreetly point in Angela's direction before slipping him five dollars and the folded napkin.

During study hall the next day, Owen's giving me unsolicited suggestions while I'm brainstorming my next sticker sheet when Angela saunters past us and drops a folded napkin onto the floor in front of me. I swipe it up before Owen can and quickly unfold it.

Then I smile.

> *Angela, please help me make this right. What should I do?*
> *A) Apologize*
> *B) Treat you to bubble tea*
> *C) Support you in the ways you want to be supported*
> *D) All of the above*
>
> *E.) Meet you at Baa Bing after school*

Because of course she would.

· · ·

During the winter, when folks aren't craving shaved ice, Baa Bing serves hot desserts like red bean soup and tofu pudding. I get there before Angela and rack my brain over what she'd like. I comb through every conversation we've had to try to remember if she ever mentioned liking mung beans. . . .

"Their red bean melee is a bestseller, so I've heard."

I flinch as Angela sidles up to me, her eyes trained on the overhead menu.

"A classic tofu pudding sounds just as satisfying," she continues, tapping a finger to her chin. "Decisions, decisions . . ."

"Bora loves the tofu pudding here," I say for lack of a better response. "She picks some weird toppings, though, like peanuts and boba."

Angela side-eyes me. "Hey, that's your best friend you're talking about."

"I know, and . . . standing next to me is my girlfriend?"

"Hmm . . . Are you sure you want to be with this insecure writer?"

"Do you still want to be with someone who called you that?"

"Maybe . . ." She crosses her arms. "Maybe not."

And like a rolled-up tube of paint, the second she presses me, I spill my heart out.

"I'm sorry, Angela. That day, I was only thinking about myself. I was mad at Josie for quitting violin, and I took my anger out on you, and most of all, I'm sorry for making you feel like you're not good enough. You're amazing. You know what you want, and I love that about you—even when what you want isn't what I want, because as long as you're happy, I'm happy. I know I have a lot of growing up to do and—"

"Excuse me." The young man behind the register clears his throat. "Sorry to interrupt, but are you ready to order?"

"No, give me a minute," I say before turning back to Angela. "As I was saying—"

Angela clutches her stomach and belts out a laugh. "I'm sorry," she says to the cashier. "Excuse us, we're having a moment." She places a hand on my back and steers me away from the counter.

Only then do I notice the line behind us, and standing among the procession of gawking bystanders is Bora. I told her I was meeting Angela here. I didn't think she'd come to eavesdrop. She shoots me a thumbs-up as Angela ushers me out the door.

Now that we're outside and I've had a chance to calm down, I want to kick myself for sharing such intimate things in public—again.

"That was something," Angela says, wiping tears from her eyes, "and you sounded so sincere, too."

"I was being honest." I tug my scarf farther up my face to hide my embarrassment. While I do regret announcing my relationship problems to the world, I'm glad Angela can at least laugh about it. It's better than making her cry. "So . . ."

"So?"

"Are you okay?" I ask. She nods, and a part of me relaxes. "Why were you absent for a whole week?"

"After our fight, I caught a nasty bug and couldn't get out of bed."

"Oh . . ." That wasn't the explanation I expected. "I'm glad you're feeling better. Does that mean . . ." I struggle for the right words. "Are we . . . are we okay?"

"We have a lot of work ahead of us," she says, closing her eyes. "You said some hurtful things, and you know what? You're right. I am insecure." I start to object until she raises a hand to silence me. "Being right doesn't justify what you did, but . . . I know myself. I'm not ready to take the leap and commit myself to my writing."

Then, with an insinuating look in my direction, she says, "One day I'll be ready, and when that day comes, you better be there." I stare at her, wide-eyed and speechless. "As for

Love Takes Root, I found us a background artist. Your original deadline is back on—and I'm assigning you some mandatory reading."

"You're letting me read Sun Hong's route?" I all but gasp. She gives me an affirmative nod, and I clap a hand over my mouth. "Are you sure? It's okay if you don't trust me."

"I'm trusting you this time. You said it yourself, didn't you? *Artists who don't take risks never get close to being the best.* Well, you're the risk I'm taking."

A sweet, delightful feeling blooms inside my chest. It's bright and yellow like the sun and feels a lot like hope. After everything I said, Angela still wants to be with me and dream with me. If that's not forgiveness, I don't know what is.

Thank you, Angela, for taking a chance on someone like me.

Thank you for believing in me.

I tamp down the surge of emotions pooling in my throat and take a deep breath. "Are you saying we can have a happy ending?"

Angela offers me a tender smile. "Perhaps . . . but why anticipate the ending when you and I are just beginning?" She entwines her fingers with mine, her eyes sparkling with affection and determination as she holds my gaze. "Love is an art, Lynda. Points to you if you can keep up."

Acknowledgments

Back in 2017, I wrote a contemporary young adult novel about Lynda Fan, a defeated artist who runs away from home and embarks on an emotional journey to rediscover her dreams. After querying that book with no success, I shelved it, thinking it would never see the light of day again. Toward the end of 2021, I decided to rewrite Lynda's story. Now, after a complete overhaul and a lot of perseverance, *Love Points to You* is finally out in the world. A heartfelt thank you to everyone who made this possible:

♥ Alison Romig, my editor, who is incredibly insightful and articulate. You see things I overlook and find words for what I can't describe.

♥ Lynnette Novak, my agent, for supporting my ideas. Without you, this book would still be gathering metaphorical dust.

♥ Ray Shappell for the wonderful art direction and for delivering a cover design that captures the book so well.

♥ Jacqueline Li for bringing the characters to life with your utterly adorable cover art. I'm so happy we could work together on this!

♥ Nicole Wayland and Colleen Fellingham for catching

my mistakes and whipping this book into tiptop shape with their meticulous copyediting.

♥ To the team at Delacorte Romance: Beverly Horowitz, Wendy Loggia, Tamar Schwartz, CJ Han, Kenneth Crossland, and Sarah Lawrenson. Publishing really feels like one big group project. No contribution is too small, and your efforts are needed and appreciated.

About the Author

Alice Lin first started dreaming up stories in sixth grade. She holds a master's degree in library and information science from Rutgers University and worked as a teen librarian for six years before publishing her first novel, *Fireworks*.

alice-lin.com
@miss_alicelin on Instagram

Delacorte Romance

IT'S A LOVE STORY.